BEFORE
ALL ELSE

FIONA HOLLAND

Fiona Holland.

SilverWood

Published in 2016 by SilverWood Books

SilverWood Books Ltd
14 Small Street, Bristol, BS1 1DE, United Kingdom
www.silverwoodbooks.co.uk

ISBN 978-1-78132-539-1 (paperback)
ISBN 978-1-78132-540-7 (ebook)

British Library Cataloguing in Publication Data
A CIP catalogue record for this book is available from
the British Library

Page design and typesetting by SilverWood Books
Printed on responsibly sourced paper

FIONA HOLLAND was born in Malta during her parents' Navy posting. School, University and Secretarial College followed in due succession, as did a variety of jobs as au-pair, wedding car chauffeur, pig farmer, potato picker and foster carer.

Her writing career was given a mighty fillip by winning the 2013 Gladstone's Library Short Fiction prize for her story Looking The Other Way. Gladstone's Library is home to the Victorian, three-times Prime Minister's book collection, and the prize was awarded from submissions from all over the world judged by established writers.

Since that time Fiona has focussed on her creative writing together with running a 5-acre small-holding in North Wales and offering a writers retreat in her hand-crafted Shepherd's Hut. *Before All Else* is her first published novel.

To find out more, visit www.fionaholland.co.uk

Before all else, live together in harmony, being of one mind and one heart on the way to God.

Rule of St. Augustine, Ch. 1.2

WINTER

The salt air creeps further and further inland from the soft-edged coast, the dewy mists captured by fewer and fewer mighty oak sentinels. The land is gradually cleared, dug, heaped. A deep rotation begins. Hand-size is no longer enough. Flint is joined with worked wood to find more flint to work more wood. No need now to outrun the wolf, the other Neolithic animals, for now we have shelter, fire, food. The dead are put without the palisade, their bones worn clean by wind and rain and rodents, the bones of them brought together in mounds. Shapes begin to form upon the landscape – rectangular, circular, man-made.

A mere hundred generations ago.

Metal works alongside flint for tools, hunting and adornment. Spaces widen between the thinning trees; wood smoke travels horizontally in the gaps, pulling towards its source traders, marauders, the curious. The collective begins. Tribes are formed. The individual good becomes the common good. Hill forts rise high, refuge is sought behind mounting earthworks; both embattled and invader have Latinate names, the prerogative of the victor. Dung.

M. Blatt

1

Cecily

Cecily closes the heavy front door behind her and breathes in the warm, familiar scent of flatulent dog, overblown hyacinths and damp spores.

Trueman, the black Labrador, creator and disperser of the worst smells in the house, ambles sleepily into the hallway. "Hello, True-bie." Cecily bends to stroke his patrician head. He wags his tail and returns to his bed in the kitchen. If he were in human form he would surely rattle his newspaper and enquire if she'd had a good night, if Mrs Green were holding up and whether she wanted him to lock up. Trueman's eyes are so similar to Henry's. A caramel brown, inclined to dart hither and thither, fringed by long dark lashes, beneath such a worried forehead.

It had been a trying day, on several counts. Funerals are always funny affairs. Shiny trousers, an unnatural humility and piousness brought on by the religious surroundings, the sense of mortality brought on by the prospect of a later-than-usual lunch, and a chill feeling on the back of the neck of one's own position in the queue advancing, of being ushered up the line faster than one would wish.

Mr Green, their old gardener, had been despatched with little fuss yet it was the sadness on the faces of the family that would stay with her. Mark, Mr Green's son, had steered her to the front door. He shook her hand, thanking her volubly for coming today. "You'll look after your mum, won't you?" She placed her hand on his arm, regretting instantly the unintended patronising tone. Occasionally it seems as if Mother's mantle has been flung about her own shoulders.

"Of course," he answered. "There's lots of us. She won't be lonely."

Mark had spoken movingly of his father at the lectern, his own young son standing solemnly by his side. As the mourners filed out of the church, the entire family stood as one to thank them for their kind thoughts in their time of darkness. Seeds blown from the one seed head.

Tilly

It's a shame she couldn't go to Mr Green's funeral. After all, the family had known him for nigh on thirty years. When Cecily phoned a few days earlier to see if she wanted to attend, she'd declined. "Can't come, darling. Good of you to let me know. Lambing. A hundred ewes. None of them with less than twins. About twenty with triplets and a few with quads. Can't leave them."

"You sound shattered."

"I am. It's a twenty-four-hour operation. Don't get much sleep January to March."

"Couldn't Lizzie help?"

"Don't ask." Lizzie, all the compassion of a saint and none of the wisdom. Working long shifts at the kennels, studying for her Diploma in Animal Welfare, living in a thin-walled caravan with that idle, good-for-nothing slug of a boyfriend.

"Oh?"

"Don't get me started. Anyway, funny to think of Mr Green gone. Do you remember when you thought he was the most gorgeous creature that ever walked this planet?"

Cecily chuckled, a laugh that rolled down the decades.

"Remember when Mother caught you and Melly ogling him?" The two elder sisters had been entwined together on the window seat, shrieking and ducking as he passed to and fro in front of the library window. "She was furious. Said it was no way for young ladies to behave."

"Bit unfair. We were only about twelve and fourteen at the time. And you, Tilly, must have been eight. Probably playing with your Ark under Daddy's desk, innocent to what all the fuss was about."

"Well, he was ancient even then."

"Must have been about forty."

"Gross!"

"We were placed under the strictest instructions to avoid fraternising with him—"

"Sexy Simon, as you used to call him."

"Sexy Simon! Yes! I'd forgotten. Mother banned us from speaking to him after that little episode."

"Anyway, Cecily. Thanks for letting me know. I'll come and visit as soon as lambing's over."

Tilly had put the phone down before she realised she hadn't asked Cecily if there was any news from Amelia – Melly. She considered quickly phoning her sister back again, but decided against it, fairly confident that the answer would be a resigned no. Rarely did they ever get any reply to their texts or emails.

Cecily

The house is empty, other than Trueman of course, yet she cannot escape the feeling of eyes watching her. Ghosts, if there are such a thing, must be crowding out this house. Not just the faint echoes of lives known to her – Mummy, Daddy, Darling Henry – but all those who had tenure in the past five hundred years. This feeling of being crowded out is always strongest at night. She has strange dreams where she is the shade, the insubstantial one. A stiff drink, that would put them all to sleep.

It's unsettling to think of Mr Green gone.

He had been a small but regular feature of their growing up. The shout of, "Can someone take Mr Green a cup of tea?" would go up from the kitchen when Mother put the kettle on. For a brief, ecstatic period, at the height of her and Melly's infatuation, his cups were festooned with handmade daisy chains, the rim held close to the breast when the empty cup was returned to the back door at the end of his shift. Yet this period was short-lived. Within the briefest time, even despite Mother's edict, he was more likely to be given a cup with the contents sloshed over or, more cruelly, left where he might find it or might not.

For it had not taken long for the girls to become fastidious in their chosen objects of desire.

By the time she and Melly had started their school exams, Simon had become a troll at the bottom of the garden. With his paunchy belly, his stooped shoulders and necrotic nose, his allure had quickly vanished. Like a once common garden bird now on the endangered list, he was only rarely and fleetingly observed, tying up the runner beans, pruning the rambling rose, washing algae off the glasshouse.

Had their infatuation been real or just a facsimile of an infatuation? A try-on? For, truly speaking, just how attractive are middle-aged men, overalls wound down, pasty skin exposed to the sun, huffing and puffing behind a recalcitrant lawnmower?

Cecily pulls a brandy balloon with a dusty bloom from the back of the display cabinet and pours herself a large drink.

Strange to contemplate that she herself has transformed from young Miss Cecily of Hingham House to Mrs Marchant, wife and now widow of Darling Henry, still of Hingham House, in the same way that Sexy Simon had mutated into Old Mr Green and then, ultimately, into compost.

Madge

While the fiery brandy courses its way down Cecily's gullet, Madge is sitting with her feet up on Mrs Green's pouffe, commenting on the day's events, most gleefully on Mandy's outburst.

"That woman's not right in the head."

Mrs Green is stacking small bowls, emptying the crispy corn snacks and cheesy balls into one large dish, thinking the hens will enjoy them tomorrow. "What woman?"

"That Mandy, who else?"

"Well, there's a few burrows short of a bunny around here."

"Did you hear her going on about 'Mr Marchant, Henry Marchant'?"

"Cecily's husband?"

"Yes. You should have seen her face too. She looked livid." Madge leans back against the spongy sofa, exhaling a plume of minty tobacco smoke. She'd seen Cecily shake Mark's hand and head down to the church. What time of night is that to be traipsing through a church-yard? "If you ask me, that woman spends far too much time moping at the graveside." But Mrs Green is now in the back kitchen roughly wash-ing the pots and borrowed mugs, muttering under her breath about how a little help around here wouldn't go amiss.

Cecily

The house is growing chilly, the heating having clicked off some time ago; it is becoming ice fast. If she closes her eyes she can almost hear the click of each ice crystal as it interlocks with the next. Only she and the dog pulse warmth within the coldness of the kitchen.

She turns a gas ring on and waits while it click-click-clicks itself alight. The rising heat is barely enough to stir the air. She puts a pan of milk on to warm through and watches the bubbles rise slowly through the whiteness, like tapioca beads. "Sod it," she says out loud. Trueman thumps his tail on the kitchen floor. It is freezing. It has been a hell of a day. Old Mr Green has shuffled off. There'd been near uproar at the wake when Mandy had wobbled in from the back garden and started on like she had. Cecily is jolly well going to have a cigarette to go with the cocoa and the brandy. There must be some in the back of the cutlery drawer, left over from Amelia's last visit three years ago.

There are two left in the soft packet. She puts one between her lips and bends to the naked flame under the saucepan. A combination of burning milk, burning hair and burning tobacco assails her nose. The side of her cheek stings.

Mandy

That cow, Cecily. No better than she ought to be. Her and her sisters. Remember how they used to sit there, on the school bus, all prim and proper, terrified that the boys would rampage down the aisle and pull their hats off?

Mum used to go up and help at the house. Why did they always need 'help'? More of them, so more hands to do the work. Not like when it was just Mum and her, in the flat.

Cecily

They'd brought Mandy in from the back yard, walking on the balls of her feet like the very inebriated do, held upright by Mr Green's son, Mark, and one of Ned's workmen. Ned had wanted to take her home but she refused. When Cecily caught sight of her again, she was sitting at a cloth-covered table, morosely and mechanically filling her mouth with maize snacks.

Their eyes locked. Holding her gaze, Mandy had shouted out into the room, spraying bright orange crumbs, "Henry Marchant, anyone?" As always happened whenever she saw Mandy, the dummy's head loomed large, its grotesque face leering at her, a torrent of filth about to pour from its mouth.

"Hush, Mandy," someone called from the hallway. "Stop there!"

"Does anyone *know* Henry Marchant?"

Cecily stood stock still as if Henry had suddenly been conjured up right in front of her, as if he were about to read the whole sad, sorry, awful, shaming truth in the dead eyes of this marionette.

"*Know* him, like I *know* him, I mean."

Cecily had the briefest notion to march up to the foul woman and slap her hard. It was an unbelievable liberty to voice his name. But to pluck his name out of thin air, scrunch it up and lob it fast and direct over the heads of all those in the room, was an insult too far. Mandy looked about her, her head moving in short, staccato bursts as if seeking validation from everyone around. The dummy's head swivelled maniacally, following the direction of her wild eyes. It seemed to be in cahoots with Mandy.

"Ned? Where's Ned? I think Ned should take her home."

Cecily felt herself being steered out of the room into a less-occupied lounge and made to sit on the flat, wide sofa.

Mandy

Ned shouldn't have left her like he did. He'd gone back to work after the funeral. "I'll just check on how everyone's getting on. I'll be back in half an hour." She knew he wouldn't be just half an hour. Knew he'd be longer than that. That he was leaving her to her own devices at the wake. Unreliable. Unreliable and late. So it was all his fault. Mostly. As per.

The family had squeezed a few tears out and shaken everyone's hands on the church steps and then the hearse had driven the coffin and the principle mourners to the crematorium ten miles away. She was one of a little huddle round the back of the Greens' house, all shivering in the bitter wind, waiting for the family to return and take the wrappers off the sandwiches.

"Funny. You'd never think Simon was a gardener, would you, looking at this garden," someone had observed. She'd stubbed out a cigarette and kicked the flattened butt into the long grass, long desiccated grass bending itself against the cold, a rusting barbecue and garden furniture tangled under a flapping tarpaulin. She'd laughed at this comment. Perhaps she wasn't the only one whose life was essentially a pile of shite.

"Hurry up," she muttered under her breath, stamping her feet and pulling her thin coat about her, wondering if anybody had thought to try the door. Then again, it hadn't seemed quite right to occupy a dead man's house. Ned should have taken her with him. She could have sat in his office, next to the paraffin heater, and kept warm and out of the way until it was time to go back together and toast the old git's passing.

She must have drunk a litre of that cheap white wine before Ned had finally come back. Tasted like maiden's water, it did. Loosens the tongue too. Apparently.

Ned had that firm set of the jaw he has when he's cross. He didn't say much.

Cecily

Cecily cradles the mug of cocoa between her two hands, stiffening in the chill air. Trueman has his chin on her knee, his front paws slipping on the tiled flooring, eyebrows triangulating as if trying to assess her mood. What is her mood? An image comes to mind of a disco ball revolving slowly in a darkened space, car headlights passing occasionally over its faceted surface causing it to throw out brief spots of coloured light. How can you truly be said to exist if there is no one in front of you on whom to radiate your colours? The dog doesn't quite count.

Someone had offered to make her a cup of tea while Ned – who had arrived just after the incident – controlled his thrashing wife out of the front door. The tea never came but someone else had patted her hand. It was too dark to see who it was. She had left shortly afterwards, kissing the grieving widow, now slightly consoled for her loss by drink. A few voices called "Goodnight" as she made her way out of the small, crowded room. Old Boy Crowther set up a wheezing cough and she slipped away under the distraction of fetched towels and a tactfully proffered bowl, hastily emptied of its peanuts, should the hacking cough lead to something altogether more productive and technicolour.

Cars were bumped up pell-mell on the pavement circling the four-sided patch of grass opposite the house. Mr Green was a popular man and his family certainly plentiful. She wondered what it must be like to be buttressed by so many people.

Mandy

She pretends to be such a Goody Two Shoes.

Cecily

Her cigarette spits and sizzles in the darkness of the kitchen. It tastes revolting, so she stubs it out in a saucer, regretting her moment of rebellion. Small flecks of burning ash rise into the air in a firefly moment, sinking back down again into grey oblivion.

"Come on, old friend," she calls to Trueman, who follows her to the back door. She leans against the door jamb and watches fast-moving clouds wipe the face of the bright moon. Trueman disappears into the undergrowth and re-emerges a few moments later with wet paws. He brushes past her on his way back into the kitchen and his bed under the stairs. She is comforted by his touch. It's on nights like this that it doesn't seem right to leave the hound to sleep downstairs.

Mandy

Ned puts her to bed. "There's a bucket and bog roll by the side of the bed." It's about all he's said to her since he collected her from Mr Green's house.

"Aw, don't be like that, love. Come here."

Ned ignores her and leaves the bedroom. From the bulb on the landing ceiling, she can see that the back of his shirt is crumpled and half-untucked. He pulls at his shirt to loosen it and unbuttons his cuffs.

"Go to sleep. You'll feel better in the morning," he replies as she calls out his name. His voice descends down the stairs. "I'm going to lock up."

Cecily

It is an old, old secret but still it gnaws away. Is it even that important now? Maybe not at all or maybe only at the Final Reckoning when we are called to account for ourselves in both the good times and the bad times. Really it's nothing to do with Mandy, but she has this way of making it hers.

Cecily knows it is guilt that drives the mechanism that twists the wooden spoon that operates the dummy's head from left to right. That over-varnished face with its mechanical jaw and parodied gaiety. It feeds on silence and grows fat on guilt. She should break its neck. Drown its splintered shards. Hold its fat, greasy face under water until the bubbles cease and its eyes pop.

But what to do with the puppet-master, Mandy?

Within her icy bed, her vaporous lover trails his long fingers along the back of her neck. He pushes his fingers between hers till they leach all heat. He blows his frozen breath on her cheek, on her eyelids, across her feet. She swaddles herself with the bedclothes and waits for him to leave.

She dreams of bleached bones.

2

Cecily

The next morning, a few cars are still bumped up on the verge outside Mrs Green's house. Relatives from afar, perhaps, who had billeted with friends and neighbours. She makes her usual way down to the churchyard. The High Street has yet to come alive, with only a few delivery vans, their back doors opened to boxes of Dutch stems, hanging carcasses, crates of milk. The pavement is still treacherous with frost, glistening under a spent moon.

The church sits upon its own grassy rise flanked by low flint walls and the one-way system. Having fulfilled its original promise to make the local wool merchants wealthy, it now sees to the occasional religious requirements of the village of Bullenden. A wrought-iron archway with its central lamp embellishes the entrance. The bulb flickers, throwing its intermittent light over inch-deep flies and spiders, each as dead as the other. Walking gingerly up the path, she makes her way over to Henry. *Darling* Henry.

He is always Darling Henry. Could never be anything other than Darling Henry. Even now, six years later, she thinks of him only with an access of pure love and affection.

Mandy

She wakes slowly. The bedroom is warm and close. There is an old, familiar, heart-wrenching smell in the air. Paris Nights. The scent is old, sour, but it belongs to a time when there had been more promise in the air. "Hartlepool Nights, more like," her Jerry had said, as she waved a drenched wrist under his nose.

Jerry. Jerry. Jerry. So different from Ned. Where are you now, Jerry?

More to the point, where's that Ned? Luckily he hadn't had a go at her last night. He'd pushed her up the stairs with his hand in the small of her back. Had she been sick again? She leans over the bed. The bucket is empty. Mercifully she'd made it out to the Greens' garden in time last night. Sharon had come out with her and rubbed her back. "Never mind, love, happens to all of us at some time." Those sausage rolls were definitely off.

Cecily

She leans against the granite headstone that marks out his dates. Even now she is only just the age Henry was when they met. He had been looking forward to retirement; she had been living in a rented farm cottage, working part-time, biding her time, although for what, she couldn't say.

What a tiny, tiny moment it was. How many factors conspired to make that meeting possible? Equally, there could have been a million reasons for them not to have met. Where would she be now if they hadn't?

She'd been cross country for a few days and was waiting for her train home, sitting at a precariously balanced plastic table, coldness seeping in through the tall, steel-framed windows, her few purchases stacked in front of her. The station was crowded with commuters returning home corralled into a holding bay with their coffees and laptops. As the screens flickered, so the next batch of travellers moved down the steps to be heaved onto their train on the platform below. Between the tilting panes of glass, office buildings glowed in the setting sun with the warmer tones of the city's Victorian industrial heritage. A mass, a press of people, of processes; no different now than a century or two ago.

The exhibition had been so-so, not that she was that interested in Surrealism, but she'd let herself wander amongst the terrifyingly skewed world of oversized and undersized objects juxtaposed in an apocalyptic landscape.

She was checking her phone – there were still twenty minutes before her train was due to depart – when the pearly light from the grimy window darkened a little. She was aware of someone scraping back a chair and sitting down. Still in the middle of the table was the exhibition's guide book, its glossy cover featuring a spinning cauldron, molten animal parts stirred by shrouded, ghostly white creatures. A hollow house with flaming windows was set on a distant hill made of bleached bones.

"Looking at that too long would give you nightmares."

She glanced at the programme. It looked not a little dystopian, even weird, fetishistic.

"Mind if I have a look?" He held her eyes with a directness and bonhomie, before reaching across to pick it up, skimming the pages, stopping every so often for a brief look. As the pages fanned past, releasing the smell of freshly printed high colour, she felt herself becoming almost mesmerised. He bent the pages back, cracking the spine. It was as if she herself were being scrutinised; all her dirty little secrets coming chattering, unreservedly, to the fore. And what was more, this man with his bold hands like catch nets and barbed eyes could, she thought to herself uneasily, become the procreator of a few of those guilty little secrets. "Not really my style," he said, replacing the programme on the table between them and shaking out his newspaper.

There was nothing she could think of to say, so returned to her phone.

Later they found themselves on the same train, heading east from Crewe.

And this is why bones rattle while houses burn in her dreams. For if Henry had ever found out, it would have knocked the stars out of the sky for him. If anyone knew, everything – the exquisite house she lived in on the High Street, her love for her sisters, her grieving for Henry, the daily visits to the graveyard – everything in her life, would be shown up to be a sham, a pretence, built on the shifting sands of hypocrisy and undeserved good fortune.

Cecily shakes her head but the thought refuses to dislodge itself. She steps carefully over the still frosted flagstones to Henry's grave.

Mandy

Jerry had gone. Good riddance. But he wasn't hers to keep anyway, was he? And then, surprisingly, Ned had come along. On the surface, it had been a pretty good swap. Jerry, with his suet butties and roving eye, for Ned; compact, local, honourable and, above all, available.

She'd promised Mum that she would give Ned a go but it had been Jerry who had lifted her higher and higher.

She counts on her fingers, although she knows the answer all too well. Fifteen years. Fifteen years since Jerry had drawn up in his wagon, asking the way to Britannia Street. "No idea love," she'd called up over the thrumming of the engine. He'd hooked his elbow over the partly closed window. "Want a lift?"

"It's alright. Can find my own way home."

"Funny place for a lass. In the middle of the roundabout."

She'd wanted to explain how she'd been out with the girls for somebody's leaving do and it would have meant the taxi making a detour into the village, so she'd said she'd get out here and walk home. The girls hadn't wanted her to, of course, but she was a big lass, could take care of herself. Seen off many a likely lad in her time.

"No, you're alright. Hubbie'll be along shortly." A lie. Mr Trucker wasn't to know that, that most of the time she felt so completely and utterly all alone in this big wide world with not even so much as a Premium Bond to her name and no friend to pull her out of the River Alyn. Ok, they were alright, the girls at work, had a laugh with them – she had that night – but she could tell what they all thought of her. Good for a laugh with a few Malibus inside her but the office ran a hell of a lot more smoothly on her sick days.

Yeah. Jerry. Jerry! Jer-rey. Fat ugly bastard who took every last penny of her dwindling savings, all two and a half thousand quid saved from her divorce settlement.

Fair dos, though, that night he'd said he'd wait until Hubbie arrived. Even when she told him to push off and stop mithering, he gave a lopsided grin, put his hands on the steering wheel, but never budged.

"I'm off. Night."

"Night, love."

"Night."

Cecily

She couldn't now remember what they had spoken about as the train pushed its way through the thickening night. Certainly the conversation revealed no impediment to them seeing each other again. On the contrary, she had the feeling that the forces of inevitability were at work, as strong and as powerful as the man sitting in front of her.

Henry put his contact details into her phone. "So you can't make the excuse that you must have put the numbers in the wrong way round." She'd walked down the aisle of the train with him and waited, staring at his back, for the doors to open at his station a few stops before her own. He turned and took a kiss from her willing lips, unbalancing her as he stepped back away from her.

"Phone me."

"I will."

Back at her seat, playful, whimsical rondos from *La Fille Mal Gardée* popped into her mind, making her smile. At approaching forty years old, it was laughingly delicious to be *The Wayward Daughter*.

Mandy

Ned ignores her on the way to the bathroom. The door closes on her, the toilet seat clacks against the cistern.

She longs to fall back on the quilted bed covers and fall asleep again but there's a vile taste in her mouth. She needs to rinse her mouth.

The night she met Jerry replays on the silver screen of her memory. She wishes she had a friend she could tell the story to. A friend who might even have the perception to ask why she doesn't hold the memory of the night she met Ned so dear as the night she met Jerry.

She'd tell the friend, this imaginary friend, how once she'd called out 'Night then' and set off across the grass verge, she'd came to a sudden halt. Couldn't move a muscle. "Get like that, I do, when I want a wee. Been like that since I was a little girl. Stock still. Just got to concentrate on holding it in. 'Cos, let a little out, and it all comes out. Not an age thing. Always been like that, I have."

"Standing there, you know how you've got to press your legs together and your arse sticks out a bit. And he's laughing."

And he's laughing. The memory is sweet. "Stop bloody laughing, you."

"Why you standing there like some kind of demented ostrich?"

"Can't bloody move, can I?"

"What's the matter?"

"Can't tell you."

"Are you alright?"

"No."

"Can I help?"

"No. I'll be alright in a minute."

He makes to look in the mirrors. "Can't see nobody coming to fetch you."

"Oh shut up." It eases off a bit. "Look, I'm alright. Just bugger off will you," because she's thinking she might be able to hop over the hedge if only he wasn't looking at her like he had plans for her. Which he had, as it turned out.

"Well, OK, if you're sure."

"I'm sure."

The loo flushes and she can hear Ned clean his teeth with the electric toothbrush. He pops his brush into the stainless cup. He can't bear to have his brush close to hers. He flushes the loo a second time. Why has she got to go through these motions, this acute intimacy, with a man she can barely stand and who seems to begrudge her her every succeeding breath?

The old familiar sadness grows in her breast, both augmented and diminished by replaying in her mind the events of the night she met Jerry. To keep the memory shiny and precious she must choke back her true feelings for the low down, cheating, thieving bastard.

If she had a friend, just one good friend, she'd have them in stitches by this point. She'd tell them how it was pitch black when she climbed over the gate. "I can hear these sheep munching away, at least I think it was sheep. Blessed relief it was, thought I'd never stop. I climb back over the gate and bleedin' Jerry comes back again. He's only just gone round the next roundabout and come back again."

"Need a hand, love? You're looking a bit precarious."

"I'm halfway over the gate by this time, trying to get me other leg over and keep me shoes from falling to the ground."

"Fuck off, I tell 'im"

"He drives the cab onto the verge, hops out, all nimble like, and gives me a steadying hand over the gate. Funny thing was, I wasn't worried. You can usually tell when a bloke's a bit threatening. He wasn't. Let go of my hand as soon as I was down. Didn't try any funny business. Which is why I thought I'd let him give me a lift home. My feet were wet, I couldn't get my shoes back on and it was two o'clock in the morning. I told him Mum would still be up.

"Having got me off the gate, he's now getting me up the steps into the cab. Heave ho.

"It was only two minutes home, but we chat and he tells me his name, where he lives, the fact that he's single, getting a divorce, him and his wife splitting up after twenty years. But he's alright about it, kids have left home. Tells me to call him if I like because he'll be passing through this way again a week on Tuesday."

Mandy hauls herself upright and coughs loudly. Stepping from the bed, her foot kicks a high-heeled shoe across the floor against the skirting board. She imagines Ned pulling the floss from his teeth and pricking his ears at the sudden noise. She pulls a vigorous V-sign at the back of the bathroom door on her way to her vanity unit.

She puts the stopper back on the bottle. Must have left it off last night. Paris Nights. Pah! She'd got her wires crossed once. Nearly given the game away. Forgotten that it wasn't Ned who called her perfume Hartlepool Nights. Looked at him like he was stupid for not remembering their little joke. But it wasn't him at all. It had been Jerry. Fucking gobshite...

Truth is, of course, whatever the seductive promise of the perfume, her silk stocking would never glide gracefully from her smooth leg like a falling feather! Nor would the man of her dreams cup her slenderly turned calf in his hand and blow lightly across her toes like pan pipes! No longer does she have the power to withhold a promise, the power to tease, to thwart, to reject; the power to disappoint.

Cecily

A week after their meeting on the train, Henry's name buzzed onto her phone screen. "Passing your way next Wednesday. Lunch?" She'd almost forgotten about him, putting it down to a flash encounter on the road to nowhere. Yet she had no hesitation to text back, almost immediately, "That would be lovely."

The village is quiet, the hush that only comes with the bitter cold. The orange of the sodium lights in the street muddies the clarity of the early morning.

When Mother and Father passed away, within fifteen months of each other, as it happened, Mother was adamant that no cut flowers were to be left on their graves. "So untidy. So common." But that was Mother. Cecily does not share the same qualms and, every week, brings fresh flowers, seasonal fruits, berries, something from the garden, a piece of Christmas cake, a daisy chain – anything. After all, Henry had given her so much in her life that this small pile of grave goods could only be just that, very small in comparison.

It was Tilly, who once said, "I've given Daddy a boiled sweet," that gave her the idea. Cecily had looked at her askance.

"How? What do you mean? Daddy's not likely to fancy a boiled sweet now."

"No. I've pushed it into the earth, so Mother can't see it. Well, I know she can't actually see anything now, but you know what I mean."

The youngest, always outwardly obedient, Tilly relished these small gestures of rebellion. "Come, I'll show you."

Tilly bent and showed Cecily a small removable square of grass. She lifted it and beneath, in various degrees of decay and stickiness, were Nuttal's Mintoes, Glacier Mints and Travel Sweets. "Mother was almost as adamant about the perils of sweets as she was about the vulgarity of floral offerings, so it's mine and Daddy's little secret."

Cecily laughed at Tilly's childish glee, her irrepressible spirit bubbling to the fore.

Cecily looked to Tilly to show her a more playful, less literal way. She envied her youngest sister for her imagination.

Henry loved this about her. Her solemnity. Her passive face while awaiting direction and instruction. Her wide-eyed cat's stare. "You are such the eldest daughter. It's as if you line up to offer your shoulders for the next burden, your back for its strength, your arms for the next load."

So she brings little offerings to Henry. And she tidies them away again before they blow into Treasured Memories of a Dear Nan, or Zenobiusz Chojnowski, or Toby Cobain, infant son, whose company Henry keeps.

She has made peace with Henry's going, in a just-in-the-next-room sort of a way. She has made peace with her parents shuffling off – just. There is just a sense of emptiness now. The sadness has drained out of her, taking much with it, but still leaving some air, some room for a breeze to blow. As honoured and exalted a role as being Henry's widow is, is it enough?

Here she is, standing in the graveyard, while the dying stars move over her head and the dead slumber at her feet. Life, it seems, is everywhere else, but here.

Mandy

Oh, she had the power to disappoint all right. As she soon found out.

No such thing as consensual in Jerry's mind. A man's right, it was. A man's right to help himself whenever and, in the end, wherever he wanted. She should have known. She should never have made that phone call the following Tuesday. Would have saved her a lot of grief and her savings.

But phone she did. Pretended that she'd dialled his number by accident. Pretended for a moment that she couldn't quite recall anyone called Jerry. Alarm bells should have gone off then, when he obviously couldn't remember who she was. "You know, you stopped and asked me the way to Britannia Street."

"Lots of streets called Britannia Street, love. Give us another clue."

"Er…" She hesitated to remind him of her drunken wobble over the farm gate, her desperate need to relieve herself.

"Come on, love, give us a clue. Oh, I know, you the lassie at the chip shop?"

"No."

"Oh, hang on. I've got you," and he asked her if she managed to get the car home.

"No. No. No. Forget it!"

"Wait a minute, sweetheart. Only joking. How are you, anyway? Everything alright?"

He'd kept her on the line. Asked her general questions. Had she really sensed a sudden disappointment in his voice when he finally realised who she was? Or was it just her bitter imagination?

"So, how are you, Jerry?"

"Yeah. Really busy, like. Never know where I am from one day to the next, you know."

"You said you might be coming through this way day after tomorrow."

"Did I?"

"Yes. You did."

The line went quiet.

"Jerry?"

"Yes, hello, love. Still here."

"You did."

"Oh, right. Yes, the thing is, see, my rota has changed. Only just found out. Would have let you know. Can't make it. Sorry, love. See you around. OK?"

"OK. Bye."

And it might have been alright. Things might have turned out very differently. OK, so she was down for a couple of days. Maxed out on the crisps and cider. Missed Mum even more. Tore off a few more strips of wallpaper from the back bedroom. Cried to a George Clooney film.

God knows, she'd been there before. She knew the routine. When the sun came up on a new day, suddenly she was no longer such an attractive prospect. By the time the Alka Seltzer had left its chalky residue on the glass, she'd become a skin-of-your-teeth escape, a tale worth telling the lads at the bar. She'd seen what the lads in the post room said about her on Facebook.

Why did she even bother?

Why didn't she leave well alone?

The list of contacts in her phone flattered her. She never deleted anyone. They were all hopefuls once. They were all might-have-beens once. Who knows?

So she got the fright of her life when her phone went off in work about two months later. Tentatively she answered it. Technically they weren't supposed to have phones at their desk, but everyone did. She caught a glimpse of Sandra in the cubicle opposite. She was listening, but pretending not to. She must have emailed Gladys and Elaine and all the rest, because when she put the phone down, they were all looking at her. Silent.

"What?"

"Who you talking to?"

"No one."

"So, you're meeting 'no one' at eight tonight, are you?"

"Never you mind." She pretended to go back to work but the nudges and winks and silent looks rained down about her like sackfuls of rose petals.

They'd arranged to meet at The Engineers. Not her first choice of pub, being as it was the wrong side of town and a bit of a dive. Finally he turned up at quarter to nine. She'd had three ciders by then and they were curdling in her stomach. A better woman would have gone long ago, she knew that. A coarser woman would have waited for him and slapped his face before leaving, she knew that too. A more confident woman would not have been there in the first place. But she was none of those things.

She'd waited quietly, hopefully, demurely, and it was a smiling face she turned towards him when he eventually approached her table.

"Alright, love? What you drinking?"

He offered no apology or explanation for being late.

He'd turned to the bar before she had chance to ask for another cider. His return was less direct. He downed a pint and then asked the barman for a second. While it was being poured, he disappeared into the gents, stopping at the slot machine in the corridor before collecting his second drink. Is this how people behave? she asked herself. What should I do? Stay? Go? Is this right? I don't know. I don't know. I don't know.

Jerry straddled the stool the opposite side of the table.

"Looking very nice, love."

"Ta."

Voices were chattering away inside her head. She couldn't think straight. Grace at work had told her to lean forward, focus on his mouth when he spoke. Eileen had said to do no such thing. He'll come on to you quick enough without any encouragement. Mum. What would Mum say to do? God, she missed Mum.

"Not very talkative, are you?"

"Er, no."

Jerry leaned an elbow on his knee and peered behind him around the bar.

"Bit of a dump this place. Why did you say to meet here?"

"I didn't. You did!"

"Oh, did I? Forgot."

She looked at his face in profile as he continued his rake of the public bar. Obviously nothing like George Clooney. More like the fat one in the comedy pair you used to see at Christmas on the TV variety show. He obviously hadn't spent two hours getting ready and half a day's wage getting a new frock and across town by taxi. But, he was there. Sitting in front of her. Exuding a masculine aura. Exuding something, at least.

"So, how have you been keeping? Been busy?"

Mandy nodded. "Yeah. Not bad. You?"

He didn't seem to hear her. Her question fell on the table midway between them. In fact, he was starting to look annoyed, bored.

Quick, quick. She must think of something to say, something that will get his attention back.

"What football team do you support? We used to live in Woolwich so I used to support Arsenal. I don't go so often now. My dad's from Bolton, so he used to take us there when we were kids, but it got a bit violent in the seventies, so we stopped. Do you remember those funny score draws on TV on a Saturday afternoon? God they were boring weren't they. Like, who would bother, ha ha. Have you been anywhere nice for your holidays? Not been anywhere myself. Can't really afford it. Went to Scarborough with my mum just before she died. My mum died, you know. Cancer. Dreadful it was. And sudden. Much quicker than you would expect. So I live on my own now. In the flat we had. Mum's room's just like it was. Haven't managed to clear it. Expect I'll get round to it some time."

He was looking at her mouth. As if each word were a pebble falling from her lips. As if she were sitting there with a pile of stones in her lap, weighted to her seat, unable to move. The more he looked the more the pile increased. Words. Words. Words. None that he wanted to hear. None that flattered him. Or flattered her. Just a stream of words. Because, after all, when did someone last sit opposite her? Nice Dr Hattersley had, but there was a big sign behind his head that said that every appointment was limited to one patient, for ten minutes, and one medical issue only. Well, how can that be? When life was so difficult? And how do you say what your *one* problem is when it's all one big problem with about a thousand opposable and independent, uncontrollable legs of its own?

"I'm sorry. I'm sorry." Mandy stood up and shuffled out from behind the table.

Jerry stared into his drink. He made no move to stop her. He didn't grab her wrist. He didn't sit her down. He didn't find a tissue and get her a nice rum and pep. He didn't put his arm round her and take her out into the fresh air. He just sat and stared into his drink while she sidled away.

So, that made it all wrong then. It wasn't Jerry who called her perfume Hartlepool Nights. Because she never saw him again. So, who was it? And who had stolen her money?

Cecily

A car door slams and a shriek zigzags through the air. Someone has slipped, lost their footing. The sound briefly recalls to Cecily's mind the events of the previous night. Everyone knows Ned has a time of it. Nobody knows why he sticks with Mandy. Is it old-fashioned integrity? Cowardice, perhaps? Probably not. He just seems a great guy. It doesn't seem fair somehow that promiscuity, jealousy, neuroses aren't barriers to holding on to a true and constant husband.

Mandy

At last Ned comes out of the bathroom. He leaves the light on and the door open. "Bathroom's free."

"Evidently." Mandy makes her uneven way to the light.

"Don't be like that."

The perfume bottle sits heavily in her hand, its contents darkened and sour like a truck driver's piss thrown from the cab in a plastic bottle into the gutter. The stopper is rimed and crystallised and won't go back in.

She hitches her pyjama shirt to sit.

"Close the bloody door, can't you."

She kicks the door shut and lobs the bottle into the wicker basket, the last few precious, heavy, greasy droplets spilling onto the floor.

Ned. Ned. After all, he had done the decent thing. Funny old-fashioned Ned. Who thought that it was a fair and honourable exchange. A woman's virtue for a man's protection. A fuck for food, basically. She'd never seen ecstasy like it. His face. It was written all over his face.

If only Ned could have been her first, like she was his first. They might have had a chance then.

He's dressed and leaving the bedroom. "Come and lie with me, love."

He turns and looks disdainfully in her direction.

"Please. Just for a few minutes. Need a cuddle."

He sighs but approaches, balancing on his right side close to the edge of the mattress. She tucks in behind him and gazes at the short hairs on the back of his head lifted by the collar of his clean shirt. She runs her finger over the sharp cut ends. They feel like Mum's false lashes.

3

Marcus

Finally, at half past four on the Wednesday afternoon, the two burly men from Reno's Removals take the last box out of their high-sided van and plonk it in the hallway.

"Nice work, lads," Marcus nods, reaching into his back pocket for his wallet. Velda had already, in her efficiency, paid the removal company's invoice, even before the move, as if to make absolutely certain that they would turn up this morning and remove this loathsome creature and his pathetic belongings from out of her sight.

The sight of a wallet, like a plate of steaming food arriving at the table, seems to magnetise the two men, who stand and stare into it. Marcus instantly regrets the thick wad of notes folded within the confines of the leather for making it look as if he has double the amount he really has. Secondly, they might think it worthwhile mugging him. After all, who knows he is here? Only one monumentally disaffected soon-to-be ex-wife and his old drinking chums from The Ambassadors. Not exactly enough to form a guard of honour, were he to be found, skull stoved in amongst this stash of unpacked boxes and in need of a hasty burial.

A sharp memory comes to Marcus of the way Velda used to mime what she called Marcus's 'forays' into his wallet, shaking her hands in the air and blowing on her fingertips as if the thing had a protective heat shield around it. 'Very funny,' he almost says aloud. Maybe he *had* said it aloud as the two fellows look rather askance at him.

"Yes. Nice work. Appreciate everything you've done. Here's a fiver." He registers their rather disappointed looks as he rifles through notes of a much larger denomination. Oh, alright, he concedes. "Each." There was a slight lifting of their shoulders, but really not much.

Well, for goodness' sake, Marcus exclaims in his head. The journey along the A304 had been perilous enough. The black oil from the van's exhaust had nearly asphyxiated him the eighty miles from London. There had been moments when he had feared for his life's possessions; only one hefty gust of wind off the fenlands would have been sufficient to topple the flimsy conveyance over, his belongings skittering down the road and into the ditches before you could even say *uważać, uwaga!* Watch out!

The burly chaps depart, leaving a pall of thick black smoke in the market square, a trail of cigarette butts between the pavement and his new front door, and grubby coffee cups lined up, helpfully, on the telephone stand in the hallway.

Marcus stands for a moment. For the first time in a very, very long time, he is surrounded by peace and quiet. Everything is stock still. Where to start? Does he really want to unpack? After all, what would he find? Over the past few days Velda had in a single act of unselfishness (or was it really selfishness?) boxed up all that she could find that was, undisputably, his. His World of Warhammer magazines. His boxed sets of rock anthems. His schoolboy football trophies. His history books. Other things, ownership a bit more vague and uncertain, were squabbled over and treated a little less roughly.

They'd bought a Clarice Cliff lookalike jug and sugar bowl in Hebden Bridge, in happier days. It had come to represent no-man's land. Neither wanted it but neither could really understand why the other wanted it. Even on their very last evening together, they spoke between gritted teeth. "Not very macho, is it?" Velda scorned. He turned the pieces over in his hands. "I just like them, that's all."

"Yes, but *why?*"

"I don't know. Just do. You've got the…" and he waved his hand airily towards the china cabinet. "Set…thing…you know…your mother's."

"The 'set, thing', as you so rightfully call it, that is now significantly reduced in value since you knocked the handles off two cups and chipped a saucer."

"That was Christmas, and if you'd not been so bloody insistent that I do the washing up, then it wouldn't have happened."

"As usual, it's always somebody else's fault, never your own."

"Oh, blow this, I'm going out."

"Run away – as usual." she'd shouted to his retreating back.

So, that hadn't gone too well. He would be mildly intrigued to find out, when he got round to unpacking, who had won that particular spat. He had gone out, as threatened, but, he had to concede, probably not much missed, and come back six hours later, cold, wet and pissed, to find a bastion of cardboard boxes in the garage awaiting collection early the next morning. Despite the acid beer and the high emotion, he had allowed himself a momentary spasm of guilt at the thought of Velda heaving and groaning as she dragged the boxes from the hallway to the garage. He was being expelled like the contents of a pustule. He had wanted to acknowledge her huge effort but, as usual, it came out wrong.

"Good on you, Velda dearest!" She had given him a poisoned look that suggested any further sarcasm on his part would likely end very badly. He took the hint. "Night. Wifey!" He watched as she climbed the stairs wondering if, even if just for old times' sake, there might be some point him climbing the stairs too. No encouragement was given, so he turned resignedly on the bottom step and made for the front sitting room and the lumpy camp bed, for the last time.

What a strange feeling it had been when he had finally awoken to the fact that the house he had called home for the last twenty-two years was no longer to be his refuge. The woman he had called his wife for the past twenty-seven years no longer felt herself to have any duty of care for him. The children, Martha and Paul, both in uni, what did they think of him exactly? Had he become, in their eyes, the silly old duffer that Velda thought him to be? The old geezer who merely came along, usually reluctantly, to carry the coats and pick up the tab?

"Yeah, awesome," he'd said to Barry down at the pub when he told him he was moving out of London and to East Anglia. "Going to start again. Fresh start. A new life, all on my own. All on my own," he repeated, as if to numb the shock. Put like that, it didn't sound too bad. But on the long, wobbly walk home, it began to feel a bit different. His head began to fill with a plethora of practical problems. Where does one buy a microwave from? He was vaguely aware that bachelor chappies lived off boiled eggs and beans on toast but even that seemed a most complicated operation. Didn't you have to prick the egg with a needle stuck in a cork that was kept in a small lidded tin in the utensils drawer in the kitchen? At least that's what Velda did. But which end? And where would you get a needle in a cork? A small lidded tin? A utensil drawer?

He was being shipwrecked, finding himself on a remote beach with a few scattered, unrelated possessions that were meant to keep him alive, clean, safe, sane and fed by dint of sheer resourcefulness and a will to live.

So, why this village and not somewhere rented just round the corner where he could keep an eye on Velda and the comings and goings of their student offspring?

Good question and one, typically, that he could not answer that precisely. "Not too good at direct questions," Velda used to say of him, even to his ageing parents, as if he were some kind of foster placement that had arrived on her sofa, carting with him all the ills of his dysfunctional upbringing. "You have to wait, until he's ready to speak." Which is why arguments were never very successful as each witty retort took time, each cutting riposte needed fashioning to be economical yet incisive. But, usually, by the time his response had been delivered, slowly and articulately so that no nuance could be missed, the moment had passed and Velda had moved on to vehemently chopping carrots or flicking the pages of a magazine.

So now the removal men have gone and the mess is all his own. Boxes teeter on top of boxes. Muddled items spill out of split and broken containers.

It will take him a little while, he supposes, to get used to living on his own again. Not only that, but living without Velda, who has been a constant in his life for almost half his life, certainly more than half of his adult life.

She'd actually looked a bit tearful as she stood at the front door. "Right, I'll be off then." He'd expected less, maybe that she would 'go shopping', or have the tribe round to shout derogatory remarks over their shoulders from the living room as he struggled out of the house with the last of his few possessions. A weighty tear trembled in the corner of her eye, about to reach its critical mass. He felt inclined to offer his handkerchief but decided against the gesture. They gave each other a short arm hug. "Take care of yourself then." The removal van was waiting on the road, the air around filling with an acrid smoke. "Just hope we get there in one piece," he joked. Velda nodded, a half-smile appearing on her face. The tear nodded too. "Maybe we could email, or something?" Velda nodded again, silently. Marcus bent in and placed a kiss on her powdered cheek and allowed himself the briefest moment to breathe in her oh-so-familiar smell.

Velda followed him to the car and stood, eyes downcast, as he reversed it out of the drive. She closed the gate behind him; he tooted the horn and gave her a cheery wave. "For goodness' sake, Velda, buck up old girl. You wanted it this way. What you looking so upset for?" He spoke aloud, as he would catch himself doing many times, her presence and familiarity a hard habit to break. He glimpsed in the rearview mirror for a last sight of Belvedere Road, NW11.

Not much given to introspection, that was more Velda's sort of thing, he did allow himself a cursory check of his emotions as he pulled out behind the van in a break in traffic. Not much to say really, he thought to himself. Funny thing, life, perhaps best summed it up.

Now, he is feeling becalmed. Gone is the passion and heat of their rows. Gone is the simmering resentment that could just as quickly return to fizzing insult. Gone is the occasional fire of reconciliation. Looking around him, goodness knows, he could do with some of that energy for the task ahead of unpacking and stowing his belongings.

Marcus wanders from room to room. He'd been lucky to get this flat, or apartment, so the estate agent, Jeremy, had told him. He'd asked Velda if she wanted to view it with him. She'd declined. He drove there and back in a day and agreed to rent it there and then. All at a very reasonable price too, if the emollient man was to be believed. A lot of interest from London these days, what with the commuter trains and all. Then he'd pulled himself up short, a little voice in his animated head obviously reminding him that Marcus *was* from London and commanded the hefty sort of salary that humble estate agents in the fens could only dream of. "Will you be carrying on working in town at all, sir?" the little creep had asked, over-playing the diminutive 'town'. Marcus had evaded the question, replying, "Well, you know, who's to say?" Jeremy had nodded emphatically and sagely.

Truth is, Marcus doesn't know what he is going to do. It is all going to take a bit of getting used to.

"Tea!" he announces to the cooling air, glad to have some purpose, even if only for the next five minutes while he makes a brew.

Except the five minutes turns into ten and then into thirty while he hunts for the necessaries. "Bloody woman, you'd think she'd have organised it all a bit better," he grumbles as he searches for a box that might, helpfully, have the ticket 'Tea Making Things' or some such. "Bitch!" he mutters as he upturns box after box in search of a kettle, or a saucepan even.

Where his meagre possessions had been corralled into random pick-and-mix boxes, set hither and thither by the since departed removal men, now they are scattered and smeared throughout most of his new living quarters.

It is obvious that the heartless woman is going to deny him even the smallest comfort of a cup of tea. Bloody serves her right that he's left her for a new and better life. She can jolly well go and stew in her own loneliness.

Blood warmed, heart pumped, Marcus snatches his jacket from where it had landed on a standard lamp, and slams the front door behind him.

"Good afternoon."

Marcus is somewhat surprised when the lady behind the counter in the post office extends her arm over the gaudy chocolate bars towards him. He tentatively slides his hand into hers and wobbles her wings.

"Madge."

"Hello, Madge. Marcus Blatt."

"Hello, Marcus. Welcome to Bullenden. Saw you moving in. Am sure you will settle in; we're all quite friendly." Madge laughs such that the rollers under her gauze headscarf rattle and skitter. "Aren't we, Doreen? Friendly. Just telling Marcus here, we're fri-end-ly," the syllables extended to allow the person working behind the scenes to hear. A voice muffled by some distance and, Marcus assumes, walls lagged with stock, replies, "Yep."

"What can I get you, Marcus?"

"Er. I'm looking for a box of tea, pint of milk, sugar, saucepan and a couple of mugs."

"Cup of tea you're after, is it?"

"Yes, you could say that."

"Dor-eeeen. Put the kettle on, Dor-eeen. Make Mar-cus a cup of tea."

"No, please, I really don't want to be any bother."

"It's no bother."

"No, really, I've got a mountain of unpacking to do and I really ought to make a start. Very kind of you though."

Madge is clearly disappointed but moves round the shelves, placing Marcus's items on the counter, perhaps slightly more emphatically than strictly necessary, one by one, naming them as she goes. "Sugar...tea... milk...There you are, sir."

Marcus notes that he has been demoted to 'sir' again rather than 'Marcus' and wonders, briefly, if he has infringed an unwritten but vital code by refusing tea with the Post Mistress. He pays for and amasses his dented packages and leaves the shop.

Not being offered a bag, and not thinking to ask for one, Marcus drops both the milk and sugar almost as soon as he steps out of the vaguely quaint and disorganised shop and into the gathering dusk. A painful but controlled stoop retrieves the items from the pavement and, ignoring the twinge in his right hip, he resumes his short walk home, uncomfortably aware that his undignified passage is not going unobserved. Balancing one knee against the front door upon which to stack his purchases in size order, he flaps his jacket pocket wildly, in search for the key which must surely be in there somewhere.

"Hells bells. I don't believe it!" The wretched keys are inside the poxy apartment. He's left them on the kitchen drainer. The first of a marriage's worth of lessons to unlearn. Velda isn't in. She hasn't gone out and left the key in its hiding place behind the Green Man. This is it. A man in charge of his own house key. Locked out on his first sortie. Triumph and humility mingle in his breast. He walks back to the post office.

"Dor-eeeen. Put the kettle on for Marcus, and get some of that lemon drizzle. We can have a good chat while we wait for Mr Edge to come and sort out the lock."

*

Marcus wakes in the grey light of dawn, his chin on his chest. His search for bedding last night had been a little more successful than his search for a kettle. The duvet he had found was only a lightweight single summer one, which he had supplemented by piling coats over his feet. These had slithered to the floor in the night, leaving his extremities blue and exposed. He groans as he elbows himself to a seated position. An urgent leavening of his bladder reminds him of the countless cups of tea forced on him by the doughty Madge of the post office. He walks the crooked few yards to the downstairs toilet, rebelliously leaving the door open and whistling while he relieves himself, watching the yellow stream with some satisfaction, finishing with a flourish. Be damned if he's going to flush and put the seat down. It's my toilet. My life!

"This is Marcus Blot. Moved into old Mrs Fawcett's place. Artist, he is." So had he been introduced to a succession of shoppers the previous afternoon.

"Actually, it's Blatt, and I'm retired. Never picked up a paintbrush in my life." He'd tired of these minor corrections to his biography after the fifth telling and resigned himself to sitting out the afternoon on a wooden school chair, balancing an institutional green cup and saucer on one knee and a crumbling yet, it had to be said, delicious cake in the other, rising awkwardly on each greeting to shake hands with an assortment of young and old, men, women, children and, on one occasion, a dog's paw, longing for Mr Edge, the locksmith, to return from town.

It is going to be a monumental game of Happy Families trying to reconcile each face, name, history, genealogy, medical record, misdemeanour on further meeting.

But that is for another time. Jobs for today include, lighting the boiler, unpacking, driving into Aylston to buy provisions and, if there is time after all this, popping into The Red over the road to check out their guest ales before lunch. Oh, and get some keys cut so that he wouldn't be caught out again like yesterday.

It had been dark by the time Mr Edge had returned from his mission up country. Marcus hadn't quite seen what he'd done to open the door, but it had taken mere seconds.

41

"There you go, Mr Blot. No, no, have it on me," he'd said as Marcus made an elaborate show of reaching for his back pocket, as if to say, *Let me pay you for your services, my good fellow.* "I'm sure you'll give me a call if you need me again."

"Yes, of course. Without hesitation. Thank you. Goodnight."

Marcus had closed the front door behind him and, too tired for supper, made his rudimentary bed and fallen into a deep but disturbed slumber.

Now, it is time for breakfast. He'd seen a box marked 'Kitchen: Cooking Apparatus' somewhere. After a brief search, he finds it in the back bedroom. Stupid bloody place to put it. The four flaps release their hold on each other as he pulls. Ah. Marvellous. Inside, a frying pan, kettle, mugs, cutlery and, inexplicably, a pasta maker. Well, who knows? Maybe he has reached a time in his life when he could try his hand at making pasta.

He carries his trophies to the kitchen before it dawns on him to question why he couldn't have found these tea-making things yesterday and saved himself an awful lot of bother, sitting around making small talk to half the village and their dog. Never mind, all is well now. Time for a celebratory cuppa.

Sugar. Sugar. Sugar, he mutters to himself, spinning round looking. Tea? Last night's lock-out flashes into his mind, together with a memory of where he had stowed his provisions before finding himself at Mr Edge's mercy. He shakes the kettle, another marital habit, checking for water. Of course there won't be any. Why would there be? He'll put the kettle on and then go and retrieve yesterday's purchases. From the flower box outside.

Placing the kettle under the tap, he turns the handle. Nothing. He tries the hot tap. Still nothing. What the blazes is going on? Possibly the water had been turned off. Isn't that what people do when they vacate a house? He rummages inside his memory to think back to what Velda might have done prior to their annual summer sojourn to Shell Island. A vague recollection of her half submerged under the sink comes back to him. Stop tap. That's what he's looking for. Stop tap. Nothing to it!

Marcus kneels slowly and stiffly onto the cold kitchen floor, bracing himself on the swinging cabinet doors to help his descent. Apart from the serpentine plumbing under the sink and a grimy swan's neck watering can, there is nothing. No tap of any description. He shuffles to the cabinets either side. Still nothing. What in the name of Moses is going on? Shouldn't places come with some sort of instruction manual?

"Velda!" he futilely shouts over his shoulder.

After a series of grunts and heaves, he articulates himself upright again. "Blast. Blast. Blast and blast!" He ponders his options, nursing his fist, having banged it on the counter top with each outburst. His options are severely limited. Severely limited to one. There is only one thing for it.

Madge would not dream of letting Marcus go back to his cold, empty house. She will call Mr Edge the plumber, and then Marcus is to sit down here and have a nice cup of tea while he waits. It had been so nice yesterday to have somebody new to chat to and there is still so much to tell him.

Marcus sits reluctantly on the chair, silently willing the multi-talented Mr Edge to please hurry up. It is a skill honed over twenty-seven years with the venerable Velda that he is able to give the impression of listening, actively if required, to every word while only really scanning every utterance for its kernel of meaning and responding appropriately. So while he eyes the Mars bars hungrily, sips weak tea and longs for a long hot bath to soothe his aching joints and muscles, he gives every impression of listening politely and attentively.

Customers come and go, greeting him like an old friend. They know his name so obviously expect him to know theirs. His hand of Happy Families cards resembles more a game of Pick Up Sticks.

Finally, around eleven thirty, the door clangs open to admit the one person Marcus could recognise as a familiar and welcome friend, Mr Edge. Hurrah!

"Can't find the stop tap," he responds rather sheepishly to Mr Edge's enquiry. "Wonder if you wouldn't mind coming round and, you know, just, you know..." Marcus waves his arms vaguely in their air. "You know."

"Sure thing, matey. No problem at all."

The two men walk together down the pavement. Mr Edge's van is already parked outside.

The bag of sugar is still in the window box, but it has been invaded by a pair of slugs. The box of tea looks intact. Not that Marcus could face another cup right at this very minute.

Mr Edge stands in the hall, as if planning a route through the strewn debris. "Sorry, it's all a bit of a mess."

Mr Edge nods, as if disinclined to dispute that point. "Right then, matey. I'll get the water on for you. Expect you'd like me to take a look at the boiler and get that started for you too." Marcus nods mutely. "I'll take a look at the radiators. They've probably not been bled in a while. Might not be a bad idea if I check the gutters and downpipes. Rain's on its way. Anything else you want me to look at?"

Marcus shakes his head, shrugs and sweeps his arm in an arc as if to say, *Do it all. Matey.*

The afternoon passes pleasantly enough. It is nice to have some company in the place. While Mr Edge heaves his tool box from room to room, leaving rusty puddles and scrunched-up flannels, spanners, ladders, things that go bleep, drills and footprints wherever he goes, the flat gradually comes to life.

Marcus wanders aimlessly from room to room, looking for a place for his glass chess set, his guitar, his weights. Welcome sounds independently percolate their way to him – the rush of water into the stainless-steel kitchen sink, the gurgle and tick of warming radiators, the whistle of the gas jet in the grill. He can hear Mr Edge calling out to him.

"Sorry, what was that?"

"You can get a half-decent bacon and cheese panini from the mini mart in the garage, you know." Marcus is about to thank Mr Edge for this piece of local knowledge, when the penny drops.

"Oh, OK. Want anything else with it?" For gratitude is spreading, unusually, into generosity.

"Wouldn't mind a flapjack or something like it."

"OK. Be right back, then."

"And a Coke? Maybe?"

Marcus flees the house, before the list grows any longer. Sheepishly, he skulks the long way round the square, lest Madge the Post Mistress should spot him and call him in to finish her tale regarding the late

Mr Duckett's half-niece by his first marriage to the nervy Sandra Jones who went backpacking to Thailand and wasn't seen for half a year... He groans inwardly at the thought of this endlessly complicated, cat's cradle of a community, wondering whether he too would wander into its labyrinthine centre and never be seen again or whether it would bounce him, reject him like a sickly, undernourished fledgling.

Nourishment. Food. An angry roar from his stomach reminds him that, in fact, he hasn't eaten since yesterday afternoon and that was nothing of real substance. He looks in at the deli's windows, wondering how a village of this size could support an establishment selling frangipanes and macaroons and, oh, how wonderful, his favourite, giant coffee profiteroles with crème anglaise. He puts these musings to one side while he enters the sweetly scented shop. No, it isn't just a shop. It is heaven. Wholemeal bread. Cheese rolls. Roasted vegetable tarts. Black pepper scones. Mrs Somebody's homemade jam. Piccalilli. Sliced ham with that lovely yellow breadcrumbed edge to creamy white fat. Oh bliss. After a stressful and taxing couple of days, he knows, he just knows deep down in the pit of his stomach, that everything is going to come right. This whole independent living thing isn't going to be too hard after all.

And, as if that wasn't enough, the nice girl behind the counter with two long black plaits, who reminded him a bit of Martha, as she had been in the sixth form, before she went off to uni and came back all weird, didn't seem inclined to engage him in any conversation beyond what was strictly necessary in the transaction, the exchange of a few delicious items for himself and the hard-working Mr Edge and something for tonight, for money.

Buoyed by his discovery and the prospect of some delicious savoury food, delighted that it required no more effort than to descend his stairs, turn right into the alley and right again into the market square and sharp right into the recessed, tiled entry of the food emporium below his flat, Marcus walks painfully straight into the closed and irrefutably locked front door of his flat. He hammers on the door to alert Mr Edge to his plight, checking his first instinct to call out for Velda. An improvement, at least.

The two men munch their lunch in silence. Satisfaction made all the sweeter by being swilled down by a pot of freshly brewed and mercifully wildlife-free tea.

Dusk falls on Marcus's first full day in his new house. Their paths cross and recross as Mr Edge sees to the plumbing and other maintenance jobs and Marcus replaces items for which there is no obvious home back into boxes, promising himself that he would get round to sorting them out. "You don't do shelves do you, by any chance?"

"Yes, sure, mate. Just let me know where you want them."

Goodness knows why Velda got her knickers in such a twist about things around the house. It is easy. You just have to know the right people to ask.

"More tea?"

"Wouldn't say no."

Marcus stands in his kitchen, his back to the sink, waiting for the kettle to boil, full of the simple pleasure of making a cup of tea. A feeling of happiness spreads through him like an ink stain. An almost animal affection towards Mr Edge moves him. Perhaps he should go to the post office for custard creams to go with his tea. No. Emphatically not. Mr Edge, after all, is just doing his job. Wouldn't do to get too pally, would it?

Mr Edge works into the evening, Marcus beginning to feel a little concerned that he might have to offer him some of the scrumptious Quiche Lorraine and Pinot that he'd earmarked for supper time. Mercifully, by eight o'clock, Edge is packing up his various boxes of kit.

He has to hand it to him. He had made a massive difference to the flat, short of actually unpacking that is. Every corner is warm. Hot water billows on demand out of the tap. He'd even added a hook by the front door, "For the purpose of hanging your keys. Mate."

Mr Edge puts his tools and equipment back in the van and hovers at the doorway. He sniffs the air. "Funny smell, mate. Can't quite put my finger on it."

"Oh, I expect it's alright. For another day, eh?" as Marcus sidles towards the lavatory door and closes it.

"Right, well, I'll be off then."

"OK. Fantastic job. Really pleased."

"Right, I'll be off."

So, off you go then, Marcus internally prompts him, already priming himself for a quiet spot of supper beside the log-burner-lookalike gas fire in the sitting room, savouring the hopefully chilled, slightly acidic wine. Be gone.

But Mr Edge seems disinclined to move from the doorstep.

"Er…"

"Yes?"

"That'll be…"

Oh, Christ. The fellow wants paying. Marcus's arm reaches round to his back pocket. Couldn't the man just send him a bill or something?

Mr Edge's price brings a look of horror on Marcus's face. "It's the going rate. Mate."

The sense of bonhomie drains fast from Marcus's soul.

"Oh, very well."

Having counted out a large wad of notes into Mr Edge's hand, Marcus closes the door behind him. To the sound of Mr Edge's van spluttering its way into the night, Marcus pushes open the door to the downstairs loo, lowers the seat and pulls the chain. *Pace Velda.*

Pouring a large tumbler of wine and taking the quiche into the sitting room with him, ready to eat straight from the paper wrapper, he sinks into a dusty armchair and falls slowly to the ground as the overtaxed webbing declines to hold his weight.

SPRING

Another millennium has ticked over and we are in the territory of the Civitas. Land clearance is now the engine of the marching army. Two thousand miles of stone and flint and gravel criss-cross Provincia Britannia linking the Saxon shore forts to the far-flung north.

The Roman town founded at the confluence of the river and two roads, within a matter of less than ten generations, sinks lower and lower into obscurity. The hearths, the graves, the smelting ovens, the quarries, the latrines, the kilns, the animal pens, ditches all stuffed and muted by mounds of earth.

And so sights are lowered; ambition reaches no more than two or three fields ahead. Wilderness trees, beech, oak, ash, birch take root among the tumbling walls; ploughs crosshatch arterial roads; a leafy canopy draws over an abandoned site; coins become baser, corrupted, post-Apocalyptic.

M. Blatt

4

Marcus

It is now a few weeks since Marcus moved to Bullenden. Is it seven? Ten? Who's counting. All is coming along splendidly. Mr Edge returned to shelve out the alcoves. Most of the boxes are unpacked. Most of his possessions have settled in their allotted places although there is still no sign of the Clarice Cliff set that they'd argued so fulsomely over on their last night together. He has grown accustomed to cooking for himself – or at least reheating for himself. The days are lengthening and he can almost feel himself lengthening as recent cares and worries lift from his shoulders.

It is a relief that the rather forceful Madge is not on duty today. Instead he is served by a hangdog-looking chap whose eyes do not rise above the level of his hand, outstretched to receive Marcus's coin.

It had been an interesting walk. He wouldn't mind betting that not everyone in Bullenden is aware that the raised pavement that runs for several hundred yards from the river meadow in through the northern boundary of the village was gifted by a local goodwoman and benefactor to allow churchgoers to attend Mass without getting their pattens wet. He had been about to offer this fascinating piece of information to a young woman gingerly descending a buggy's back wheels down the sheer face of the granite edging tiles but something about the grim set of her face had deterred him. Obviously significant was the observation that the pavement widened and the road narrowed somewhat as they approached the church, thus allowing drovers and traders opportunity to slow down and offer obeisance to the Almighty as good business practice demanded.

Perhaps this would be a good topic to offer up to the local History Society. He could offer them a short presentation on – well, all sorts of topics really. The Viking village. East Anglian watermills and fish ponds. Monastic land clearance. The view from the back lanes. Local brick kilns. Prehistoric tracks to turnpikes. If anybody is interested, that is.

Maybe this is why he has settled in Bullenden. This sense that he can look around him and gain glimpses, paraphrasing Hoskins, of the last ten centuries in 100 acres. But really, man-made history reaches back much further than just 1000 years. For more than 6000 years it has been lurking just under the surface, waiting to break into the light of day. Still-sharp Neolithic adzes for working and smoothing wood shoulder their way to the surface. Pea-size shapes of porous ore, emptied of their lead content, tumble their way upwards from ruined Roman smelting works. Grassy banks split open in heavy rain to release the rubble of peasant farmsteads abandoned at scythe-point during the Black Death. So much that lies hidden beneath the accumulated layers of hummus and debris. The very thought thrills him. It occurs to him that the process of unpacking the discards of his marriage followed a similar process of rediscovery.

Among the surprising things that Velda had packed for him is an album she must have created, entitled, ironically enough, *Velda and Marcus, the Happy Years*. He'd found it in amongst 'Towels, Miscellaneous' (not the best ones, he noted, but the ones he remembered for their seventies rust, orange and mustard hues) and 'Cushion Covers, If Required', which hailed from the same optically- and chromatically-challenged era, their early married life.

He'd placed the album on the coffee table a while ago where it nestled under a growing pile of menus, receipts and old newspapers. Maybe he owes it to Velda to look through it. After all, it seems as if she had gone to some trouble. And, now, as time moves on, perhaps he could just bring himself to have a look. With a cup of coffee on the chair arm and his feet on the coffee table, he places the album on his knee and creaks open the pages.

The album moves forward chronologically, a page or two devoted to each decade. Him and Velda with the babies in their arms. In the park, throwing snowballs with the teenagers. Grandparents. Holidays and, more recently, the touring photographs. Given the haphazard way the photos are positioned on the page and the creased and crumpled nature of the protective plastic sheets Marcus guesses that the images had been chosen and slapped in place at one of her late-night sessions, legs tucked under the coffee table, the terrier on her lap, wine rings spreading over the table like ripples in a pond.

Those 'nights' of hers. Some of them solo, some of them with her chums from the Mindfulness Centre. He shudders as the memories come back to him.

A common theme on such nights was 'When I finally woke up and realised what had become of the man I married'. The sitting room would go quiet as all the tribe prepared to exercise their sisterly indignation. Sitting on the camp bed in the box room of the marital home, he could practically hear the bosoms within the kaftans gear up to heave in outrage.

"For pity's sake, Velda," he would moan to himself, head lowered, tapping his feet in isolation, boredom and imminent humiliation.

One night he actually shouted down, "Go on, Velda dearest. Tell them all our sordid little secrets. It's not just me, you know."

The sitting room door closed loudly on the sound of clucking and outrage within.

He would hear the cackling as Velda, building up to a crescendo, denied to him on that particular day, it had to be said, told the assembly of how she wandered into the garage, in all innocence, looking for a spanner.

"There I found him. Leaning against the wall. Bloody three o'clock in the afternoon. There he is…" and her voice would dip, as she mimed the scene.

So, on that particular sad day, he had wandered into the garage and, having forgotten what he had gone in for, his eyes fell upon the poster 'Melanie and her Honda CB400N Super Dream'. It had been on the wall of various properties he had lived in for the past thirty-five years, a fold-out from a magazine back when he had freedom of the road.

During their post-discovery recriminations he could offer no real explanation of what had come over him.

"What were you thinking of? What if someone had wandered in?"
"Well, they did. *You* did."

"Don't be so bloody facetious." It occurred to him to defend a man's right to euphemise in his own garage but knew that whatever defence he offered would wither under the effects of her scorn. As he, indeed, had at the time. "What did you think you were doing?"

"I'd have thought that was pretty obvious," was the best retort he could manage. He could offer no real explanation. Was it the poster? Was it pent-up desire? Was it, more likely, a simple need for comfort, the inner two-year-old putting their hand down their pants?

Even those who had heard Velda relate the story many times added to the gasps and ooohs. He could hear her voice pick up again. "Not only was he, you know…" Here she was evidently waggling a downcast index finger to indicate the unaccustomed state of freedom of his member, "But he was also…" Marcus flung himself back on his bed, knowing, just knowing that now Velda would be miming the action. "Noooooo," drifted up the stairs. "Yes!" she replied emphatically. "Although, perhaps I should say…" as she modified her actions to a much reduced length and girth. The cackles were positively fiendish.

As the coffee cools beside him and the redness of remembered shame leaves his cheeks Marcus turns the pages of the album, each one a new discovery, a returning memory. Along with the pleasant rediscoveries comes the thought that there wasn't just one single fissure that tore them asunder, it was more a crazed and cracked pattern that spread and multiplied till it undermined their entire foundations.

Some of the photos were taken outside their caravan, bought as a joint project.

"Be lovely. We can get out and about. Go places. See new things," Velda's tone largely persuading him that she had already made up her mind. "And you can take in a few of your beloved churches." So, lovely it was to be, then. For a few years, mostly once the children had grown up, they trundled around together. And in the way people ham it up for the camera, the shots in the album did show a moderately happy couple, larking about. Velda hanging upside down on a horizontal pole. Marcus with a white, frothy moustache and a pint of real ale in his hand. Only an insider could see the line of tension in Marcus's jaw, the look of sheer determination in Velda's furrowed brow.

He turns the pages one by one, a gathering sense of nostalgia and loss building in his chest. The sight of one photograph stops him. Nothing like being cooped up in a caravan on Whitstable sands on a blowy bank holiday for exposing the creaks and the cracks and the faults. He peers closely at the lopsided image. A figure in a blue windcheater walks crablike into the wind. A chip paper has flattened itself against the caravan wheel. He remembers sitting inside the caravan, powerless against the elemental forces outside.

"For pity's sake, Marcus." He adjusted his gaze slowly from the back window – onto which the rain was throwing salt and sand like buckets of gravel – to his wife.

"What?"

"You need to *do* something."

"About what?"

Velda drew breath and stretched out the fingers of one hand as if to enumerate the first five items at least of a comprehensive list.

"Well, there's the loo for a start. It stinks. Think it's backing up. And then there's the wind whistling through the window frame. You could patch it up."

Marcus turned his head in minute degrees to the source of the whistling sound. A green mould seemed to be insinuating itself under the glass and into the caravan. Maybe if he prevaricated for long enough, it would completely envelop the van. They would slowly suffocate and have to be chiselled out and put on display like the Pompeii people. Sludge Man and Gloop Woman caught in the final millennial moments of having a domestic meltdown.

"Are you listening? You're not listening, are you? Marcus!"

"I'm listening, my precious turtledove."

"Hmmm. And while you're at it, we need some more milk from the shop."

Marcus shrugged on his coat. Velda had already returned to her magazines, flicking the glossy pages with an irascible air. No cheery wave then. He turned up the collar of his coat against the raging wind and stepped outside. He could hear her rap on the window with her grotesque ring. Max, the ironically named Yorkshire terrier, yapped synchronistically. He ignored them both.

He returned half an hour later pulling the roller barrel full of water behind him and a tube of mastic sticking out from his coat pocket. Revived by the bracing air and the success of his shopping trip, Marcus stood at the caravan door to shake the raindrops off his coat. "Brass monkeys out there." He chattered on for a moment about the number of empty bays, the state of the tide, his surprise at finding a tube of mastic in the site shop.

"Did you get the milk?"

Velda closed her ears against the profanities that coloured the air blue and returned to her crossword puzzles while Marcus forced his arm back into a wet sleeve now stubbornly inside out. Striding back to the campsite shop, the bitter squalls outside matched the bitter squalls within his heart. A gull called out in the skies above. It seemed the most lonesome sound on the planet. It was singing just for him.

Milk purchased and the wrapper of a consolatory chocolate bar stuffed in an inside pocket, he returned to the van. Velda's head was tilted to one side, propped by a bent arm. She had fallen asleep against the window. Her face had slipped and he could see one eyeball skitter under an incompletely closed eyelid. He closed the door quietly and tenderly covered her and the mutt with a blanket.

For the last five years of their marriage, the caravan had stood on the drive, gradually acquiring a greenish hue, the tyres slowly deflating. One of the kids had drawn a Banksy-esque cartoon of the two of them in profile at the window, Velda's bouffant layers picked out in the dog's own pelt. He'd slept in it on occasion, mostly when returning home drunk and finding the front door locked and barred. It was always cold and damp and seemed to be a required sojourn in purgatory before he was allowed back in the house.

The arguments followed a well-worn groove, centred around defects in his personality, understanding and sensitivity, personal hygiene, ambition, DIY skills, drinking habits, ability to moderate his tone when angry and the volume on the hi-fi.

The thing is, he can't really find much to criticise Velda about. Okay, she isn't quite the girl he had married, but one might expect that after twenty-seven years. Youthful peachiness had turned to voluptuousness had turned to a bit of embonpoint which had turned to middle-aged spread and thence, admittedly, to hints of gargantuanism. If she is partial to one custard cream over the eight, well, for goodness' sake, let her. And if the old girl wants to dabble in a few interests – great! In the early years, it had been macramé. Twisted, knotted cords hung from every spare hook stuffed with motley plants, pasta packets, car keys. Yoga, Reiki, even paganism followed. Then animal rescue – that was a particularly taxing period, he would admit. Cages everywhere filled with small, furry, scurrying things as she made it known that she could provide a loving home to ferrets, weasels and stoats. Well, he could put up with that. No phase usually lasted more than a couple of years. Vegetarianism, veganism; he wouldn't mind if he never saw another sprouted mung bean again. But they lost weight, even if flatulence was then added to the list of his personal defects.

The process of emptying him out of the house completely started about two years ago. All the objects that are now stowed on Mr Edge's shelves, in the wardrobe and chest of drawers in his new bedroom, and those still in the box room, had begun their slow journey to this point all that time ago; a process, once started, seemingly impossible to halt. Maybe their irretrievable breakdown and subsequent divorce had been one of her 'projects' – how to declutter your life and rediscover your inner child. Decluttering began with transferring boxes of his possessions from the house to the caravan.

Subsequent to each argument and night spent in the cold, more and more boxes found their way to the caravan, stuffed unkindly in the kitchen cupboards, piled randomly in the grimy shower, left in haphazard order under the bench seats. Boxes of defunct telephones, music cassettes, penknives, matchbox cars, wizards...

At first, Marcus, once he had regained entry into the marital home, assumed the boxes had made their way into the caravan as a form of protest, a measure taken to make a point known and understood. Having fully taken on board the fact that he was personally defective and less than adequate as a husband and a constant disappointment, Marcus assumed that it would be perfectly in order to return said items to their rightful places in the house.

"Where are you going with that?"

"I'm putting it back."

"Back where?"

"Back in my office, where it's always been."

"You can't do that. I want to make your office into a snug."

"What for?"

"We need the space."

"Space? There's just the two of us in this house. What do we need more space for?"

"So that I can...*think of something.*"

"Why can't you do that in the living room?"

"It's just not...not...conducive."

"I'll give you conducive! These are staying put," Marcus insisted.

Any victory had only been short-lived. As time went on, he seemed to fall out of favour with greater speed and regularity. The caravan filled up with boxes which, even he had to admit, contained a lot of useless crap. He gradually lost the will to march them back up the drive and into the house, so allowed them to accumulate, the cardboard gradually softening in the damp air and folding in on itself.

Finally, the number of boxes in the caravan outnumbered Marcus's possessions in the house.

During those periods of awkward detente, his clothes still hung in the wardrobe, his shirts were still ironed for him, albeit with more of a slapdash lick than he'd been used to. A plate of food still appeared in front of him every evening, although the portions were less in his favour than they used to be. They'd long ago, laughingly, told the children that Dad sleeps in the small bedroom now because he snores like a rutting rhino. The small courtesies and politenesses were more often observed than not, such as two glasses accompanying a bottle of wine, a cup of tea, a collar tucked in. What else was a marriage built on? It's not as if one really expected the grand passion to survive two children now packed off to university, one redundancy, one prostate scare, thread veins, myopia and all the rest. What did the old girl want? Was he really that terrible a husband?

"This is bloody ridiculous," he'd said to Velda one bright spring morning. "I feel like I've got no place in my own home."

"Well, if you treat it like something between a hotel and pigsty, then maybe you haven't. Got a place. In this house." He looked at her while

60

marshalling his arguments. Something was different. She looked more…
more…striking. Was that the word? A flush rose to her cheeks under his
scrutiny. She lifted a hand to her face. That was it. Eyebrows.

"What have you done to your eyebrows?"

"Nothing."

"Yes you have. They look…" He searched for the word. Bigger?
Bushier? Brassier? She'd always had virtually non-existent eyebrows,
plucked to oblivion when such was the fashion. Now she looked as if
they'd been reseeded with Miracle Gro or reapplied with a marker pen.

"That is so not the point." He was gratified, nonetheless, to see her
blush darken. Another row was obviously brewing and it was pleasing to
have scored a point so early in the debacle. "That's just so bloody typical
of you. You are always trying to do me down. At least I make an effort.
Have you looked in the mirror lately?"

Marcus knew that little annoyed Velda more than a straightforward
answer to a rhetorical question and so interrupted her tirade to answer,
"Yes, this morning. When getting dressed. In the mirror behind the door
in the smallest room in the house which I pay for and which I'm happy to
call my own when not banished to the caravan. If I stand in the two-foot
square of carpet allotted me and bend over backwards like some contor-
tionist, then yes, I can just about see the top half of myself. In the mirror."

"And what did you see?"

Marcus held out his arms, as if offering himself for inspection. "Me."

"Well, shall I tell you what I see?" Velda fulminated.

"No, really, please don't bother."

"Well, I see—"

"I said don't bother."

Marcus stood up, knocking the kitchen chair over behind him. "At
least my eyebrows are my own."

Velda stood too, pushing her chair back with a scrape. "At least I don't
have to go into the garage to get a cheap thrill."

"Where do you go then?" Marcus jibed over his shoulder as he left
the kitchen.

And that seemed to be that.

They were on their way.

Marching towards divorce, singledom, packet suppers and one-bar electric fires.

"Make sure she doesn't fleece you, mate," Brian Cattermole had cautioned during a long session at the Cock and Bottle. "Get yourself a good solicitor. Pays for itself in the long run. Cunning, these women. Don't imagine that she won't have clocked all your little policies, pensions, pots for rainy days. She'll know exactly what you're worth. Better than you probably."

Marcus stared gloomily into his beer. "There's not much anyway. Never really gone in for saving."

"Fifty-three percent. That's what the former Mrs C got her hands on. Fifty-three percent. Never did a hand's turn throughout our entire marriage."

So it was that Marcus came home one day to the brown envelope on the hall table. Carden, Coddington and Clutton Solicitors, acting on behalf of Velda Imogen Blatt née Cartwright, advising him to give his instructions at his earliest opportunity in respect of Mrs Blatt's request for a divorce.

"What's this all about?" he'd puzzled, wandering in to the now appropriated snug where Velda was welding bits of copper wire.

"I've had enough, Marcus. I've served my time as your wife, cook, housemaid, nursemaid, bottle washer. I want to be on my own. I want my own space." She'd looked vengefully up at him over the top of her glasses.

"Is there nothing...I can do...say? What about those marriage guidance Jennies?" His heart was racing. A weakness overcame his legs. He wanted to sit down before he collapsed but didn't feel he could in what was no longer his room.

"I've made up my mind. There's no future for us. It's not as if we even love each other any more." Marcus felt rather inclined to argue this point but the wind had gone out of him. So, sadly and dejectedly, the next day he made his way down to the solicitors on Queen Street for his initial half-hour free consultation. Once he'd put both feet on the treadmill, it seemed the process was unstoppable until he was ejected, staggering, at the other end.

5

Amelia

Amelia leans against the door frame, her back to the first-floor balcony, watching Enzo. He is sitting in 'the office', a small space between the kitchen and hallway, staring short-sightedly at the computer screen, tapping an occasional key as if making a labyrinthine selection. She carefully folds Tilly's letter and places it in her back pocket.

She waits for him to ask who the letter is from. Smoke wreaths from his over-full ashtray. He continues to tap, tap, tap and takes no notice.

The last time she had spoken to either of her sisters was when Cecily had rung several months ago to invite her to Mr Green's funeral.

"Why not come over? You said yourself it's not a busy time." Cecily's voice faded in and out.

She'd promised she'd see what she could do. "Better go now," she said, knowing before the call was finished that she wouldn't go, that it wasn't worth the arguments. As she snapped the phone shut, beyond the extraneous noises of the long-distance call, she had caught a tiny resonance of home – the long-case clock chiming in the hall, a dog barking, a kettle whistling. Since when did Cecily have a dog?

Let them bury Mr Green. Did she care? Not a lot. He belonged to a distant time, a distant place. This is her life now.

Yet, what sort of life is it? How had it come to this? What had happened to the free-spirited traveller who had the world at her bidding? She'd been run into a corral ten years ago, and then held fast, held tight, given no way out. The more she struggles, the more the constraints tighten.

He will ask her, eventually, who the letter is from. A trick of his, to spring a question, a conundrum, a crisis, just when she thinks she is in the clear. As with everything involving Enzo these days, every move, every word, has to be considered in the round, calculated, benefits weighed against pitfalls.

A noise catches her attention. She turns to look down into the street where a vegetable seller is in heated conversation with a customer. Both hold on to the same bunch of tomatoes. Is it an argument or are they in vociferous agreement with each other? It is hard to tell in this country. A police car whines along the shaded, dusty street watched by two old men sitting under a tattered awning.

Not that it had always been like this but it is strange to think that, over time, even illicit love affairs are no more proofed against ennui, fatigue, disappointment than more conventional ones.

It had promised well a decade ago when, early morning, she'd stepped off the small island ferry. She'd walked along the harbour wall towards the old town, past coils of rusting chains and frayed ropes, sidestepping lobster pots. A gentle on-shore breeze stirred the smells of the sea and human habitation.

"Pretty lady. Come. Come. I insist."

A young man dressed in black trousers and white shirt was sitting at a pavement café, idly running a laminated menu through his fingers. She ignored him and fixed her eyes on the anglers perched on tumbled boulders casting their whip-thin rods out past the buoys.

A gap in the concrete box shops, beach towels, crab nets, lilos and sharks swinging from their fixings, led up a steep cobbled street. Her plan was to ask at a few of the smaller hotels for work.

"Excuse me. Sorry." As she turned the corner to go uphill, she stumbled into a man sitting on the paving, leaning against the low wall of the Excelsior Hotel, watches, mobile phones and wallets spread out on a square of black material on the ground. He did not move but sightlessly let Amelia rearrange the goods she had kicked out of place.

The street twisted and turned in shallow cobbled steps, narrowing as it rose between high stuccoed walls. A shallow-angled sun caught the top of the walls, turning them bright with colour. At ground level, the shade was still dark and cooling. On either side, she glimpsed secluded courtyards shaded by slender palms, soothed by gentle fountains. A man in overalls, bare-chested, hosed a veranda. "Any work?" she shouted through the elaborately wrought gate. He shrugged, palms lifted heavenward, as if such a thing could only be the gift of a higher authority.

After a climb, the hill opened out into a medieval square and then continued upwards into a flight of graduating stone steps to a flat-fronted church. Three old women painfully made their way up the steps towards the elaborately carved doors, pulling themselves up, humble penitents, on a metal handrail.

Amelia sat on the bottom step, stretching her bare legs out into the sunshine. A starved unkempt cat stalked towards her, her three wretched kittens dropping from her empty teats. "I have nothing to offer you." She allowed the cat to writhe round her legs before shooing it away with the thought of scabs and fleas.

Tall timber-framed houses occupied one side of the square, an antiquarian map- and book-seller's, a solicitor's office and a kitchen supplier squeezed together along the other side. No obvious work opportunity here. Better to head back to the harbour's tourist area. Maybe ask that waiter.

For a few moments she allowed herself to sit and watch, tired after the overnight crossing. Long cool shadows fell across the square, deepening the colours, lending a more moderate, refined air to the area than the gaudy harbour front. The church bell rang out above her in a thin, querulous tone, creaking against its fixings. She moved herself into a corner, out of the way of the few approaching worshippers who nodded to her as they passed. Once the bell stopped, she gazed out to the sea beyond the bay. The ferry was pulling away, tumbling the foamy water behind it, gulls following like bonded courtiers.

"Hey. Miss. Come. Come. I insist. Sit down." She walked towards the waiter who had called out to her earlier, fixing her eyes on his steadily as she approached, assessing him. He was young, aged about nineteen, tall, slender in his overlarge shirt. A natural ease and fluidity about his movements, straightforwardly good-looking, he was surely simply offering her a cup of coffee. He pulled out a chair for her. She would observe the due processes and enquire after work, either here or elsewhere.

"Coffee, lady?"

"Yes please."

"You travel alone?"

Amelia studied the menu, ignoring the question. "Just coffee please."

The waiter left her after an elaborate show of securing the cloth with steel clips to the table edge, returning after some considerable time with a glass of iced water, the ice cubes already smoothed to resemble sucked lozenges, a piece of green and yellow mottled lemon floating on the top. She did not look up or offer any thanks. She waited, watching the dampness from the frosted glass spread outwards onto the paper cloth, hands folded in her lap.

Someone switched on a radio. Euro-music, derivative and catchy, blared from the dark cavern of the restaurant. A shout went up and the music quietened. A middle-aged woman hummed as she swept the dusty floor out onto the pavement, scraping the lightweight metal chairs to one side, clattering them back into place. Sparrows hopped on and off the decking locating crumbs. The woman glanced at Amelia and shouted through to the back. A man's voice shouted back.

"I apologise for my aunt. She is not the quietest first thing in the morning."

Amelia looked up as he brought her a large cup of coffee. "Compliments of the house," he grinned ruefully, putting down a pastry onto the table. He didn't voice what they both knew, that it was yesterday's anyway.

"Thank you."

The man seemed hesitant to go. The seconds lengthened and ballooned. She felt crowded, watched, as if the atmosphere was turning slightly hostile.

"That's very kind…"

"Do you mind me asking…"

Both spoke at the same time. Both laughed. The normal pace of life resumed.

"Go ahead."

"I was asking if you are a visitor for long time here."

"I don't know. Have to see how things go."

He folded his arms and leant against a wooden support. "I am returning for the summer. This restaurant belong my uncle. In October I go back to Hamburg to continue my studies."

Her hand shook slightly as she lifted the coffee to her lips. It smelt stale, as if it had been kept on a hot plate all night. She took a small sip, holding it in her mouth before allowing it to trickle into her throat. She glanced from the oily film on top of the dark coffee to the sugary coating on the cake. It seemed rude to eat or drink too gustily with him standing above her, but she was starving and parched.

She motioned to the chair opposite.

"No, I must not sit. I must be busy. My uncle, he is…er…he make us work hard, not sit down and chat. He say, 'Don't let the goose eat your cherries.'" The waiter shrugged with a wry smile.

Amelia laughed and nodded. She was being invited into his life, entrusted with a small detail about a tyrannical uncle with the typical work-hard attitude of a self-made man who only wishes he had half the privileges of the modern generation.

"Does your uncle need any help by any chance? I might be looking for work."

A door slammed at the back of the restaurant, and the waiter glanced anxiously into the darkness of the café. "Come back this afternoon. I will ask." The warmth of a confidence shared had gone.

Amelia put coins on the table and stood to go. The young man helped her down the wooden steps to the pavement before hurrying away.

And so it was that the Café Paradiso became her workplace and Uncle Enzo became her lover.

He looked on her almost as a gift from God, a *dono di Dio*. A week earlier they had buried his father. Time for him to emerge into the light, bestow upon himself certain fruits. He put her up in a flat, one of several he owned on the road out to the industrial sector. There he visited her. She knew he was married. His wife never came into the café. Maybe the aunt with the broom kept her sister informed of Enzo and his new *amante*.

Enzo had never made sex a condition of the job and the flat. But he had been hard to deny. After her first week at the café, he asked her to stay behind. The last drinkers had left at about three o'clock in the morning.

She'd passed the time sitting on a high stool behind the wooden bar reading a phrase book, turning the words and phrases round her tongue like a warm worm. A string of naked bulbs danced in a line along the roadside, pinpoints of light in an otherwise velvet dark night. The waves had receded far out from the shoreline like players bowing out at the end of the night. All was quiet. Enzo pulled up a bar stool next to her. She was surprised to see that he had her rucksack from the hostel. "What are you doing with that?" she'd asked him.

He turned her hand over and drilled his gaze into her palm. It tingled. His fingers were icy and damp from the two glasses of beer he'd poured for them. His head was slightly bent and she could see past the back of his neck down into his collar line. He seemed to be pleading with her, mutely. His shoulders were strong and still. After a period, during which Amelia swept her eyes over and over his bulk, noting every detail, he lifted his eyes up to hers. She nodded. He smiled and leant back, satisfied that a contract had been offered and agreed. They had an understanding.

He reached behind the bar for a bottle of almond liqueur and two small glasses, pouring clumsily. He licked the spillage from his fingers in a matter-of-fact way, talking as he went on. He told her how his parents had come here forty years ago when the resort was newly opened, how it was important to work hard, pay the official taxes and the unofficial taxes. This place was his life. He and his wife had six children as well as other members of the family to support. And that she was oh so English.

"What do you mean?"

"You look as if you don't approve. I have a flat," he continued in his matter-of-fact tone.

In the early days, he revelled in her. He didn't want her to cut her hair, insisting she let it grow so he could count how many revolutions a single lock could make round his ring finger. He watched her hair lighten and her skin darken. He smiled, indulgently, as she tripped over her new vocabulary. Rough winds had blown her off course and he nurtured and cared for her as might an explorer on the *Beagle* with an as yet uncharted find.

He made her write out a list of all the jobs she had done, simultaneously searching the list for any hint of moral decline while delighting in the range and versatility. "OK, so chambermaid. Waitress. Bar work." He pointed to each item on the list, his English faltering. "Tennis coach…"

"Sous chef. Courier."

"That's it. Then tour organiser. Stone polisher. Fruit picker. How am I doing?"

"Great. Keep going. Fruit packer. Dog walker. Nanny. Teacher of English. Reflexologist. Crystal healer. Clown."

"Clown?"

"Children's parties. Go on."

"Er. Time share. Gardener. Basket weaver. Pool attendant. Cage dancer. Fish filleter. Salt panner. Zoo attendant. Roman centurion. Potter. Here, here, I've run out. Give me yours." He grabbed her hands, counting out on her outstretched fingers. "Henna artist. Hair braider. Hostess. Manicurist. Water cooler supplier. Air-conditioning agent. Oh, I give up. Too much."

Later that night she lay in bed and completed the list. Tour guide. Kiosk manager. Line dance caller. Bingo caller. Magician's assistant. Rental car agent. Beggar. Wood carver. Runner. Decorator. Sand sculptor. Handbill distributor. Hawker. Amanuensis. Goat herd. Beachcomber. Living sculpture. Companion. Dance partner. Personal shopper. Yoga teacher. Condom supplier. Film extra. African drummer. Fire eater. Chalet maid.

What was it that singled her out for the precarious, unpredictable life of a traveller? Just how had it happened? Some people she had met around the world looked on travelling as a totally immersive experience as if they wanted the experiences, the encounters to change the colour of their blood, cause it to flow the other way. To her, moving from place to place, country to country was a lantern show. She was the lens through which images flickered and faltered. The world moved, whorled and danced, like the spume of the ferry, the tumbling of the gulls. The lens – she – was immutable, unchanging, apart.

Now she wants Enzo to leave the apartment so she can open the letter from Tilly. It is unlikely to be very important, just a page or so of news of the farm, her husband and her daughter, sale success at the sheep market, the British weather. Why does Tilly continue to write? Amelia has yet to write back. What would she write about? The games that she and Enzo play? Their code, their understanding? How strange it would seem to any outsider.

They are nothing but professional when working together in the café. He is the Patron, at night snapping his fingers at her to bring a tray of liqueur and six tumblers to his most esteemed guests. In the tight corners between tables, he expects her to squeeze herself out of his way. He shouts over conversations, allies himself with the customers, never her. A man who walks on air fanned by the wings of his domestic angels.

Never does he put his arm round her, introduce her to his associates. Never does he look at her in any way that could give any hint of their afternoon intimacies. She knows she is a fool for looking for any special recognition. There is too much to lose, too much at stake.

He is rarely in the restaurant during the day, when Amelia serves the lunchtime customers and makes preparations for the evening. "It's as if you don't even know I'm here."

"Of course I know you are here. But, we have to be so careful, so discreet. We are all playing a game. There are players, who are not just the two of us. There are players beyond us. We can play the game as long as we respect the rules. The day we challenge the rules is the day the game stops." From this, Amelia understands that the sanctity of his marriage is being honoured, in his own particular way. He will protect his wife from any and every embarrassment, from any contact or association with this British woman who is simply an orbiting moon, whose brilliance, even, is a mere reflection.

Is it for this, then, twenty years ago, that Cecily, who had forged every path that Amelia had travelled up to that point, had sent her on her separate way with her blessing? "Go. Do it for me." Cecily was about to marry Henry. She would miss the wedding. "Don't come back till you're ready."

And Amelia's part in this? Her arms move, her body moves, images on a carousel, shadow dancing against the wall. Once the show is over, she will leave without trace. Just as a candle flame has no shadow. Maybe head north, spend a ski season in the Alps, edging home a few hundred kilometres at a time, nonchalant, haphazard, non-committal. Aloof.

Yet the danger is, this aloofness that she wraps herself in for protection is also her undoing. Her comforter and her assassin. She knows she is going nowhere – fast.

Enzo switches off the computer and pushes back from the desk on his chair, lighting another cigarette despite one still smouldering in the ashtray.

"I'll be in for eleven o'clock. Will I see you?" Instantly she regrets her question for it seems to spin a silken thread round the two of them. Enzo is hunting for his keys and taking pages off the printer. There is no way she would ask about his correspondence, so why is she defensively asking bright questions to bat away his curiosity about hers?

"Possibly. I'm not sure."

"Tomorrow? Still going up to the mountains? You did promise." She cannot stop herself. Even with nothing to hide, Enzo's bullishness, his extreme jealousy, his possessiveness tip her into a pit of guilt and guile. She becomes petulant, pushy.

"We'll see." He kisses her hurriedly, grabs his jacket and leaves, slamming the flat door behind him.

She watches from the balcony as he strides up the street towards his car. A memory comes back to her, of their first outing as a couple. Enzo had collected her from the flat and they headed out of town up into the hills. The road was being made dual carriageway. They edged slowly past heavy machinery, a temporary gantry and queues of traffic going the other way. Yellow dust quickly covered his car, like creeping guilt. They said very little to each other. She rested her elbow out of the window, wishing for wind in her hair and the smell of olives, citrus, aromatic herbs, not this heavy sultriness and bitumen from the roadworks.

Will he look up and wave before he drives off? She leans over the balcony, primed to wave. Already she is forgotten. He drives off at speed.

Tilly's letter contains the final plea, "When are you going to come and visit, Melly? We all miss you."

Since being with Enzo, she had only visited home twice. Once for Mummy's funeral; once for Daddy's. On her first visit, Cecily had seemed apologetic yet defiant, defensive. "I've put you up at the pub," Cecily had told her.

"Why can't I have my old room?"

"Uncle Denny's in there."

"Well, why does Uncle Denny get my room and not me?"

Cecily gave Amelia a steely look. "Because I didn't know you were coming."

"Well, I'm not staying anyway. Going back on the nine o'clock flight."

Cecily had sighed and walked away, leaving Amelia to step over the door into the hallway.

Cecily had phoned eighteen months later to say that Mummy was really ill, not expected to last. Which came first? Her protest why Mummy had declined so far before they let her know? Or a sharp, guilty little spasm – why do I need to know this? If you hadn't told me, then... She left unvoiced the unthinkable thought of not coming back for her mother's funeral. Sorrow and regret danced a macabre dance in her heart.

Yet it had been different when she'd returned home for the funeral. They'd maybe gone too far the last time in their resentment and anger. This time the sisters were more careful with each other. Softer.

"I've put you in your old room this time," Cecily had told her after hauling her out of the airport taxi and holding her in an extended embrace. "It's not exactly the same, obviously, but I thought you'd be comfortable there." She lay down on the narrow bed, her eyes following the familiar lines of the gable windows, the dust between the rug and floorboards, the gap under the door, the shadows of people's feet as they passed in the corridor. The room had been hers throughout her childhood and early adulthood. How she wished she could scrape away the patina, the accretions, cleanse her eyes, remove what fogged and smeared her vision, could turn back her clock, go back to when things were so very different.

"Stay for a few days," Cecily had urged. "It's ages since we've seen you. You've changed so much. You must have some great stories." She gripped her arm, imploring her with a long, solicitous look. "Tilly. Tell Amelia she can't go yet." Tilly stood on her other side.

"Come on, sis. What's the rush?"

Amelia felt hemmed in by a bodily conspiracy of sisters. Enzo had said he would be at the airport waiting for her in less than ten hours. He had stood behind her as she booked the flights, pointing on the screen which ones to select, giving her a pass out of less than twenty-five hours. He didn't offer to accompany her and she had not thought of asking him.

"Oh, I can't. You know, got to get back to work. Would love to, you know I would." Cecily and Tilly looked at her doubtfully, both sharing the same tilt of the head, the same pull of the lips. If she let loose one tear, let fall one single negative word, then all would come tumbling down. Best just pay her respects, hug each sister long and hard and be back on that plane. "I'll come back for longer, I promise."

Mummy was laid to rest next to Daddy, their gravestones identical. "Don't stack us, darlings. You know me and your father. The only thing that kept this marriage going is separate everything. Alongside is fine." Mummy, for whom the funeral of her husband of forty years was no excuse to be anything less than gracious and courteous. Tears were for the weak. Amelia agreed with her.

If Amelia thinks of Cecily now, it is almost without sound or vision. A presence in the house that they'd grown up in. A caretaker of people. Of other people's spaces.

Is she ever going to make it back home again?

She quickly rereads Tilly's letter before tearing it into small pieces.

For too long now her wandering star had got its co-ordinates stuck.

73

6

Marcus

Marcus places milk and a newspaper on the kitchen counter before making his way into the living room. The late morning sun is pouring through the window, turning the carpet an African red. Pleasant smells of salamis, rich cheese and fresh bread waft up from the deli beneath. Within half an hour, the doors to the pub will swing open for business. Could life really get any better?

As time moves on, life with Velda is becoming simply a strata, an episode banded by other episodes, a distinct period set in the context of what came before and what will come after, a way station on the way to somewhere else.

Well, that is on a good day. But it still grieves him to have to put Velda in the past. He'd always assumed she'd be around for good, seeing him off when his time came, and then probably starting a new life of her own in Eastbourne, within a bus ride of her sister.

The children had been fine, thankfully. A couple of days after moving in, he'd received a text from Martha. "Hi Dad. Just checking you got there OK and are settling in. See you soon xxx". Nothing from Paul, but he hadn't expected there would be. Both son and daughter had seemed fairly equitable about the split. Weren't things meant to be a bit more heated than this? Weren't there supposed to be tears and recriminations? If not from the parents, then at least from the children?

He and Velda hadn't really established a protocol for contact post-separation. He'd have to just see how things go, how she wants to play it. He will always be there if she needs anything. Wouldn't let the old girl flounder but, and he sighs as he considers the fact, it had all been her idea. If she wants to go it alone, then so be it. He has a fleeting image of Velda sitting in the middle of the rug, the tribal sisters all around her, incense snaking into the air. There would be wooden beads and incantations, drum beating and arm waving and exhortations. She'll be fine. He can see her point. What more use could she possibly have for a defunct Quantity Surveyor with one foot in Grimes Graves and all the sensitivity of a rutting rhino? Or was that more to do with his snoring? What does it matter now anyway?

He can only stand by as the big red book of their marriage, age-spotted and careworn, neglected and overlooked, relinquishes its dry glue, pages fluttering one by one to the floor.

Time for a cup of coffee. He leans against the window frame, looking down onto the market square. A quiet, purposeful energy suffuses the place. Isn't that what Velda would say? She went on quite a lot about 'energy'. Her thing was sub-kinetic energy. The tick-tock of the universe. Tosh! But it's proving quite a struggle to rid Velda from his mind.

But the energy thing is true. The small town has a genteel feel about it. Cars manoeuvre sedately round the market place, drivers looking for somewhere to park. People greet each other across the street. There is a bustle, comings and goings. He chuckles to himself. That would be a good name for a shop, Cummins and Goings. He might even think of opening a little establishment himself. It seems that sort of village (or was it a town?): an antiques shop, an art gallery, a deli of course, two pubs, an Indian, a supermarket, a post office (run by the redoubtable Madge), a bookshop, an ironmongers. People happy to support local businesses. How much better here than that ghastly place on the outskirts of London he'd just left behind him, house numbers up to four figures, muggings, having to lock everything up, wheelie bins taken for a joy ride every Friday and Saturday night, vomit in the front garden.

He has time now to just watch the world go by. And sleep! He has never slept so well, every night dreamless oblivion coming like a fast-acting narcotic.

Today really is the first day of the rest of my life, Marcus announces to the empty room. What might he do? Good question. But not one that needs answering today. He can take his time. Because it *is* his time. He can go backwards, round and round, come to a crashing halt for all anyone cares now. He relishes each word as it comes to him. There. Is. No one. To. Tell. Me. What. To. Do. No targets. No deadlines. Nobody else's agenda. Freedom. The very idea of so much freedom is enough to make a chap giddy, so he sits down hard at the table in front of the window to ponder.

A shop. That would be rather splendid. Leaning against a worn wooden counter, passing the time of day with his regulars, sharing a joke, allowing the odd indiscreet comment to pass his lips such that they would think him a jovial sort of cove. One who doesn't take things at face value. The sort of chap you could rely on for a pithy comment on the issues of the day. Nobody's fool. Trouble was, scan the shelves as he might in this glorious daydream of his, he can't quite see what items he is offering for sale. The village seems pretty well catered for. What does he know about anything anyway? Apart from a patchy interest in local history, there isn't much that he could bring to the party.

Business is already looking brisk at the Red. He might check that out later, perhaps for an early supper. His eyes sweep along the buildings opposite. Not much action at the insurance office. Lights dim in the solicitor's too. The street continues down the hill in a haphazard, jumbled fashion.

He watches as the woman opposite steps over the cobbles and up the stone steps to her front door, bending over a few faded potted daffodils on the way.

His phone beeps loudly and vibrates itself a few inches across the table. The sender's name comes up as Velda but there is no message. Silly woman. She'd never managed technology very well. What does she want? Should he text her to ask if she is OK? But what can he do about it if she isn't?

He reaches for his notebook. Last night, Wagner on the stereo and a bottle of fifteen-year-old port to hand, he'd started to write a few notes. Somewhat euphorically perhaps he imagined himself flying high in the sky, reeling and circling above an ancient landscape. To the marshalling music, a sonorous voice had narrated his words:

The salt air creeps further and further inland from the soft-edged coast, the dewy mists captured by fewer and fewer mighty oak sentinels. The land is gradually cleared, dug, heaped. A deep rotation begins.

It goes on, but much is largely illegible. He will look at it again when he's got more time.

There is a sound of honking in the square. A large white van with an image of a wheelbarrow on the side reverses out of one of the parking spaces in the centre of the square, hitting a lamppost. The passenger wing mirror drops shards of broken glass onto the road. A small car hurriedly reverses out of the van's way.

Maybe he is still affected by the creative pulse of the previous night, sitting at the table into the small hours, writing, writing, writing, but he can still recall that feeling of floating in free space, sipping the nectar of endless possibilities, buoyed by a joy and an optimism denied him for so long. The feeling rather surprises him.

This calls for action.

The box marked 'Desk Drawer' contains a ball of Blu-Tack. It is dry, cracked and contains a surprising number of short hairs. Unfolding the glossy poster, he relocates Melanie and her Honda CB400N Super Dream to the back of the loo door.

They have both been given the freedom of the road.

Cecily

So that had been a rather fruitless search for elderflowers. What had she been thinking of? She drops the dried daffodil heads she'd collected on her way in into the compost bucket by the sink. Stupid woman!

Time for some lunch and then she'd have a think about what to do to pass the afternoon. Perhaps she could start to write that history of the house she'd been thinking about. Get down to the library and do some research. Print a little pamphlet. Have an Open Day with scones and cream. Oh really?

The odd murder or scandal or skeleton somewhere lurking in the woodwork would appeal to the Out and Abouters. Plain scones or fruit? Cream with that or the dairy-free option? English Breakfast or Berry Burst to refresh your curious mind, with a side order of wronged maidservants, captured highwaymen, disgraced nobility? That would be £2.50 please. It would take a lot of tray bakes and cups of tea to fix the lead flashing in the chimney or arrest the rising damp in the back kitchen.

Can she strip back the layers and reveal the house in its many subtle and its more extreme mutations? Can she see herself pointing out the seventeenth-century beams, fashioned from decommissioned sailing ships by Roger de Willoughby, former cloth merchant – while keeping an eye on the more portable of her possessions? Could she recreate for the visitors the conditions inside the Victorian Bethel Missionary School for children of proselytising and absent parents? Or what it must have been like for the twelve-year-old Jewish refugee from Poland, billeted on the Stour family resident at Hingham House at the time of World War Two?

But that all belongs to the outer pulse of the house. There is another pulse – the inner life of the house, *her* life in the house. Such that, after his naval service, Dr and Mrs de Mare acquired the house within a decade of the end of the Second World War – the Jewish refugee having left East Anglia, presumably to start the uncertain task of finding her family, leaving only her name and date and place of birth carved in a sill in the cellar. Hannah Metzger, 1929, Kraków. Their three daughters, Cecily, Amelia and Tilly were brought up here, each leaving for respective careers and marriages. Upon Dr de Mare's retirement, the eldest daughter, Cecily, moved back to Hingham House with her husband, Henry Marchant, and his two sons, Michael and Thomas, from his first marriage. Dr and Mrs de Mare were cared for by Henry and Cecily Marchant who retained the title to the house upon their death. Henry Marchant also deceased.

True but bland. A potted history that said nothing about the adder in the garden, bringing newborn babies home, the trusty Christmas tree fairy, the triumphs and tragedies of school and first love, tearful departures, joyful reunions, the delicate negotiations involved in combining two stepsons and two ageing parents, the day the two-year-old Tilly came screaming in the house with a stag beetle in her hair, planting the orchard, parties, wakes, the conversions to vegetarianism, the returned wedding dress, the myriad Hammies and Jerries and Sookies buried in the garden, violin practice, trips to A&E, midnight feasts, the ash tree that fell on the greenhouse, the flood, sliding down the bannisters, finding the George

III penny, the arguments with the Parish Council about the Sky dish, driving lessons, slammed doors, plaster casts, each trip to the consultant that seemed to bash Daddy like a nail further and further into a piece of wood, colour schemes, colour TV, fibre optic, microwave, camping in the garden, bonfire nights...

The wash and rinse and spin of so many lives lived in this house. Within the last sixty-five years, three generations, albeit dog-legged, could call this house, Hingham House, their home.

And what of her ghosts? Ghosts which come out when it is quiet. Which it is too often these days.

Henry is at the forefront. Others flicker in and out, invited or not.

Henry is everywhere. His tools are in the shed at the bottom of the garden, pretty well as he'd left them, nails and tacks in rusting tobacco tins, paintbrushes in jars of slowly gelatinising white spirit. Sometimes a shade only appears during a particular time or function, such as the closing down of the house at night-time. The slide of the bolt, the turn of the key, the extinguishing of the light, the placing of the key in Henry's coat pocket that still hangs amongst hers in the hallway. At times it feels as if Henry's hand is still on hers. Steadying her, making her go through the motions, ensuring everything is secure, guiding her.

Other ghosts rattle noisily around the house at the imagined click of the catches of his briefcase, the imagined clatter of his work boots on the hearth after a hard weekend's work. Occasionally she strains her hearing to the sound of his voice in the passageway.

But then, people do not have to die to have ghosts. Amelia and Tilly still walk this earth and have left their younger selves behind in the house. Henry's sons, Michael and Thomas, weekend and holiday visitors, tall, awkward, fearful of being in the way, ever obliging to their father's parents-in-law, by this time inclined to wander, to shout, to choke. But this was never their home, and their real selves no longer reside here.

Ghosts have secrets too. Daddy's penchant for garden bonfires, to hide his occasional Benson and Hedges habit. Boxes of shoes in Mummy's closet, their soles unblemished, labels still attached. A fragile, almost transparent love letter. Pills in packets. Booze.

Daddy had a fascination with the Black Prince and all things heraldic. When the girls emptied out his study, they found boxes and boxes of hand-painted lead figures. "A last bastion of manliness," Tilly observed. "Imagine living with us three *and* Mummy! Would drive anyone to toy soldiers!"

Ghosts have movement, they have secrets, and they also have an aroma all of their own. The scent of roses, where once, all summer long, Mother had arranged gloriously extravagant blooms that dipped their heads and their earwigs onto the hall table. Bonfires. The occasional, elusive, heart-breaking whiff of Henry's soap on the pillow.

For Cecily, the question is, does her real self reside in this house, the house she has lived in as a child and as a wife and as a stepmother, and as a widow? Or is it a gilded cage? Can there be any escape?

Might there be a lighter, more carefree life for her beyond the confines of the bars? A life less hamstrung by obligations to the past? Or would she be like Amelia – once out, never finding her way back in?

Tilly, surprisingly, has it right. Tilly, the youngest by a good many years, scoffed at, overlooked, occasionally petted and then put down, has it bang to rights. Married the first man she slept with, a man still rugged but suave, a dry wit but not depressive, who worships the ground she walks on, even after twenty-five years, in her docker's wellies and torn tartan fleece.

Cecily rises to begin preparing lunch. A tiny unopened white-green waxy flower falls from the sole of her boot.

The Village

The crowd that has taken over the corner of the pub while Marcus is tucking into his early evening steak and ale pie is made up of members of the Village Summer Fair Committee.

"Right. Has everyone got a drink? When we're all seated, we can start. Well, *get* a drink, Brian. No, there isn't a kitty. Hurry up about it." Stanley Mercer, owner of Hammer and Tongs, the ironmongers, is the self-appointed Chair of the committee. There is a good turnout. Too good, in fact, as there proves to be more bums than seats and some squashing up required. Cecily Marchant looks decidedly uncomfortable to be sharing a hard curved-back chair with Madge from the post office. "Cecily. Cecily.

Over here. Come and sit by me. You need to be close at hand in order to take the minutes, anyway." Cecily gratefully shuffles between the round pub tables and knees, apologising as she goes, to Stanley's side.

"Thank you, Stanley," she whispers, and places a tonic water in front of her before pulling out a large pad from her bag.

"Right. If everyone's present and correct, I'll call this meeting to order. When I call your name, if present, please say 'Aye'."

"Oh, come on, Stan. Just get on with it," shouts Peter, on the margins of the group, rocking on his heels, arms crossed, holding a pint glass in his hand. "I've got to get back to milking."

"Right. Well, as I was saying. Following the success of last summer's fair, or should I say, 'fay-re', I take it we are all in agreement that we should take it upon ourselves to repeat the experience this year." Stanley looks round at all the faces nodding agreement. "You should all have sight of the agenda, namely items for consideration in the planning of this year's fair, or fay-re." There is a collective stretch as people reach for the pieces of paper on the tables in front of them. "Item One. Situation. Major Welding has kindly agreed that we can use what is known as the Town Field this year, on condition that we undertake some remedial works, clear up after ourselves and arrange for separate parking. I think we owe a debt of gratitude to Cecily Marchant for negotiating this deal following the refusal by the Borough Council to let us use the playing fields, as has been the tradition for the past four years."

Stanley pauses for a small trickle of applause. "This leads on to Item 1A, a proposal that we ask Year 6 children from All Saints to be our litter-pickers. Agreed? No objections? No? And Item 1B, that we write to the landlord of The Hare for permission to use the car park. Are we all happy with this?"

The assembly nods, some mutely asking their neighbours how long this is all going to take. "I'd forgotten what a boring bastard he is," someone whispers. "This is going to take forever." Stan glances across at the dissenters.

"Be quiet. He can hear you."

"But there's fourteen items on the blinking agenda. Why can't he just say, you, you, you, do this, do this, do this, and be done with it?"

"Because it needs to be organised. Now shut up."

"Right, well, if I could call this meeting to order again and ask that if there's anything you wish the meeting to be aware of, that you address your comments through the Chair."

Marcus

Marcus is contentedly making his way through a golden suet crust, deep rich gravy, satisfying chunks of tender beef, silky mashed potato and strong, earthy kale and carrots while the meeting progresses through the items. He is surprised how many people he recognises. The woman across the road, who is busy scribbling away, presumably taking the minutes. The frightful woman from the post office, Madge, who greets him like a lost friend and clutches his arm while waiting at the bar for her drink. The proprietor of the delicatessen.

Is there a similarity amongst them? Any old family names, he wonders? Names and blood corrupted over the centuries. Good old ruddy, rustic folk with roots reaching through the Suffolk soil. Or are they mostly retired professionals like himself? Hard to tell. He returns to his newspaper. Doubtless he would find out.

"Right. Item Eight. Ticketing. Do we part with convention and offer e-ticketing, as has been proposed or do we stick with tradition and sell printed tickets? Your thoughts please."

A general groan rises up from the assembly. Marcus becomes aware of a movement and a press against the bar. He shuffles himself along to make room, taking his roly poly with him.

Stanley's voice rises over the hubbub. "Well, I'm sorry you all seem to feel this way. But the devil is in the detail."

"The devil's dancing round your hat, mate."

Marcus looks through the now animated crowd around the bar. It appears that only four people remain of the Fair Committee, one of whom is arguing vehemently with Stanley. Even the note-taker has put her pen down and her hands in her lap.

A husky voice breathes past Marcus's ear. "Over here. I'm next. Over here. Large vodka please." The two bar staff, a lad with his shirt tail hanging out at the back and a young woman with piled-up blonde hair, are busy down the other end of the bar. A strong scent of cheap perfume assails Marcus's nose and makes his eyes water. "Hopeless they are in here." He turns to smile non-committally. His first impression is of a small woman, lines deeply etched in her face, dark-ish hair combed and lacquered into a type of helmet, the grey roots showing through like underlay. The hand clutching the twenty-pound note which she waves in some obvious distress is puffy and blotchy. Her elbow digs sharply in his side as she places one foot on the rung of his bar stool to heave herself over the edge of the bar. Leaning between the pumps, she shouts towards the two young people. "Garcon! Miss! Vodka!" Marcus simultaneously fears for his pudding, his pint and his balance.

"Busy tonight. I'm sure they'll get to you as soon as they can."

"Not seen you here before. Visiting, are you?" Marcus feels disinclined to offer too much information so nods once and returns to his newspaper. Out of the corner of his eye, he can see her rap her fingernails on the counter. They are honed, chipped and terrifying.

"What can I get you?" The lad appears in front of them.

"'Bout time too. Vodka. Double. Splash of tonic. No lemon." She grins at Marcus. "Mandy. Married to Ned Gallagher. We have a nursery out on the Lowestoft Road. We supply garden centres in the area and Ned and his team do gardening and landscaping jobs." Marcus smiles weakly. The lad, whose name badge announces him as NATHAN FOOD AND BEVERAGE, places a tumbler of clear liquid in front of Mandy.

"Eight pounds fifty please."

Marcus, assuming that there might have been a companion to Mandy in the pub, is surprised to see her hand over the twenty-pound note as she takes a mouthful. "No. No. Wait. Give me another one." She retracts the note and takes another large swallow. Nathan returns with another highball glass. Marcus wonders if he should offer to pay but takes heed of the mute warning in Nathan's eye and decides not to. Mandy puts the first, empty glass on the counter and turns to Marcus. "What did you say your name was?"

He offered his hand. "Marcus Blatt." To pre-empt any further questions, he asks, "Do you live in the village? Are you part of this committee?"

"Yeah, we live over there." Mandy waggles her fingers in a vaguely westerly direction. "Ned said to come along as he's supposed to be clearing the field for the fete. Typical of him. He'll do it for nothing, I know he will. It will take him days to clear all that rubbish and bramble. He said it's good advertising. Last year we had a banner round the cricket pitch. Stan won't pay a penny. But that's men for you. Men. Short for 'mean'."

Marcus watches, half enthralled, as Mandy chatters on. After a few minutes, it becomes apparent there is no need to offer any reply or feedback. His eyes zero in on her constantly moving lips, fascinated as a small ball of, he assumes, lipstick transfers itself from her bottom lip to her top lip and back again. It is like watching a game of bagatelle. "And then my *second* husband, God rot his soul, turned out no better. Ten-year stretch in Ipswich Prison, two years still to go." Mandy pauses momentarily to study the bottom of her glass. "But you seem a nice enough chap. What did you say your name was?"

Marcus excuses himself and slides down from the bar stool, making a hasty retreat towards the door. As he retrieves his coat from the stand next to the slot machine, he can hear a conversation between Stanley, the woman from the house opposite him – the note-taker – and a tall chap whom he had observed lobbing in comments from the margin of the group and who now seems to be objecting to some player in the upcoming fair.

"I still don't understand why we have to use the Major's field. Think it's a bloody cheek, I do, that he expects us to clear the field. It's not been used for anything for decades. It's full of nettles and thistles."

"But, Peter, if I can interrupt you there. Ned Gallagher has said he will arrange for it to be cleared."

"Well, that's a bloody liberty, if you ask me. We don't know him from Adam. He buys up the Hall and then expects to be involved."

"You'd complain if he *didn't* get involved. Listen, Peter. Cecily has been in correspondence with the Major's team for the last few weeks. You've got no reason to suspect anything untoward, have you, Cecily?"

The woman shakes her head.

Marcus shrugs on his coat and pushes the door. Cecily. So that's her name. He wonders if he should call round one day and introduce himself. Giddy thought.

Mandy

Ned had told her to come to the meeting. Where is he for Christ's sake that he can't come to the meeting himself? Damned if she can remember. He's always leaving her for some sort of errand or other. She'll get the gist of it anyway, from the bar. She'd taken a couple of notes from his wallet so she'd have some lubrication for the night.

Nice chap that Marcus. Bit old. Not her type really. Did she even have a type? Still, Ned, for all his faults, provided well. Never home, that was his bloody problem. She'd offered to give him a hand in the business. Would give her something to do. He always said he'd find her something, but never came up with the goods. Happy to have her at home. Old-fashioned that way.

God, the vodka tasted good. That first hit. Like it could blow your tits off. Nothing like it. At least nobody could call her a secret drinker when she was in the pub, surrounded by everybody.

Look at that bitch sitting over there, cosying up to the committee, clipboard in hand, taking the minutes. No better than she ought to be.

Probably not more than five years between us. Well, that would be about right, wouldn't it? Big house and only Cecily in it. Everybody else has buggered off. And who can blame them? Who'd want to live with that miserable cow?

Thinks she's so special. I've seen her, down at the graves every other day. It's all fake, you know.

And I know it's fake. Because I've seen her. Coloured bright red she did when she saw me sitting across from her at the clinic. No such thing as patient confidentiality there. Obvious we were in for the same thing. You'd think butter wouldn't melt.

Marcus

The night air is crisp and cool. A warm light emanates into the street from behind his red curtains. It isn't home yet but it has promise. His footsteps echo along the alley towards his door. Holding his phone to shed some light on the lock, he notices there is a text waiting for him, from Velda. It says, simply, "Marcus?"

7

Tilly

Tilly drives through the flat landscape of the fens. The sheep are feisty and unsettled, forcing the trailer to kick and buck sideways. For a brief moment, she imagines them all tipping into the ditch, the wheels of the Land Rover spinning, Moonspell's heavy metal anthem 'Wolfshade Masquerade' blaring out from the speakers over the misty fields. "Steady, my girls," she shouts into the rearview mirror. Pip the sheepdog pricks up an ear and stares lopsidedly from the boot.

Lambing is finally over for another year. Already the early ones have reached weight and gone to market. The auctioneer had winked at her and held on to the bidding until top price was reached. She'll send him a bottle of whisky at Christmas. In the trailer now, four prime Border Leicesters from a breeder in the Midlands. They will augment her flock in a fine way.

Her phone rings, muffled within the layers of clothing required for the unpredictable spring weather. "Hold on. Hold on. Give me a minute." Tilly thrusts her hand inside the torn pocket of her jacket and snags it on the belt of her jeans. "Wa-a-a-i-t." She reaches into her jeans pocket and grabs the phone. Cecily. "Hiya. Not far off now. Can just see the sugar factory. So, what, thirty-five minutes? OK."

It is a roundabout way home but she's been wanting to see Cecily for ages, having missed Mr Green's funeral in the winter.

Tilly takes the last few bends into the village carefully, her mind full of Amelia. It seems all wrong that she is out there in the world, so far from her family, so out of touch. Would anybody think to contact the family if anything was amiss? She pulls onto the cobble frontage outside the house and waits, hazard lights flashing, for a number of cars to pass her. "Come on. Get a move on," she mutters under her breath. The pace of traffic is slow and considered. The four new ewes start up a protest of their own, baaing loudly, the steel trailer acting as a kind of boom box. The trailer jolts and jostles and Pip barks in alarm. "Quiet, girl. Enough now." The dog emits a little squeak and lowers her muzzle onto her paws, every small correction a massive telling-off. "It's alright, Pip. Not cross with you. Just hush now."

The traffic clears and Tilly swings a sharp right to straighten out the Land Rover and trailer, nudging her nose towards the cars parked around the market cross, before starting a careful and slow manoeuvre backwards, repeatedly checking both outer mirrors. There is about six inches to spare between the alleyway walls and the sides of the trailer. One wrong move and she will be wedged.

A flash of white catches her eye. Someone shouts, "Watch out!" Tilly stares, mesmerised, as a large white van hurtles towards her, the driver remonstrating, both hands, alarmingly, off the wheel.

"What you doing in the middle of the road?" he shouts through his open window.

"Naff off," Tilly shouts back. The bonnet of the van is mere inches from her door. He mouths something inaudible in reply.

Cecily comes down the front steps onto the road and waves cheerily at the driver.

"Who the heck is that? He nearly hit me broadside. What you doing waving to him? He's a danger."

"Oh, don't worry, it's only Ned Gallagher. He rarely actually hits anything. He's always in a rush."

Tilly takes in the wheelbarrow logo on the side of the van. Gallagher's Garden Services. "Bloody menace he is." The van's engine has cut out; the driver folds his arms and stares sullenly at the two sisters. "Quick. Help me back. Want to get out of this maniac's way."

She continues her slow passage backwards down the cobbled alleyway until lined up with the wooden gate the colour of verdigris, the colour it's always been, in the brick and flint wall. Climbing out of the back of the Land Rover, Tilly jumps down to position Cecily and Pip. The van driver seems to be having trouble restarting the van which, finally, thrums and judders as if sharing the driver's impatience and clatters on its way.

Tilly opens the back door of the trailer and whooshes the sheep into the back garden. They jump and slide down the ramp, barging and knocking, propelled more by the urge to move rather than any actual endpoint. Within minutes they are contentedly tearing at the long, lush grass as if all life before had been but a dream.

Tilly sees Cecily glance anxiously towards the borders. It would not do if they chowed down on the prize hostas. But then maybe it would be worth it, just to see the look of horror on Cecily's face. Tilly swallows down this unworthy thought and sends up a silent prayer that the sheep confine themselves to the grass. Cecily is too easily upset, far too easy to tease.

The sisters go into the house through the back door, straight into the kitchen, leaving Pip in the garden to alert them of any misadventure concerning the sheep.

Tilly walks through the downstairs rooms, scanning for the subtle changes. A picture added or removed. New fabrics. A rearrangement of the furniture. Cecily's taste is not dissimilar to Mummy and Daddy's, who were themselves skilled at matching period to, say, Terence Conran. Perhaps they all share the same taste; she is aware of some features repeating in her own house too – the deep-seated sofas, rough-cut shelves heaving with treasured books, a well-chosen painting or bronze, kilims, musical instruments, objets trouvés, family photographs. Different clutter. Different mementoes. But definitely a familial style.

There must be some sort of memory creep, Tilly supposes. Each time she goes 'home', she has to reconfigure it from the enduring images of before she left Hingham House as a young bride, to the present day. Home is the arena for childhood experiments, dark dens, dressing up, hide and seek. Home is the repository of so many hopes and ambitions and memories. Home, strangely, now belongs to Cecily. There is a necessary adjustment to this fact, to the here and now, every time she walks through the door and smells the beeswax polish, hears the syncopated tick and chime of the long-case clocks, sees the old coats, dusty round the shoulders, hanging in the hallway, like the discarded skins of the departed.

She shivers when she sees them. Horrid to think of Mummy and

Daddy gradually diminishing from the giants who could pick apples out of the trees, rescue stunned birds from the gutters, retrieve catapulted socks from the top of wardrobes, to the stunted, needy little gremlins they became. Horrid to think of Henry gone, and Cecily's almost unbearable grief and loneliness.

Cecily calls through, "Coffee's ready."

"Coming."

Tilly walks through to the kitchen and hesitates momentarily. Should she wait to be invited to sit down? Gone is the automatic tenure she had as a child. Children don't think, do they? They just walk in, expecting the house to be just the same as when they left it that morning. How does it work nowadays? Does she have the same right to flop in the armchair with her feet up the wall as she did when she was fourteen? Or should she wait to be invited to sit and then take the less comfortable seat?

"What are you waiting for? Sit down, for goodness' sake!"

Cecily

While Cecily waits for the kettle to boil, she is conscious of Tilly wandering from room to room. It is a little unnerving. And a little irritating. Of course Tilly has every right to be here. It is her childhood home after all, but why does she have to pick everything up, touch everything, like some visitor to an interactive museum? She will have to go round later and put things back in their place. What's mine, she asks herself? What's really mine, mine alone? She elbows away her vexation.

She always said Tilly had the blessings of the third child, their parents having thrown away the rule book by the time she and Melly were past the cradle and the potty. After a sulky first child and a rebellious second child, there was little time or energy left over to trouble Tilly greatly. So she had been left to enjoy so much more freedom, so much more self-determination. Tilly, carefree and joyous, had just got on with things. Cecily told her once how jealous she was that Tilly just knew how to be happy. That Tilly, being happy, led a happy life.

"How did you do it, sis?" Cecily asked her. "You marry the first man you sleep with. He turns out to be totally gorgeous, he worships the ground you walk on, two gorgeous blonde-haired talented kids, nice house. The works!"

"Dunno. Just luck I guess."

"And Mother and Father just adore everything about your life because it's what every parent wants for their child."

"Don't give them sleepless nights, you mean?"

"You mean I do?"

"Well, you *used* to."

"What do you mean?"

"OK, where do I start? You go off to uni and rarely come home, let alone phone or write. No. No. Let me finish. You marry straight out of uni and that marriage lasts eighteen months, tops. Amelia has to tell them you're getting a divorce because, for whatever reason, you won't come home to face the music. Then you disappear completely off the scene for about seven years and no one really knows where you are. Then you pop up with another husband. He's given a bit of a run for his money and is dropped just as suddenly. Then we are introduced to Darling Henry."

"But it isn't all my fault that I wasn't around. I just didn't match up to what they wanted or expected of their eldest daughter. There was just too much expectation to be well turned out, have impeccable manners, leave nothing on the plate, have excellent school reports, Grade 8 piano. It was like their model daughter was supposed to be modest, charming, helpful, vivacious, polite and never flirtatious, sentimental, overbearing or clumsy. I never really matched up. And they made it known. Well, Mother did. Daddy was a bit more easygoing. They were no better at keeping in touch with me."

"Fault's not really the issue when it comes to apportioning blame though, is it? Doesn't matter whose fault it is. That's the way it went. Then you pull an absolute blinder, turning yourself overnight from black sheep into holy cow. Turning up with Henry, like that. Tall. Handsome. Educated. Successful. And loaded. And with the kindest heart in Christendom. Suddenly all Mummy and Daddy's little money problems are over. Henry buys Hingham House. We all get a nice cash injection. Mummy and Daddy live out their days in the annexe."

"And I get to be Head Girl again!"

"It was quite a pill for the old folks to swallow."

"Whereas you, Tilly, get things right first time. A lot less bother.

It all comes so naturally to you, and to Sophie and Lizzie. Anyway, it's lovely to see it all working out so well for you. Couldn't happen to a nicer person."

"Now you're being mawkish. Shut up."

"OK."

Tilly

Conversation ceases for a few minutes while they devour a large pot of coffee and a plate of home-baked cookies round the kitchen table.

"Bit like the sheep, aren't we?"

"What do you mean?"

"In the way we're going at the food." The two sisters laugh. Ahead of them, at least a couple of hours to be together, in the company of someone of the same blood. "It's funny," Tilly eventually says, scraping a stray chocolate chip into her mouth.

"What is?"

"I don't know, really. It's just funny being here."

"In a good way?"

"Oh yes, definitely in a good way."

"Good. Anyway, Tils, fill me in on all the news. Haven't seen you for ages. What's the goss?"

"Where shall I start?"

"Edmund."

"Yeah, Edmund's good. Still trying to make a go of it with the Shepherds' Huts."

"And the two of you still good?"

"Oh, you know me and Edmund. Hopeless without each other."

"And the girls?"

"Well, as you might expect, there's more to tell there. How long have you got?"

"Forever. More coffee?"

"Thanks. Well, Sophie's fine. One more year at sixth form, then she'll be off on an art and design course somewhere. Did I tell you she's saved up enough to go to New York in the summer? Going to do all the galleries and museums. Got a nice boyfriend. He seems to spend all his time writing poetry for her and giving her the big calf eyes. So she's OK."

"It's Lizzie you're worried about then?"

"Yes. She seems to have lost her way a little bit. She's talking about dropping out of college. Said she isn't ready or it isn't for her. She's missing so many lectures."

"So what's she doing instead?"

"She's working in the kennels."

"Sounds OK. She's only young. Be good experience for her while she decides what she's going to do."

"Well, that part of it's OK. I agree, she's got time to look around and find something better that suits her. Trouble is, she's met this guy called Billy."

"Is that his only offence? His name?"

"No, silly. It's not his name we object to. He's eight years older than her. Again, not a crime, but it's quite an age gap for a twenty-two-year old. She says they met at a festival in Somerset. He just seemed to follow her home."

"Are they both living with you?"

"No. They live in a caravan on the kennel yard. Honestly, Cecily, I've been there. It's absolutely rank. She's out all hours at work, and occasionally college, and as far as I can see, he just sits on his fat arse, well, skinny arse actually, in the caravan, buying and selling vinyl on the Internet all day."

"Does he make any money out of it?"

"Who knows? He doesn't tell Lizzie if he does. She's borrowing money from me to pay for food. He's not contributing a penny. He wants a baby. I'm so worried that she'll just go along with it or it'll just happen by default. Apparently he's had a child with about three different girls."

"What does she say when you talk to her about it?"

"Nothing. She just clams up. But I honestly can't see what she sees in him. He's, like, got this hair."

"Well, that's not so unusual."

"Be quiet. No, this hair," and Tilly screws up her face, "it's like rolls of orange and purple cotton wool, which he ties up behind him or shoves in this sort of crochet hat."

"A rasta then?"

"No, no, nothing like that. He eats sausages and drinks like a fish. He doesn't look cool, he looks like some kind of psychedelic nightmare. He's a self-avowed skip rat, never buys anything new, just wears other people's discards, so his clothes are rags. And none too fresh-smelling either."

"Kind of the eco-warrior look then?"

"I wouldn't say he's any kind of warrior. Don't think there's a principled bone in his puny little body. Do you know what he's actually done! I don't know if it's illegal but it's certainly a rotten thing to do. He's got some kind of ugly Staffordshire terrier which somebody abandoned at the kennels. He's only gone and got it tattooed. On its rump. It's got this balled fist and 'England Expects' underneath. Vile!"

"You're beginning to paint quite a picture. What does Lizzie see in him?"

"God knows! I think she's got into this bind that some girls get into. A guy comes along who is so arrogant, so full of himself that he, momentarily at least, convinces the impressionable that there really is something about him."

"They usually get found out in the end."

"Do you know just how arrogant he is? He actually suggested to me that..."

"What?"

"Oh, I can't even tell you."

"You mean he made a pass at you?"

Tilly nodded, pulling a face of absolute disgust. "Except 'a pass' has a sort of old-fashioned, roguish quality to it. 'Lunge' would be a better word."

"Did you tell Lizzie?"

"Nah! She'd somehow say it was all my fault or I'd imagined it and then I'd lose what little of her that's still connected to her old world."

"What did you do?"

"I slapped him. Hard. And, do you know what, the little rat, this gleam came into his eye and he came at me. Bloody hell, Cecily. I'm twenty-five years older than him."

"No barrier for some."

"Disgusting."

Cecily puts her hand over Tilly's. "I'm sorry, love. I'm sure it will sort itself out, though." Tilly snatches her hand away.

"And, another thing! He tried to blackmail me. Said that I should give him five hundred pounds or else he would tell Lizzie. I told him to get lost. But then three days afterwards, Lizzie comes to me and says that Billy needs money, to buy stock ostensibly, or else he would have to leave. I refuse. She rows with me and says she's given him all the money she's saved for college. She earns precious little as it is. I just cannot believe what an exploitative, manipulative bastard that man is. Or what Lizzie sees in him. He's not even that good-looking. He's got a fat belly, weak eyes and small feet. And heaven knows what germs and parasites he's harbouring in his busy little cock."

Tilly sighs and reaches for another biscuit. "I just want her to be with someone who shows her some love and respect. Somebody who... I don't know...somebody who hangs his clothes up at night in a wardrobe."

Cecily laughed. "That sounds a bit bourgeois. But I know what you mean. Somebody like her dad."

"Isn't that what every girl wants?"

"Well, only if they have a fab dad."

"It just breaks my heart to see her give her love away so easily, like it's not worth anything."

"Haven't we all got to do that at least once, give our love away to somebody completely worthless?"

"I don't know. Did you?"

"Yeah. I guess." Cecily stands abruptly and rinses the cups out under a fast stream of cold water. Droplets spray out in the sun shining through the window, forming fleeting rainbows. Tilly watches her back. Is Cecily on edge? By moving to the sink, it feels as if Cecily has moved a stone out of the magic circle. "Sheep are OK." Cecily wipes her hands on a towel and returns to the table. "But you never know if you are going to reach the stars or not. If you knew you were, you might not stop off at the lesser planets on the way. You know, if you were Lizzie's age and knew that sometime in your twenties or thirties or fifties, or whenever, you were going to meet the one person who made your life complete, you might live a very different life. If you knew you weren't ever ever going to meet that one special person, then you think to yourself that at least you might pick up some moondust, if you can't have the stars."

"Don't know what you're talking about, Cess."

"No, neither do I really. So, go on, Tils, who was your undesirable love?"

"Well, I never had one, did I? Perfect man comes along before any sullying or disillusionment had time to take place. I've been spared all that crying into my Chardonnay, group hugs with the girls and ritualistic burning of love tokens."

"Was there nobody in school? Must have been."

"Nope. Too busy with early milking to be bothered. Too knackered. Oh, but hang on..." Tilly searches the air around as if she could reach back through time. "Do you remember that letter?"

"What letter?"

"You know. Daddy went ballistic. Thought I'd been making eyes at the boys on the estate. Turns out it was the paper boy who fancied me and wrote this little note suggesting that he could be my boyfriend and we could go and sit on the church wall together. Except he didn't know my name, so he said 'the girl in the tree house'."

"Oh, I remember. Then he must have got fed up 'cos then he sent the same letter, this time to Amelia, 'the girl with a scooter'. Daddy called him a randy little scrote."

"That's funny. Daddy soon saw him off." Tilly sighs, her thoughts returning to Lizzie. "It's as if Billy's stripped out any sense of rightfulness from her. She waits on him hand and foot. It turns my stomach to see her looking at him with such adoration in her eyes. Edmund won't have him in the house. Which means she won't come over. Which means I've got to go to the yard to see her. Can't meet her in town or at college, because she's always hurrying home, or for what passes for home in her altered life.

"And she's changed so much. She's got love bites on her neck. She's cut her hair off one side of her head and dyed the rest orange. She wears these rebel clothes. My beautiful little girl. Where's she gone?"

"She's not gone far. She'll be back."

"And she's gone and got a tattoo."

"Well, she'll look back on that one day and it'll remind her of the time that she had to challenge all her mum's wisdom. Had to go and find out for herself. Best get that little lesson out of the way good and early. You know, the one that says the bad boys, they are nothing more than empty calories. And, maybe…"

"What?"

"Maybe she's having this little rebellion for the two of you."

"Eh?"

"Well, as you said, you've led the perfect life. Never put a foot wrong. Whether through luck or good judgement, who knows. This really is the closest you are ever going to come to experiencing a bit of the bad stuff. At one remove, I know. In a way that causes you pain, I know. But, you'll see, she'll come back to you one day."

"Promise?"

"Promise."

"Like Amelia, you mean."

"Yeah, well, different matter."

8

Marcus – and Cecily, perchance?

Marcus stirs under the duvet. The sun is rising earlier and earlier these days and now part-wakes him just before six am. Strange to think that this time last year he would have been hastily shaving, jamming toast in his mouth, hoping to slip out of the house to catch his bus to the station before any edicts were issued from the once-marital bedroom.

The whole point of indolence surely is to enjoy it, to enjoy the lack of purpose, to revel in very little. He pulls the lumpy duvet up under his chin and rests the back of his head in his cradled hands, drifting back to sleep while pondering the unfinished business of his marriage.

In a former life, the married-to-Velda life, even if it didn't turn out to be married-to-Velda-*for*-life, his days had been marked out entirely by purpose. Railway timetables. Project deadlines. Shopping lists. The diurnal variations. Family events. So, now it is all rather odd having very little purpose. Odd but delicious. Delicious but a bit bewildering. Bewildering but…what is the word? The only words he can think of are Velda words, like 'empowering', 'liberating', 'grounding'. In a funny sort of way, he does feel connected to something. Maybe, God wot, it *is* to the 'Universe', in a way that he never was when he was rushing through Waterloo on the 6.55 or driving Velda to her Chakra Dance classes. Maybe the old dear hadn't been too far wrong with all her chanting and arm-waving and incantations. Odd way to go about things, but maybe she had a point. More to the simple, mortal man, and all that.

Over the past few weeks, he has really come to like his little bit of the universe. Down to the deli for takeaway coffee and bread rolls for breakfast. Taking his time over the morning paper. A drive out in the afternoon. Back to the for supper and a pint and a chat with whoever is at the bar. Catch the news with a glass of whisky. Write up his notes. Off to bed.

The sound of a delivery van reversing cuts across his thoughts. He stiffly lowers his bent arms and sniffs. A mushroom smell, which he suspects isn't emanating from the deli below, prompts Marcus's decision to change the bedclothes. That will be his simple purpose for the day.

"Crumbs. Forgot!" In a flash, swifter and more fluid than he might have thought himself capable of, Marcus leaps out of bed and stands dithering on the sheepskin rug as various and self-cancelling prompts to action reveal themselves to him, like a card-sharp's shuffle. How could he have forgotten? Today is Tuesday. Tuesday! No time for indolence or contemplation. Martha and Paul are coming today. This morning!

He bends down, legs passing for straight, to see if he can touch his toes. Isn't there some sort of sun salutation thing that people do when they feel themselves connected, in the right place at the right time? He grunts. If he ignores the pain in his left buttock, he could just about slide his fingers to the first joint past his knees. Maybe he isn't totally tuned to celestial resonance just yet. Would have to work on that, but not today.

After a hasty tidy up, he watches for them from the living room window. They did say eleven o'clock, didn't they? He glances over to the mantelpiece clock. Maybe it was half past. Even that makes them twenty minutes late. He would send out a heartfelt bid for their safety while travelling, if he only knew which nameless, faceless, desert-wandering, pilgrim deity to address it to. Perhaps it would be less obstructionist if he goes and dries the dishes, thus releasing any blocked energy? Or is it only patient and faithful watchfulness that will ensure their safe delivery? Oh, blow it! He'll have another cup of tea and leave others to worry about the mysteries of the universe.

There is time for Marcus to marry up the crisped socks forming a line along the kitchen radiator and to float the desiccated roots of his Maidenhair Fern within its brown plastic pot before Paul and Martha emerge from an unfamiliar car, Paul hauling a rucksack onto his back,

Martha reaching into the boot of the car to bring out multiple bags and baskets. They both stand by the car for a while, looking around. Marcus rushes down and calls from the alley entrance, "Over here."

"Dad," they both shout and walk their shiny, youthful confidence over to him. He opens his arms and they take a quadrant each, squeezing him hard, making him wince slightly. "Hey, Dad, you look great."

"It's me who should be checking you out. Let me take a look at you both." Passers-by hop out of the way as the two step backwards and occupy the pavement. When did they become so tall? It isn't just their bags and their accoutrements that make them take up so much space. They just look so abundant.

"Sorry," Martha apologises as a lady walking past with a white Scottie dog is forced off the pavement.

Whereas once Marcus would have chided his children, now he is totally enamoured by Martha's charm and ease. Even still, he can't resist a, "Mind out."

"So, are you going to show us where you're living now?"

"Sure. Come on up." He feels a strange little anxiety that the children won't like his new place. Also, a strange tilting of the balance in that, living here, he is not providing a home for them. Even an empty nest is still a nest, one that could be squatted or occupied if the need arose. He has no means to put them up. They would need to look to their mum to provide a home. He could only provide a crash pad. The thought makes him simultaneously a bit uneasy, as if failing in his duty as a father, but also places him, thrillingly, a little alongside their own youthful lives and experience.

"Hey, Dad, it's great." Martha heaves the bags off her shoulders and onto the kitchen table. It seems she might have bought him presents. He hopes there aren't any ghastly *objets* from home. Home? Paul moves straight to the sitting room and slumps on the sofa. While Martha goes round the apartment surveying and touching, Paul fiddles with the TV remote.

"Coffee, anyone?" Marcus busies himself in the kitchen, feeling slightly crowded out.

"Can I smoke in here?" Marcus glowers through the doorway at his son.

"Since when did you smoke?"

"Don't let him, Dad. It's vile."

"You can talk, Miss Goody Two Shoes."

"Children. Children. Stop bickering."

"Sorry, Dad."

"If you want to smoke, you can lean out of the side window. But don't drop your ash on Mrs Owen's pelargoniums." Paul looks too comfortable to move and satisfies himself by reaching out an arm to accept Marcus's offered cup of coffee. "Martha. Stop nosing and come and sit down."

"Righto, Dad," she calls from somewhere out of sight.

Marcus rips open a paper bag containing cake. He'd bought what he thought, from memory, the children would like. They both lean in hungrily, but laughingly reject his offer of a gingerbread man and a pink fancy. "You're alright, Dad. Thanks all the same."

He leans back on his armchair. "So." There seems to be so much to talk about. How have they been since he last saw them, before he moved out? How's Mum? Do they think any less of him, upping sticks and moving to East Anglia? Has he totally wrecked everything? All these vital questions seem trapped within a smooth, weightless orb, spinning and humming in front of them. "Soooo…"

Luckily Paul and Martha do not appear to suffer from their Dad's reticence. Whereas he thought that they may have been sent on a mission by their mother to check him out and report back on any evidence of female occupancy, signs of distress or mismanagement, it seems that is not their intent. Rather, to report to Dad on their own activities of late. With a jolt, he remembers a dream from the night before, Martha wearing bright yellow rubber gloves and holding up a scrubbing brush in the kitchen, shouting out, "Dad, it's infested with maggots." He is fairly positive that no such wildlife would be found but makes an urgent note to self to check when unobserved.

Paul describes his continuing internship at a PR firm in a smart part of London, his eyrie of a flat in a less eximious part of town, elbow fights with commuters and the price of beer. Marcus envies his youthful bravado but is nonetheless glad to be out of that particular game. The impression grows stronger with each anecdote that his son inhabits a totally different capital city to the one Marcus travelled to and from, day in and day out, for thirty-five years. Doubtless they must have glimpsed the same monuments, travelled the same Tube lines, even bought a paper from the same kiosk, yet Paul's PR talk is at complete variance to Marcus's experience as a quantity surveyor for a small building company. Should he admonish or admire as Paul laughingly tells them of arriving at work, late and still inebriated, after an all-night party in Clapham? Had he, Marcus, ever been to an all-night party? Ever not had a full night's sleep? Paul's life is out of balance, askew, crazy, but he is loving it. Marcus's life has always been balanced – nutritionally, financially, emotionally – but ultimately, boring as buggery. He is glad that Paul is running at full pelt. Time to worry about wiser things at a later date.

"What about you, Martha?"

"Oh, you know, Dad. It's going well."

"Still in Edinburgh?"

"No. Didn't I tell you, I've just got a great job as a buyer for a company in Cork." Martha name-drops an interiors shop saturatingly advertised in the colour supplements. Achingly trendy and overpriced would have been his verdict, if asked. But he had learned, over the years, to hold his counsel on such matters.

But of course Martha hadn't told him. Nobody had told him. He had sort of assumed that the children would side with their mother and he hadn't wanted to upset any apple cart. There was a wavy line in terms of culpability depending on whether one moved out or one was ejected. Or, put another way, whether one had finally had enough of one's boring eejit of a husband or whether one had a right to start a new life of one's own. So, he had just sort of slipped away, wanting to avoid upsetting the children. Although, looking at Paul outstretched and overhanging the sofa by half a mile, and Martha, sitting so self-composed, maybe it is no longer appropriate to think of them as 'children'. And they don't look particularly upset either.

Brilliant that they are here and brilliant that Paul feels he can sprawl and brilliant that he does not have to nag him to get his feet off the coffee table. He can sprawl and put his feet wherever he wishes. A quiet little thought though, which he keeps to himself for fear of spoiling the atmosphere; it might have been better if the boy thought to take his shoes off first. Something unsavoury appears to be lurking between the treads. But he won't, for the life of him, at this point in the proceedings, say anything. At all. He smiles as Paul imitates his Liverpudlian boss shouting at his intern to "Stop pecking me 'ead, will ya?"

An electrical charge runs between the two children. He watches in paternal amusement as they verbally leapfrog each other, outdoing each other with tales of near escapes, drunken mishaps, unreliable landlords and skanky girlfriends/boyfriends. Absentmindedly, they reach out for the previously rejected cake and talk through half-chewed crumbs. He could not love them more.

After a period, they seem to have worn each other out. A conversational lull ensues. He wonders if now the true purpose of their visit will manifest itself. He waits in readiness for the pointed questions like, "So, Dad, any regrets?" "Can you still get down on bended knee?" "Too proud to beg?" But it seems that the hiatus only reminds them how hungry they are and how near lunchtime it is getting.

"I wonder what you fancy doing. Do you want to drive out a bit? There's a great pub in Clarendon. Could show you a few of the local sights. Or we could go across the road to the Red." What is one supposed to do? Velda usually managed the itinerary on their visits home. Last time he had been truly in charge of their programme of activities it had been driving them from football training to skateboarding, from horse riding to gymnastics. Now they are autonomous, adult, and the thought scares him. He has no automatic right now to any love or respect or obedience. It all has to be earned, all over again. He is on his own. They seem happy enough to let him decide. Maybe they too feel a bit displaced. What does it matter? They are here now and they look like they are intent on enjoying themselves. It doesn't look as if they are about to run off or sulk or slam any doors.

The decision being his, he decides on a quick round trip of the nearest villages, stopping at the Ox Tail for some of their excellent beer and sandwiches. "Come on then. Let's go."

In the warmth of a beautiful May morning, they obligingly peer down wells, gaze up at wrought-iron village signs, listen to his discourse on round church towers versus square ones and profess an interest in

Saxon shore forts. He takes them to one. A solitary wall rises from an embankment overlooking the tidal river. Its grey mass pushes down into the grass with the weight of an almost mythical tyranny. The Roman terracotta tiles layered between bands of cut and mortared flint are a persistent echo of the warm Umbrian sun failing to warm the chill of this hard, grey, sea-bound place.

In many ways, the children haven't changed so very much. Paul could never sit in the passenger seat of any car without fiddling with all the dials and controls within reach. Marcus grits his back teeth as Paul moves the radio dial from classical to country, from current affairs to pop. "What you looking for, son, exactly?" Marcus cannot prevent himself from asking, as Paul empties out the glove compartment.

"Don't know. Just looking. Got any travel sweets?"

"No." A tiny irksome question frets at Marcus's brain, whether Paul would allow him to rifle through the glove compartment of *his* car, or whether that would be considered a paternal snoop too far? Why is it that some privileges only go one way?

Marcus glances at Martha in the rearview mirror. As she gazes through the slightly open window at the flashing countryside, her dark blonde hair blows in ribbons across her face. She is oblivious to this in her contemplation of the features of the landscape, her eyes tracking right to left as a water tower approaches and flashes past. His heart nearly stops for love of her.

He mulls over their earlier conversation. Paul now in London, Martha in Cork. That is it. They are all going through changes. Life doesn't stand still. At twenty-three or at sixty-three. Perhaps they have more in common than just the traditional bonds of fatherhood and childhood.

But beneath this metaphysical revelation, two questions continue to gnaw inside his mind or 'peck his 'ead', as Paul described it. When are they going home? And how indeed is Velda? Could any ganging up be construed in the three of them being together? But then, he realises, that makes three questions and with the fabulous fifteenth-century Ox Tail less than two miles away, the matter of whether to sample the mild or the pale ale first becomes a far more pressing matter.

After a three-course lunch made all the more succulent by the children's evident enjoyment, they are on their way home again, Paul mercifully quietened by some activity on his phone and Martha fast asleep in the back of the car.

Between concentrating on the sharp bends and the sunken ditches, his mind moves ahead to the meeting tonight. Both Madge and Mr Edge had asked if he was going. If he is honest with himself, he had thought that being a relative newcomer gave him immunity to the travails of his chosen resting place. So he had not heeded the call to all to attend the village fair action meeting. But it seems that others had different ideas. "Fresh blood. Fresh ideas." "More the merrier."

Dull as, Marcus thought quietly, but feared to appear disobliging.

So, he will have to go to the meeting. He will offer the kids a quick cup of tea and beans on toast and hasten them on their way home. Maybe then time for a bit of shut-eye and down to the Red for the 7.30 start.

As he parks the car alongside Bob's Garage, Paul and Martha stir and stretch. Paul lets out an impressive two-tone belch while a look of startlement distorts Martha's face before she realises where she is.

"Cuppa, anyone?" Paul and Martha resume their places, Paul on the sofa to watch a football match and Martha on a dining chair, elbows hooked behind her around the maidenhair fern on the window sill, as if the previous cultural and gastronomic tour had been but a brief interlude. Already they are staking their claims to their separate pieces of furniture.

Time is getting on. If they don't get a wiggle on, he won't have a chance for a bit of shut-eye before he has to leave again.

Maybe Martha is thinking the same because she rises from contemplation of her toenails and goes into the kitchen. "Brought some stuff from home for you." She empties the contents of her many bags onto the kitchen table. Marcus groans inwardly for she has indeed come bearing cast-offs and rejects from the former marital home. "Mum wondered whether you wanted this." Martha offers a garish plaster of Paris doll, circa 1930 by the look of the cringeworthy greens and yellows. "She wasn't sure if it was your mum's or hers but she says she doesn't want it." For the life of him, he wouldn't let her see his rejection. One good tap against the kitchen table when everyone is gone, and the head would come off, sealing its fate forever.

"Thank you, darling. Very kind. Anything else?"

Nothing of real practical benefit emerges from the bags other than an asparagus steamer and a pair of secateurs. Might there be a subliminal message in the pair of close-quartered blades? Maybe not. No sign of the Clarice Cliff. It must be assumed that Velda's claim was the greater.

The question that burns in his throat is, 'How's your mum?' Or would it be friendlier, less confrontational to ask, 'How's Mum? Everything at home alright?' But, actually, does he really want to know? What could he do if things weren't 'alright'? On the day's evidence, the two of them are doing fine and that should be satisfaction enough.

"Dad, come and look at these." Paul cranes his neck over the back of the sofa to call through to the kitchen.

"What's that, son?"

"Photos. Of today."

"Budge up then. Get your feet off." Paul raises himself above the horizontal. Martha comes through from the kitchen and arranges herself along the sofa back. He feels himself touched on all sides. Paul holds the screen up and flicks through the shots of their afternoon. Most are selfies, he explains, and show Paul and Martha grinning and gurning behind his back. They seem particularly amused by a shot of him pointing to the remains of a Neolithic flint mine while Martha, with her forefingers stretching her mouth wide, pulls a monkey face. "Did you pay a blind bit of attention?"

"Er, of course we did, didn't we, Mar?"

"Every word, Dad."

"Mmmm. Likely thing." Neither feels his disapproval too keenly or contritely.

"I'll post these so you can have a look at them later. You are on social media, aren't you, Dad?" Marcus shrugs. "Da-ad. You're so behind. Get with it. If you 'friend' Martha and me, you can keep up with what we're doing. And we can keep an eye on you too."

Marcus rather thinks that being a father is somewhat superior to being a 'friend', but indicates grudgingly that he will think about it. It would, after all, plug the gap between their meetings and bring them a little closer to him, virtually, if not actually. He pauses before saying, not without some regret, "Anyway. Sorry to say, but I've got to go to a meeting tonight. Er…"

"Where at?" asks Martha.

"Just over the road, at the pub. There's some sort of village fair going on in the summer and it seems beholden upon the more community-minded to join the committee. There's a retired colonel or some such just moved into the Hall who is showing great munificence by allowing the villagers to use his field. He's also sending along his sidekick to 'help out'. Seems that Stan the Man, who runs the local ironmongers, and who was chairman, has taken umbrage over this turn of events and has resigned. At least that's the official version. Been booted off, more like. Think I've just been invited along to represent the silent majority. Could just make you some beans on toast or something before you, I mean, before I go."

"That's alright, Dad, we'll come over to the pub with you, if that's OK."

"Right. Lovely. More tea?"

Marcus heaves himself off the sofa, disturbing the equilibrium, causing Martha to crash into his vacated place. The children tickle and pinch each other. Their laughter ricochets off the kitchen walls as he puts bread into the toaster and checks the scrubbing brush for maggots. He thinks back to the photos on Paul's phone. Gluck's aria, 'O del mio dolce ardor', comes into his head. He hums loudly and expressively. It has all been quite splendid.

There is no time to wash up before they are due at the pub. People are already starting to arrive, moving from the darkness outside into the orange glow within. "Are you sure you want to do this? Won't be terribly exciting for you."

The children hoist on their coats and scamper down the stairs behind him. He feels a bit harried, wary of losing his footing to this herd of two.

Cecily

She pays for her drink and leans past other drinkers to place the change in a collection tube for the hospice, the coins making a dull thud with their small drop. She picks up the canister and lays it in her handbag.

"If I didn't know, I could have you stopped and searched!"

Old Bob is standing behind her with a froth-rimed glass in his hand, ready for a refill. "Should be a good forty quid in there. It all makes a difference." Barry, the barman, appears in front of them.

"Shift that other canister over here, Barry, would you?" Bob demands. Barry parts the jars of honey-roasted peanuts, chilli almonds and olives and places the empty canister in the centre of the bar. Bob picks it up and inserts it between the cash till and people reaching out for their change. "Come on. Divvy up. Good cause." Most do. "Good man, Henry. Too long gone." Cecily squeezes Bob's arm in tender affection, grateful for the instant of closeness brought by the mention of her Henry's name.

Oh no, look who's here! she murmurs to herself as Mandy pushes her way to the bar. The two women exchange a glance. To Cecily, this woman is as unnatural as a black beetle upon a white breast, a needle in the eye. During Henry's last week in the hospice, while all stepped back discreetly and tactfully, this monstrous woman danced centre stage like a houri, holding his hand, leaving sandwich wrappers on the visitor's chair, pink moisturising cream smeared on his feet, the lid unscrewed. What gave her that right? Mandy's iron-hard look as she stares back at her over the bar gives a mighty impetus to the word spinning round Cecily's own head: bitch!

Twice this siren allowed herself to be glimpsed. Once holding Henry's inert hand. The other, leaving the car park after the dawn phone call that summoned Cecily from her briefest absence to his deathbed.

Ned could not apologise enough. His utter embarrassment was as fulsome as Cecily's shock and awe at Mandy's audacity and disrespect were word-less. She could not blame Ned; he was far too ruddy and robust to have the faintest idea what drove his wife to hijack another woman's sorrow.

It's obvious the woman is unbalanced. Stalking her, since that day they sat opposite each other in the anodyne clinic, each hoping for ano-nymity in the big town. Except it isn't stalking exactly. Mandy's is a persistent, ominous, hostile presence, one she can't rid herself of. The bruise that never heals. Was it something about the soft tones, the soft colours of the hos-pice that resembled the quietness, the professional efficiency of the other place, the clinic? Two doors, two exits, side by side. Both ushering out the dead. But very, very different. One door for those who had a chance of a life, who'd reached full term or at least nearly. The other for those who hadn't even had that chance.

It's an appalling image and one that ambushes Cecily each time she claps eyes on Mandy. She pushes it to the back of her mind and, picking up her drink and notepad, squeezes her way through the crowd before the toothless gums rattle in her ear and the dummy shrieks its obscenities through its dropped jaw.

Marcus

Marcus buys drinks for himself, Paul and Martha, and looks around in case he might offer a drink to anyone else. From the corner of the pub, the meeting is called to order and people drift from the bar to squeeze themselves onto the banquettes and chairs in the corner. Marcus finds himself next to the lady from the house opposite, the note-taker for these proceedings. On her other side, a tall young man with curly blonde hair with whom she shares a packet of crisps. Paul and Martha sit near to but not part of the group. Paul has two pints in front of him and is pouring one pint down his throat without, apparently, the intervention of a swallow reflex. Chain drinking.

"Good evening. My name is Cecily."

Marcus draws his attention back from Paul's thirst and shakes her hand.

"Marcus. I live above the deli. Just moved in a few weeks ago."

"Yes, I know. I live opposite."

Marcus just holds on to the words, "I know. I've seen you," before they spill out of his mouth. He nods enthusiastically instead. Presumably the person sitting in the large wheel-backed chair, a few feet away, determinedly apart from the surrounding hubbub, demarcated by an open laptop and three phones on the table in front of him, is the Colonel's sidekick, co-opted to manage this rabble and present a glossy image of the village to the world.

Madge had been hopping between outrage and barely suppressed excitement when he'd called into the post office a week or so back to pay his newspaper bill. "Have you heard? Have you heard what's happened?"

The question had evidently been a rhetorical one for she barely allowed him the time to compose his face into one that conveyed even the slightest bit of interest before she was off again. "Bloody disgrace, I call it. Stan the Man's chaired that summer fair committee for donkey's. Shoved him off they have. Without so much as a by your leave."

Marcus waited with a crisp ten-pound note valleyed around his outstretched forefinger, hoping that it might arrest the flow of Madge's voluble indignation long enough to pay his paper bill and exit. 'By your leave', an old-fashioned courtesy that was not, it seemed, to be extended to him; he would just have to stop and listen to this tale of woe undiminished despite being oft-repeated.

"I said to Bill, and to Doreen, and Mrs Turnbull, for all that's she's as deaf as a post. I said to them, 'That's no way to treat a man of standing. Stan's been the Man forever.'"

Marcus tutted sympathetically. It would seem that this parvenu of a Colonel had been throwing his weight around. Just because he'd bought up Haughton Hall.

"Bill said he'd heard that the feudal rights that went with the Manor extended to more than the estate and the millstream and a few town fields, if you know what I mean. I told him not to be so filthy."

Marcus stood patiently while the Colonel's plans were trumpeted from the inexpertly drawn lines of lipstick on Madge's mouth until the doorbell pinged for the next customer. He seized his chance.

"Must dash. Bye."

Despite some disaffection in the village over the replacement of the *ancien régime*, it seems that most had decided to swerve any revolt and just go along with things for a quiet life, despite Madge's fervent outrage.

Nothing quiet about this chappie's outfit though, Marcus observes, his jacket resembling more one of Velda's macramé creations than anything practical and serviceable enough to offer protection from a squally easterly breeze. A high-browed baseball cap sits atop his chiselled face. Or at least Marcus assumes that the face of someone confident enough to wear string would have to be chiselled, a fact masked by an abundance of Squirrel Nutkin facial hair.

"Nice to have you on board," Cecily leans in to him and whispers *sotto voce.* Marcus turns to her and grins, allowing his eyes to briefly sweep over her face. Big fringe, dark eyelashes. She draws her hair away from her cheek, revealing elaborate earrings. He wonders whether she is one of Velda's crew.

"Right, everyone. Let's get this show on the road. I'd like to introduce myself. Chris Eveans. Spelt E-V-E-A-N-S," he emphasises, "pronounced Evans, as in Good Evans."

The tightly packed committee blinks, in unison. No one laughs although one or two allow themselves a tight smirk. "As you all know, Major Welding has kindly contracted my services to this village of...er... er..."

"Bullenden," someone pipes up from the other end of the table.

"Er...yes...Bullenden. Thank you for that. In order to maximise our social mapping and create a buzz around...er...er...Bullenden, as it were."

Marcus glances round the table. Mr Eveans's words must be as incomprehensible to the rest of the committee as they are to him; even Cecily's pen is still.

"So, I think it might be appropriate if we go round the table, as an ice-breaker exercise, telling everyone our names, a little about ourselves and perhaps mentioning something that is unique. Unique to you. A thing perhaps or a possession or an ambition; something that no one else has. So, who would like to start?"

Inevitably no one volunteers. Instead, to a certain amount of grumbling and chair-scraping, half of the putative committee break away and edge towards the bar. Perhaps there is a revolt after all.

"Ridiculous. Lived in the village all my life. Why do we need to do a bloody ice-breaker exercise, whatever one of those is?"

"If we don't know what makes each of us unique by now, then we never will."

"I'm not telling my secrets to no one."

During the exodus, embarrassed as he is for Mr WhateverHisName-Was, Marcus wonders if he could signal Paul to fetch him another pint of beer, his glass being devoid now even of froth. Paul's attention, however, is being held firm by the women's national football team at large on the TV screen. He leans forward to try and catch Martha's eye but she is stuck fast to the side of the young man who had been sharing Cecily's crisps. She looks animated.

Eveans glances across at the breakaway group, brow furrowed crossly. Cecily turns to her left to pat the young man on the knee and gesture him to be quiet or to go and be noisy elsewhere. With a degree of knee-knocking, he and Martha choose the latter option. The remaining members of the committee busy themselves with writing their names onto labels and sticking them onto their lapels.

A loud laugh rises from the bar. "Spelled P-O-N-C-E, more like." Oh dear, frets Marcus. It is beginning to look rather that Stanley from Hammer and Tongs had a better way of dealing with the local crowd than this rather effete-looking strip from up London.

"Right. Well, I think I understand your concerns, ladies and gentlemen, but before reporting back to Major Welding, I would like to make some progress with the agenda at hand. If we could turn to Item One…" Marcus is relieved that the young chappie seems to have finally got his hands on the reins and is making some headway.

An uncomfortably full sensation makes itself known to him. Oh no, that old trouble again. Warning sign. Ten minutes and counting to find the Gents. To his increasing chagrin, there is no way on God's earth that he can exit now, given that the committee has been massively culled to five members strong. Bad enough the young ones had broken off like a melting iceberg. Another inappropriate image, as he weights his knee down with his left hand to stop it jiggling in desperation. Fancy Pants Chris would totally throw his dolly out of the pram if he excused himself now. Trapped!

Distraction. What could he distract himself with? He glances at Cecily's pad. Her pen is busy fashioning emoticons that jump and giggle their way across the ruled lines of the page. What is he doing here anyway? Hardly been in the village ten minutes and here he is squashed between two locals attending a disorganised meeting about some event that is likely to go off like a damp squib overseen by a clothes horse that has escaped from London Fashion Week.

"Item Two on the agenda. Conveniences." Marcus groans inwardly.

Nothing like the image of a row of Portaloos to make one's own situation more desperate.

Mercifully, the agenda items are dealt with swiftly. Within fifteen minutes, Any Other Business looms. Marcus's attention is taken by watching Paul swallow his third pint, oblivious to the oppositional conflicts taking place within his father – a dry throat and a full bladder.

With a start, Marcus realises he has become the object of Eveans's focussed intent. "Just wondering if there was anything Mr Blatt would like to contribute." Chris Eveans looks at the unfurling label on his jacket with, is it menace, in his eye? Has he marked him down as an interloper, a spy? Good Lord. It looks as if he is being called upon for a bright idea. Had he inadvertently called attention to himself by shuffling around in increasing discomfort at his over-loaded bladder? Marcus picks up the empty glass in front of him and seeks inspiration within it.

"Er."

The row of faces look at him.

"Um."

Cecily sits poised with pen in hand.

"We-ell."

The ladies reach for their handbags, the men into their jacket pockets.

Eveans stares resolutely at Marcus. The meeting cannot be called to an end until Marcus has come up with a good idea.

"What is it?" Marcus struggles to remember something Paul had shown him that afternoon.

"What's it called?" The Chair drops his head slightly to one side as if to say, Don't expect me to help you, Buster.

"Social – er, social media. That's it. That's what we need." Marcus recalls the photographs Paul had posted of that afternoon and the discourse he had given of the use of such social media in the promotion of blah blah blah. Truth be told, he hadn't really been listening. But he must have taken on board enough to allow the following thought: "We could advertise our event online, get everyone involved, post pictures, get contributors to put their information up, keep everyone informed of progress. Er…that sort of thing."

"Splendid." A few round the table nod their approval.

"Right, well, Mr Blatt, we shall leave that to you, shall we? I now call this meeting to a close."

The meeting is suddenly and gloriously over. While Marcus ponders what it is exactly that he has let himself in for, and what he might have thought his qualifications are for the task, Eveans busies himself closing down his laptop and selecting a pocket, of which there are many, for his multifarious phones.

The corner empties.

Should he offer to buy Cecily a drink? Would that be considered a bit forward? A loud bark comes from the games room. Martha is cueing up. That young man is pretending to drop chalk into her drink. She prods him with the end of her cue. In contrast to their laughter and movement, Marcus feels wooden, awkward, and even more desperate for the Gents. Cecily stares ahead, also watching the antics in the games room.

"They don't have any of our hang-ups, do they? None of our inhibitions."

Marcus smiles weakly, too polite, too inhibited to excuse himself.

Eveans lifts his buff rucksack to his shoulder. With a curt nod, he walks through the exit, his knee-high Roman sandals clacking slightly on the stone flags.

"What the blazes was that? Did you see what he was wearing?"

"Kazuo Ortega."

"Beg your pardon? And what's that got to do with bunting and bangers?"

"Kazuo Ortega. That's what he was wearing. His *Folie de Pierre* collection. Premiered on the London Student LoSt Show last year. Destined to become a big name in the international fashion arena."

Marcus gazes on Cecily in awe. She definitely isn't one of Velda's lot. Might even be worth putting up with the village's marrow envy or whatever it is that compels them to put on this wretched summer fair, to get to know her better. Just a crying shame that faulty internal plumbing should strip him of that opportunity at this very moment in time. He shuffles awkwardly past her. "Excuse me. Excuse me. Sorry. Sorry," leaving her alone at the table, staring fixedly towards the bar.

9

Cecily – and Marcus? No chance

Cecily leans against the work bench in Gray's Garage. Young Bob cleans nozzles with a rag while Old Bob voices his opinion from underneath a car, knocking away at a crank shaft. "Doesn't bring his cars here for servicing, does he? If you live in a village, you should support that village, that's what I say." Cecily is inclined to agree but, looking around at the ivy making its way in through the skylight in the asbestos roof, the old analogue instruments rusting away on shelves and the oil-drenched drawer that serves as a cash till, she has to acknowledge that the Major might not feel that his top-of-the-range SUV is best served in this small, rural garage that still has three decommissioned Fina petrol pumps on the forecourt.

As with most of the village that day, they are spending a pleasant half hour discussing the events of the previous evening.

Old Bob compares the Major – not Colonel, as it turns out – to an irresistible force of nature. "He has no respect for the old way of doing things. Was a time when you waited to be invited to do something, especially if you were an incomer. You'd be quietly given the nod. Told that you'd be given favourable consideration if you were to, I don't know, put in for something."

And why is Eveans, 'spelled P-O-N-C-E' – the two Bobs had laughed when she relayed this joke – even bothering with such a small event as their summer fair? There was a time when the village's ambitions amounted to no more than a run on a few pots of jam and giving the headmaster a soaking in the stocks in order to sponsor a child in Africa and buy a few silks for repairs to the kneelers in the church.

It feels like the ably assisted Major is organising the Queen's Jubilee Thames Regatta all over again. Isn't that the trouble when men take something over, Cecily wonders quietly to herself? When Gladys and Iris Petty ran the show it sorted itself largely, almost like clockwork. This trumped-up Chairman, with his ABC in Events Management, his logarithms, Gantt charts, flow rates, pieces of coloured paper, is proving a bit rich for the old-timers. Rather like Long John Silver's parrot, Captain Flint. And Stan the Man is looking decidedly deflated these days, all agree.

Cecily isn't sure where she stands in relation to the fair. She doesn't want to be thought of as stuck in her ways, for sure. On the contrary. Given that she is about to give Marcus a lesson in social media, she is even ahead of the curve. For once in her life.

But she isn't looking forward to the morning closeted with Marcus. He is a nice enough chap, but he's obviously a bit of a worrier. Might even have a touch of St Vitus's dance the way his leg jiggled and bounced at the meeting last night. Perhaps a bit slow too. He'd offered to buy her a drink, which she'd accepted, *par politesse*, and it had taken him a good few minutes to gather himself up off his seat. What was that all about?

"Has anybody set eyes on this Major character?" asks Bob Senior, still only identifiable by a pair of bent legs and his fourteen-eyelet Doc Martens.

"Apparently he works two days in London. Used to work in Monte Carlo but told Madge that the centre of gravity of the financial sector is no longer to be found in these discrete, sequestered principalities but must be located in more open, transparent and regulated operations."

"Wha'?"

"No, I don't know what that means either," confesses Cecily. "But Madge, for once, was impressed. Apparently he has the regulation Botox bunny for a wife and thread veins on his nose. And he's a Major. Not a Colonel. Gets very cross if he's called Colonel."

"Oh. Right."

"Well, can you keep my old jalopy on the road for another year?" Young Bob casts a sneering glance towards the rusting Volvo waiting its turn in the MOT bay.

"Given half a chance, I'd condemn it."

"Don't be mean, Bob. Good for another hundred thousand miles your dad said, last time."

"And so it is, Robert. Mind what you say to our customers."

Cecily puts down the mug of coffee Young Bob had made her, trying to wrest her gaze away from the tannin-stained interior, the oily thumb mark and the gobbets of plastic milk spinning on the top. "Right, better go. Got a computer lesson."

"Bye, Cecily. I'll give you a call when we've done the necessary."

She picks her way over the cold concrete floor, strewn with trolley jacks and tool boxes. When Marcus brought up the topic of social media at the meeting last night, Chris Eveans had reacted as if, finally, somebody was getting the message. Poor Marcus looked as if he were a sprat that had inadvertently wandered into a lobster pot. No way out and trapped on all sides with a hungry and angry-looking crustacean. When she'd leaned over to him and whispered, "Don't worry. I'll help," he'd looked at her gratefully and given her a limp thumbs up.

Nonetheless, it is a bit annoying that she will now have to spend the morning in close quarters with someone she hardly knows. But this seems to be the way that Mr Eveans operates. Networking. Issuing different coloured Post-it notes for different areas of responsibility. Some poor folks at the meeting looked like they'd been caught in the crossfire at a paint-balling event. "There you go," Chris Eveans had said, leaning over the table and slapping a coloured square in front of Marcus. "Lime for IT. You're the man."

Who exactly is this Marcus? Last night at the pub, she had been trapped between him and the wall. With that odious Mandy twisting on her left stiletto and describing parabolic shapes at the bar in animated self-projection, she had not wanted to leave her seat. Oh dear, did he think she was riveted by his company? He had rather turned on the full force of his attention. It felt like she was being interviewed or in conversation with a quiz master. Question after question after question. How long had she been in the village? Did she have any children? She saw him drop his gaze to her left hand. Was he looking for a wedding ring? He laughed too loudly and too emphatically, seemingly more so once his eye had landed on her gold band. She might have told him about Henry and introduced him to Henry's son, Tom, who had called in long enough to wrestle with her over a bag of crisps and flirt with a random girl in the pool room on his way to Amsterdam, but hadn't felt inclined to. What with Mandy and the discontent in the village over the fair and one thing and another, everything seems fractured, broken, out of sync.

She won't offer him biscuits. She will put the laptop on the kitchen table. Offer him an instant coffee. That would be it. And keep the phone by her and the back door open in case she needs to holler for help.

Oh, it is all just a bit too wearying. What is she worrying about? He had looked a bit pathetic, to be frank, not predatory at all. Did he really only have the one jumper? It would be time for him to think about buying another one soon as this one seems to be unravelling past the cuffs. She recognised in him the air of the newly separated. A certain gung-ho zest for the ordinary, as if buying basic provisions had never been so fascinating. The rapid scanning of a crowd looking for that one special person (or their potential replacement). Ingrained habits, like the courtesy of opening a door when no one is following, over-ordering, a steadying outstretched hand when there is no one to protect from oncoming danger.

She should know, after all.

Young Bob

Young Bob picks up the mug Cecily left. It has the faintest streak of lipstick on it. "Just going for a smoke, Dad."

The small meadow at the back of the garage is overrun with emerging buttercups softening and illuminating the piles of rubble and tyres scattered about. Bob no longer beats himself up for not clearing up this patch of land; it has become an old, tired regret, worn thin. Nature could do his work for him. Before long there will be the new season's nettles and thistles, tall, on the move in the gentle breeze, thrusting themselves in the gaps between the debris.

He sits heavily on the wooden bench and pulls his cigarettes from the top pocket of his overalls. Shaking his lighter, which refuses to flame, he curses out loud. It always unsettles him to see Cecily. She has that unmistakable de Mare stamp about her familiar to him since schooldays.

The same bearing, the same sense of the absurd, kindly eyes. But, whereas Cecily's face has become harrowed over the intervening years, her style more assured, it is the memory of Amelia at the age of nearly twenty that he reaches for.

The scene always comes back to him of the two of them at the railway station at Bremen. It's on a permanent loop. How long ago is it now? Twenty years? More? A gap year they would call it now. Then it was just an adventure. They'd been travelling for nearly three weeks. They were going to see Europe, travel through North Africa and maybe head back on up to Turkey. No time constraints, just take off. When he looks back now, he yearns for that optimism, courage, happiness that bound the two of them together. They were so unbelievably naïve, bombproof.

He'd turned to her on the platform, the hand holding his yellow phone card trembling. He felt sick and had to sit down on the wooden bench, dropping his rucksack to the ground. "I'm sorry, Melly. I'm so, so sorry."

She knelt beside him, her hand on his shoulder a small and pitiful offering against the storm raging inside him. He lifted his head but his eyes didn't see hers. His hand didn't cover hers. She was already out of the picture. "I've got to go home. Dad's not well. It's all too, too soon. After Mum, and all."

They sat on the bench together for two hours. She watched the pigeons hop and peck and squabble. He pressed his hands into his belly and rocked back and forth, tears spreading over his cheeks. The sleek trains became fewer and fewer, the sleek commuters fewer and fewer, till the station was taken up with night staff: shift workers, postal workers, security guards. They fell asleep. Where did all the pigeons go?

He wanted her to come back with him. Get Dad settled again. Give him a few more months. After all, they had all their life in front of them, didn't they? It had obviously hit Dad hard, Mum going.

It had been hard to catch Aunty Jane's words over the hiss and clang and chatter of the railway station. She said his dad had had some kind of a breakdown, just sat in the chair and stared at the cold fireplace. If you asked him to do anything, he would do it, but in such a low-key way. "Bob. Come to the table and eat your tea." "Bob, bedtime now." He'd gone docile, not senile. He wasn't asking for his son to come home, but what could he do?

It was long after she'd gone, left him on that platform to make his own way home while she continued on her way, that he began to doubt her feelings. Maybe she just hadn't loved him enough to postpone her plans for a month or two. Hadn't they been inseparable at school? Hadn't their discovery of each other meant the discovery of Love in its whole mystical entirety? Hadn't they both been each other's key to the Wonderland?

She hadn't said very much, just waited for him to come to his decision. Her decision must have been made in the inner space of her own mind. She would go on. Or maybe she would have come back with him, if he'd asked her to. But he wouldn't. It was something she had to volunteer. Which she didn't.

Both battling simultaneously; both arriving at different outcomes.

Cecily

At eleven precisely, there is a firm knock at the front door. Trueman barks loudly in response, matching the rhythm. "Shh, boy. On the step." Trueman lugubriously makes his way up the stairs, sitting on the fourth step, resting his front paws on the third. "Quiet!" He looks at her with apparent disdain for failing to understand his purpose. She kisses the top of his head, reiterates a silent warning with the end of her finger and opens the door to Marcus, who makes an elaborate show of wiping his feet. Trueman jumps to the hall floor in one bound and curls his lip, silently, at the intruder.

"Oh, my goodness. What a...what a...dog!" Marcus pants. Perhaps Trueman understood the situation better than she had given him credit for. By standing between the two of them, this removed any obligation to offer the man a kiss or a handshake.

"Come through. Don't mind the dog."

"Er, perhaps easier said than done."

Cecily, making her way down the hall towards the kitchen, turns to see Marcus still firmly planted on the doormat reluctant to move past Trueman sitting on his haunches, technically quiet and technically still but nonetheless emanating a degree of menace.

"He won't hurt you. Soft as a brush. Basket!"

A flash of insight passes between the dog and the man. Trueman, happy that he has made himself understood, lowers his upper lip, barks once and leads the way into the kitchen.

Marcus sits at the square wooden table and accepts Cecily's offer of a cup of coffee. Cecily notes that he has taken the seat furthest away from the dog basket and seems reassured by the distance and quantity of woodwork between the two of them. "Lovely morning."

"Yes."

Cecily fills the kettle, bracing herself for what promises to be a long and difficult morning. It is going to have to be the good coffee to see her through and, despite her earlier intentions, she reaches for the cookies she'd made the day before. "Would you like one? They're maple and pecan." Marcus takes the two largest ones and starts to chomp before she can offer him a plate.

"So good of you to give me a hand with this. Don't really understand how I got co-opted."

Cecily smiles her understanding and is about to offer some reassurance before Marcus takes off again.

"As you know, I've only been in the village a few months. Wasn't sure if there was anything I could do to help. It was my son, Paul, who put the idea into my head. We'd been out that afternoon and he'd taken some pictures of the local sights. And posted them on this site he uses."

Cecily listens to Marcus as she pours the coffee. He seems unstoppable, as if he hasn't really spoken to anyone for ages.

"Paul's our eldest. He's twenty-four. Then there's Martha. You might have seen them? They popped up a couple of days ago. Nice really. Their mum and I have separated. Thirty years together. Married for twenty-seven. It was her decision. Didn't really have a say in it."

Cecily sits back in her chair and absorbs the flow of words. A picture builds in her mind. *Velda as Tribal Mumma. Marcus whittled away till he is stick-thin. A flash of ethnic print. Earrings like chandeliers. Marcus as failed warrior. Children leaving to catch their own wildebeest. The end of his civilisation.*

"It's not as if I didn't provide for her and the family. Don't think anyone really realises what it's like journeying up to London every day, the crowds on the trains, nowhere, nowhere, nowhere to just be, to breathe, to walk in a straight line. Bloody awful it was, for years. I know Velda didn't have it easy, what with the kids and everything. I know they can be a handful."

So, as Marcus clickety-clacks up and down the track, the track moves over the face of a clock until at the pre-appointed time, the train stops, Marcus steps down into the terminus. There are no more trains. There is nowhere else to go.

Marcus leans into the table and pours himself another cup of coffee and grabs two more cookies. Cecily slides a side plate under his chin, but he doesn't notice. "Strange feeling, when you don't know where you belong any more. I've always liked this part of the country, but I sometimes get the feeling people look at me as if I've landed from outer space."

A scorched patch of earth, a strange craft disappearing into the disturbed sky, Marcus standing with a suitcase in his hand.

Trueman is now under the table. He stretches his back legs luxuriantly and releases a fart. *Rocket fuel.*

Cecily opens the laptop and powers it up. "Shall we take a look?"

"Yes. Sorry. Am aware I've been going on a bit."

"Not at all. It's good to—"

"It's just that, I don't know, you see people all the time but you don't really connect."

Cecily sees herself with a wad of tissue and an old-fashioned letting dish, mopping Marcus's tears.

"It's absolutely lovely to be sitting here with you."

Any small instinct she might have had to tuck in the threads of his fraying cuffs disappears instantly at the thought that Marcus might be enjoying some sort of 'connection' at this very moment.

"Right. Let's get on." she says briskly.

Marcus does not appear to have heard her. Even as the laptop jingles its way into life, he continues to look mournfully across the table at her. "Anyway, tell me about you."

Anybody who says, "Anyway, tell me about you," in Cecily's experience, has usually only been either drawing breath or been told in some previous socialisation training that it was only polite to let the other person speak. Neither was a terribly promising start to a stimulating two-way conversation. He'd obviously forgotten the Q and A session of the previous evening. And anyway, her terrors were too private and too deeply buried to be lifted immediately into view. It took time, and persuasion, and wine to exhume them.

"I can show you what I know, which isn't an awful lot, but it would be a start for you to get going on, and then we can have a look at what we can do to help publicise the summer fair and keep Mr Eveans sweet!" Cecily smiles at him a cheery smile and wishes inwardly that he would just cheer up.

"Yes. That sounds great. Thank you so much." He shuffles his chair round to Cecily's side of the table. Trueman lifts his head and surveys this new proximity. "Any more coffee, by the way?"

"I'll make you some. Have a look at this while I put the kettle on."

Cecily moves to the sink and turns the tap on full blast. It sprays water everywhere, the force of it seeming to express some of the tension rising within her.

"I think you've got a message."

"Sorry." Cecily turns off the tap. "Can't hear you."

"Think you've got a message. And you've splashed yourself, by the way."

Cecily turns the laptop towards herself, wiping droplets of water from her jumper. Tilly is sending her a private message. "Excuse me a minute. I'll just reply and then we can get back."

Hi Sis. You online? Unusual.

> Hi Tils. Yes. Just about to give a
> computer lesson. Moi!

Ha ha. Phone me when you've
finished.

> Righto x

x

122

Marcus

While Cecily is fiddling on her computer, he makes his way back into the hallway, easing his way past the recumbent hound. The exposed vertical stud beams partitioning the hallway from the downstairs rooms, blackened and fibrous with age, remind him of the acres and acres of forest cleared for dwellings, for fuel, for pasture over aeons of time. Beams embedded within the walls, some short, some long, some bent, some die straight, seem to represent in their varying angles the slow stages of fall and decline of all organic matter, while yet in their antiquity representing solidity, constancy and a link with the past.

When Cecily returns with a full pot of coffee and a replenished plate of biscuits, she finds Marcus gazing at the two dragons carved on the corner braces above the arch through to the kitchen. Tiny flecks of paint remain from a revivalist return to Tudor splendour when the creatures spumed red fire and flicked their sour green tails.

"I don't really know if they are friend or foe."

"Perhaps they cancel each other out," he offers, looking at the creatures coiled within their confined spaces. "They don't look too friendly but maybe that's because they are in some kind of face-off. Perhaps one dragon would be more dangerous, less preoccupied."

"Well, as my sister Tilly points out, they are facing sure and certain extinction if their only diet is vestal virgins."

Maybe that is it; with no dragons to slay, we turn upon each other.

Something about Cecily's house moves Marcus; the age of it, the fabric of it, reaching like a hand deeper into the soil from whence we came, its timber frames symbolising a passing forwards from one man's rib to the next man's rib to the next and the next over the generations; the pargeting like the painted ladies of court; the irregular lofty rooms and low-brow rooms and musty cellar, all tiny fragments from the torn documents of history caught in a second of time.

The long rotation forward and back. The long rotation downward and up.

Cecily

The lesson, such as it is, passes well enough, although it is not long before Cecily is confirmed in her suspicion that she is only marginally more *au fait* with the technology than Marcus. Oh Christ, she thinks, after the lesson appears to have stalled, is he expecting lunch?

"Right. I think we've covered everything. Must get on."

"Yes. Yes. Certainly. So good of you to point me in the right direction. If you could let me know which of your contacts might be favourable to adding me as a friend, then we can get a page of our own going. Excellent." She is pleased to note that he rises a good deal quicker from his seat when under the watchful gaze of her dog than he did last night in the pub.

Trueman rises too, his gaze fixed steadily on Cecily's visitor. He tentatively pats the top of the hound's head with two fingertips and heads down the hall for the front door.

"Let me get the door. It sticks." Marcus stands on the doormat, his notebook clutched to his chest, his gaze sweeping over the pictures lining the stairwell, the oak console table, stroking the fringe of the kilim with the toe of his shoe. Is he going to say something? She desperately hopes not as it would possibly be of an embarrassing nature. Anyway, she wants to chat to Tilly. "OK. Good luck."

"Thanks. I know where you are if I need you."

"Indeed."

Finally, he squeezes himself through the gap of the part-opened front door. "I'll be off."

"Yes. Indeed. Off you go."

"Cheerio."

"Bye."

"Bye."

Oh for goodness' sake, she thinks, just go. She watches as Marcus makes his way down the steps to the pavement. He turns and waves once more like a departing lover. She pretends not to see and closes the front door on him. She settles Trueman and dials Tilly's number.

"Hi, Tils. You still there?"

"Hi, Cecily. Yes."

"What's up?"

"Really worried about Lizzie."

"What's happened?"

"It's that vile piece of work she is living with."

"What's happened?"

"Told you before things were not going well."

"Yeah."

"He says he's leaving."

"Is that a bad thing?"

"No, except he's claiming what amounts to half her earnings."

"How come?"

"You know we set up the kennels for them?"

"Yeah."

"Well, legally he can claim half the earnings. Less costs."

"But he doesn't do anything!"

"I know. Lizzie, poor child, has been working her socks off, setting up the business. She's really beginning to make a go of it. And she's at college part-time."

"How can he claim anything?"

"He says it's his right because his name's on the paperwork."

"But you've said he just sits on his worthless arse all day..."

"Faffing on the computer. Lizzie thinks he's sold her college books, some jewellery and bits and pieces."

"Joking!"

"No. And another thing. He's claiming some of the good will in the business."

"What a total scrote. Can't you just tell him to eff off?"

"No! Says he's entitled. Sits in that caravan. Squatting. Smug git. Lizzie gets up at five thirty every morning. She feeds the dogs, cleans out the cages, takes them for walks, pets them, then she's on her way to college. Same again when she gets home. Then she'll start to get the caravan tidied, clothes washed, tea made and cleared up. Then she goes and sorts the animals again. It's a sixteen-hour day and it's supposed to be a partnership."

"Hasn't he any shame?"

"No, and poor Lizzie's in pieces. Sleeps at home now. Feels like he's won. Makes my flesh creep."

"What does Edmund say?"

"Not really told him. He'd go ballistic."

"Sounds like somebody should go ballistic with him."

"Probably. He's the sort of person who backchats women but runs scared of men."

"Well, why don't you tell Edmund?"

"'Cos I don't want to upset him. He's got enough worries with the business. He thinks they've just had a spat and will get over it."

"Even so, you shouldn't be dealing with this on your own."

"If I told Edmund, he'd probably march him out with his arm up his back."

"Good."

"Then, knowing the little fuckwit, there'd be repercussions."

"Like what?"

"Sudden outbreak of fire. Burglary. Slashed tyres. Dog nobbled."

"Surely not!"

"Wouldn't want to risk it. Got to get rid of him somehow though. Poor Lizzie. He's a liability. Keeps leaving the gas on in the van. The one time she was late at college, she asked him to feed the dogs, and he got it all wrong. Vomit and squits for three days. Three escaped."

"Useless prat. What did Lizzie see in him?"

"Goodness knows. But now he's in, it's bloody hard to get him out."

"Oh, Tils. Bet you can't bear to look at him."

"Makes my flesh creep. Inside I turn into this screaming harridan. Want to knock his block off. Squeeze his little pips till he squeals."

"Why don't you?"

"Anything I do would come back tenfold. He's a bully. He'd take it out on Liz."

"Don't know what to say."

"Do you know what I think it is? He's one of those blokes who are better-looking than they deserve to be."

"Mother always said everybody got the face they deserved."

"Think she was talking about beauty regimes, not bone structure. He goes for the Easy Rider look. Well, he used to. Now when he puts a pair of jeans on, it's his idea of dressing up. He just slobs around in these orange sports shorts and cut-away vests. Comes a time in a man's life when he should put those away."

126

"Yeah, when they get underarm hair!"

"Eeeww! It's probably crawling."

"Don't."

"Not even sure he wears boxers."

"Ew. Ew. Ew."

"Mind you, he's getting to that point when there's a bit too much belly fat. His chin wobbles. Even his knees are sagging."

"You paint a gross picture."

"He is gross."

"What are you going to do?"

"Pay him off."

"You can't!"

"Nothing else for it. I just hope one day he'll get his comeuppance."

"No use hoping for a miracle."

"No, he'll lie and cheat and shag and manipulate and exploit his way through life."

"Karma."

"What karma?"

"Well, one day maybe he'll get duped, ripped off, done over, his heart broken, his bank account emptied, dreams destroyed."

"And crabs. I really want him to have crabs."

"And crabs! At the very least."

"Great. Good to know. Anyway, gotta go. Vet's on her way."

"Hey, Tils. Hang in there. It will get sorted. Promise."

"Love you."

"Love you too."

After the sugar and caffeine overload, Cecily is too wired for lunch. She drifts into the back garden and starts to make a mental list of jobs that need doing before summer arrives in full. Last year's bulbs, stored in a box in the greenhouse, poke naked little claws out in hopefulness. It would be kinder, if a little futile, to plant them rather than leave them even though it is so late in the season. A cobweb catches her hair as she leaves the mugginess of the glass house. She flaps at it with both hands but it inveigles itself into her hair, dusty ends blowing up her nose. A sense of panic grips her heart.

She weeps for Lizzie. Her young dreams of love shattered. So young and so perfect. Her life pulled out of orbit by an encounter with a dark star. From now on, when she hears a sad love song, she will stand still to listen to the lyrics rather than singing lustily and melodramatically into her hairbrush. She'll find it that bit harder to trust the next guy. There will be a wistfulness where once there was innocence and joy.

She weeps for Tilly. Seeing her young daughter crushed under the weight of her first bad choice. The slender reeds of first love, generosity, hope torn from their roots. A verse from Serge Gainsbourg comes to mind:

Car c'est lui qui vous baise
C'est celui qui vous baise
A l'aise

And so it goes.
And so it goes.
You just get fucked over.
So easily.

She kicks over a rotten log. Tiny white snail eggs cluster in its crevices. They will hatch in the warm weather and make their slimy way over to the young lettuces she had yet to plant. They would fatten on them and then begin their slow and stately copulation to make more eggs, hunkering down in the sides of the planters under the soil level.

Each shiny egg bears the face of niece's despoiler. She picks up the log and throws it into the hen pen. "Here you are, chuck chucks." As an act of murder, it is clean and neat and disposes of the evidence. Today's eggs, tomorrow's eggs.

What would Henry do? How would he sort this situation out? No doubt about it he would remove the little runt from out of their lives. And make sure he never came back again. He would bring the smile back to Lizzie's face and joy back into her life. But just how he would do this is impossible to answer. Back then, Henry in their lives, was a golden time. Nothing seemed to go wrong that Henry couldn't fix. Difficulties and conundrums and dilemmas abounded before and since. How come Henry just managed to *sort* things out? Everything he did and said and thought was a mystery to her. The workings of his mind, his logic, his understanding, were all foreign to her. But it all mapped to reality. And it all worked. She was just in awe of him. Her love for him was based on shock and awe.

And since? Survival without Henry is a hand-to-mouth affair, a stumbling in the dark, a bright light behind her throwing her shadow forward into multiple directions.

The Cat

Just how did curiosity kill the cat? Who can say? This fable, this exemplary tale, has been reinvented over generations immemorial. Differing each and every time, the nature of the misdeed, the scolding and punishment best suited to the misdeed, the consequences of the misdeed, the remorse and the tears. But the central fact remains. It was curiosity that did for the cat.

Maybe in these enlightened times, it is no longer appropriate or necessary to underline the morality of a tale by the demise of the feline. Maybe it suffices simply to punish the cat in some way appropriate to the misdeed, thereby illustrating that it is the behaviour of the cat, not the cat itself, that is disapproved of. So we can be reassured that the cat in this story will come to no harm but will, by dint of curiosity, have a major part to play in its unfolding.

The cat arrives with no name, no known provenance and simply jumps, unseen, out of the back of the builder's van.

Eric, the builder in this tale, not the cat, walks into the deli, hungrily eyeing the stilton, port and venison pies. He'd worked through his lunch break on the last job and there is a low-grade ache in his belly that jumps to high intensity at the intricate aromas in the shop. Luigi comes round from behind the counter and grips Eric's shoulder like an old friend. "Come. Come. I'll show you the damage." In the small courtyard at the back, Luigi points to the downpipe. It is broken like a knee injury at a rugby match.

The cat pauses at the door to the deli but knows that entrance would be denied – on many levels – so continues to pad along the High Street towards the Town Field. For there she will find small rodents for food, green water and a part-concealed, ancient space where she may give birth to and shelter her kittens.

10

Ned and the Village Contingent

Maybe Mandy is right. Maybe it is time to buy a new van. Well, *of course* it is time to buy a new van. That time came and went months ago. "Easy enough to say, but tell me where the money's supposed to come from!" he snaps as she tugs at the precariously attached bumper. "Don't do that!"

"It wouldn't matter if you didn't drive everywhere like a bleedin' maniac. Look at it. It's a wreck! You terrorise half the town and nigh-on obliterate the other half who don't get out of your way in time."

Ned pulls with all his body weight on the sliding door. It is still an inch off closing. He heaves and wrenches. No reason why it shouldn't shut. Was fine last night when he had loaded up all the equipment needed for today's field clearance. He curses mightily under his breath at the syncopated sound of spades, barrows, hoes and strimmers sliding inside the van, jamming the mechanism still further.

"What's that noise?"

"Nothing, Ben. We're going to have to repack the van, that's all."

"Wha'?"

"Just grab hold of these and make a neat pile." Ned hands out the first of twenty or so spades to the lad who slowly and methodically lines them up against the garden wall. Hurry up, Ned grumbles. The sooner they get started on this ridiculous venture, the sooner they can all get home again.

Thanks, in no small part, to Marcus's rallying call on the village's social network site, upwards of fifteen people had volunteered to clear the scrubland ready for the fair. Despite Chris Eveans's earlier confidence, pinning down Major Welding's watertight and binding permission to use the Town Field had taken a deal of tact and negotiation. For a time it seemed it might have been necessary to cancel the fair altogether for want of a venue.

At the last hour, Chris Eveans, who had given the impression of a man sorely pressed between a rock and a hard place, produced a half-page document for the remaining committee members' inspection. Beads of sweat shone on his forehead as, with a mute appeal to the assembly, he said, "If you can agree to the conditions of this definitive document, we can go ahead."

So it was that, on condition the field be cleared of ragwort, thistle, bramble, bindweed, dandelion, vetch; the grass be mowed to a uniform 3mm length; molehills levelled; rhododendrons, gorse and birch cut down to within 10mm of ground level, a cross-hatch made in the stump of no less than 3mm and the stump painted a fluorescent yellow to indicate a trip hazard; hedges trimmed to a height no lower than 2.5 metres and no higher than 4 metres; no produce, fruit or berries to be removed or consumed without the landowner's permission, including eggs; adequate toilets provided together with litter bins, clearly marked parking bays, marshalls, coconut matting if rain should exceed 10mm within four days of the fair; refuse and any other accoutrements appertaining to the gathering removed before dusk of the following day, then Bullenden would be granted, by gracious permission of Major Welding, use of the Town Field; a field which, many assumed, belonged to the town anyway.

"So, basically, our overlord's getting an acre of land cleared for the privilege of his name appearing on the programme with humble thanks from all his serfs," said Stan from Hammer and Tongs, who had overcome his displeasure at being knocked off the Chairman's spot for the vicarious pleasure of seeing someone else struggle with the role. The struggle, being mighty, made for pleasurable viewing.

Eventually there is enough floor space around the van door to allow Ned to slide it in place. It shuts perfectly.

"Come on, Ben. Jump in."

"But, Mr Gallagher..."

"Jump in, Ben. We haven't got all day."

132

Ben shrugs and, tonguing the inside of his cheek and with double-handed concentration, returns the spade to join its fellows against the garden wall. Just as he manages to close the passenger door behind him, the van speeds off down the road. Over the noise of the much-taxed engine, there is a clattering sound as the contents redistribute themselves at the first corner while ten spades remain standing, sentry-like, against Ned's garden wall.

So it is, on the appointed day, with just over two weeks till the day of the fair, a small crowd has assembled on the field between the old watermill-turned-antiques-emporium and the river.

A group of five robust ladies are sitting on benches in the car park, pouring steaming coffee into small beakers. One of their number breaks open a packet of custard creams while a cluster of blokes looks on enviously, blaming themselves or their wives for being less than adequately victualled for the arduous day ahead.

"No sign of the manicured Mr Eveans then?"

"No. And where's Ned?"

For the moment they lack a leader but are content to sit for a while and sample the balmy air. "Typical Ned. Never arrives anywhere but he's late and in a hurry."

"Stand back, everybody! He's here."

There is a collective marshalling of feet and bags as Ned's white van hurtles through the gate and comes to an abrupt halt, the back wheels sliding to form a fan-shaped gouge in the ground. The engine pops and black smoke belches through the exhaust pipe. "Aye aye. Here's Napoleon."

"Good morning, everyone. Goodness, what a good turnout. Excellent." Ned claps his hands. "Right, everybody. If I can have your attention please."

Ned has to wait while refreshments and phones are stowed away in safe places and the volunteers gather round. He looks around at the task in hand. Bloody ridiculous, the whole thing. He'll be losing a day's pay and is expected to pull off a minor miracle. The only advantage to the land he can see is that it is flat. Good job it has been a dry spring as one good deluge and the place would be flooded. Someone has obviously had a go at putting in drainage at some point, as there is a scattered line of bricks and shards of reinforced concrete, which will all need to be collected and placed in the skip, adding to the rigours of an already demanding day.

At last he has the crowd's attention. First with the motivational stuff. "I've got to say, it's very good to see everyone, and I am sure many hands will make light work. We can all take pride in the sense of community that has brought us here today. This year's fair promises to be one that we will not forget."

"You can say that again!"

"Just like that programme off the telly." Madge nudges her neighbour.

Ned waits for the murmuring to die down.

"Given the scale of the task ahead of us, I think we should divide ourselves into separate work details. You can organise yourselves into groups and select which tasks you want to undertake. There will be breaks every hour for ten minutes and a lunch break at midday for half an hour."

"Not so much *DIY SOS* as *OAP Boot Camp*," Madge's neighbour nudges back.

"I have to remind everyone that you are all here at your own risk and that neither Major Welding nor any of his agents can accept any responsibility for loss of or damage to persons or their property."

"Get on with it, Ned. Haven't got all day."

"Right, then. What I've done is divide the jobs into four sections. There's Rubble Clearance, which means picking up stones, bricks, pebbles, debris. There's Trimming and Strimming, which means cutting back overgrown hedges and brambles. There's Edging. Which means clearing and marking out the paths. And there's Levelling. Bit like knocking back the divots at a polo match, filling in any obvious dints and flattening any obvious bumps. So, if you'd like to get yourselves into teams of five or six, we can begin."

Ned pulls out the items from the jumble in the back of the van until against a crumbling brick wall stand a variety of brush cutters, strimmers, chainsaws and petrol cans, all of which seem to hold Ben's rapt attention.

For now the volunteers are keen and eager. But how will they be after a few hours of hard labour? It is going to be a hell of a day. He is going to have to keep a really close eye on Ben. "Can I have a go with this, Mr Ned?" Ned gently prises the strimmer from Ben's grasp.

"No you can't. Now just go and stand over there and don't touch anything. I'll be along in a minute." The youth rocks off, his hands in the pockets of his black jogging pants, chewing the end of the pull cord in his sweatshirt in a consolatory manner.

"Fuckin' unfair, that's what it is."

It is going to be a minor, not to say major miracle if they are all going to get through the day without injury or amputation.

"Madge. Madge. Over here!" Madge turns round and round in a bewildered fashion, looking for her companions. They are standing next to the table with trowels and trugs. "We're on Levelling Duty. Come on." The five doughty ladies grab their tools and set off like a team of scene of crime officers.

"Can I 'ave a go on the chainsaw, Mr Ned?"

"No. Wait a minute, Ben. I'll get you sorted in a minute."

Cecily and Marcus and Bob Junior from the garage are amongst those hovering around the table with the empty plastic animal feed bags, sturdy gloves and small garden forks. "Rubble Clearance, that's us," says Marcus to the group, all of whom look just as enthusiastic and pumped as if co-opted to a day on a chain gang.

"Me mum says that I can have a go at anything, so long as it's not got petrol in it."

"That's very good, Ben. We'll find you something to do in a minute. Tell you what. See those wheelbarrows over there. You can be in charge of fetching the bags of rubble out to the skip on the car park. What do you think?"

Ben surveys the big yellow skip, its short edge levered down, planks set in place. "Yeah. Looks alright." Ned is relieved.

Several men gather in one group to eye the mechanised equipment. They casually jostle and rearrange themselves as if on a ready, steady, go command they would be closest to their instrument of choice. "OK, fellas. You all look like you know what you're doing. It's the brambles, the elders, the sycamore saplings. Cut up and burn. Give Ben a shout if you want anything barrowing."

"By the way, Mr Ned, Mum says I'm not to do anything with matches either."

Ned knew this actually, having already encountered Ben's pyromaniac tendencies during a trip from the school to his nursery, when about two hundred plastic trays stored under the work benches mysteriously melted and melded together. Forty-three children and several teachers and nursery staff had had to evacuate the long greenhouses as black smoke billowed out through the open vents. No further action had been taken, at least not of a punitive nature.

Several days later, Ben's mum, who in addition to being Ben's mum was also a helper at St Giles' school, returned to the nursery with a bottle of whisky.

"This is from the children," she'd said, proffering the wrapped bottle to Ben.

"Er. Bit young for that, aren't they?"

"No. You know what I mean."

"Oh, cheers. Thanks, but you really didn't need to."

"Well. It's from me really. I think you know why. I'm Ben's mum. And I'm really grateful. And sorry. For, you know, what happened."

Her boots were too big for her slender legs. She reminded him of a cartoon character on TV from his youth. Her golden hair tumbled from a single clasp behind her head. She looked pot-bound. He had to restrain himself from reaching down to snip off a few shoots, a few tendrils, to tidy her up, to put her in proportion.

"Hey. It's fine. We always have too many of those bloomin' trays anyway." They stood facing each other, their eyes wandering.

"Well, you're very kind. I hope you enjoy the bottle." He turned it, thoughtfully, in his hands for a moment. She watched him. He had big hands. Capable hands. Despite the chipped nails and engrained grime, they looked intelligent hands. Sensitive hands.

"Right."

"Right."

Ben's mum turned to leave. "Tell you what." She turned back again as he gave voice to an uncensored thought. "Would Ben like to come and lend a hand at the nursery? Might teach him a few skills. Nothing difficult, mind. Just a bit of potting up. Making tea. That sort of thing. I mean, I'm sorry if I'm speaking out of turn. Sometimes it's a good thing, you know, sort of making reparations. And I can see he's not…he's not…er…" Ned's heart sank as he felt himself about to make the most monumental gaff. How could you describe this boy of hers?

She just stood there, with her head on one side, weighted by this great mass of hair. Luckily she was smiling. She seemed to be willing him to find a word, smiling quietly at his discomfort. He flapped his hands in the air, the tissue paper coming away from the bottle, as all words eluded him. "Er…"

"No, he's not very 'er', is he? But that's the way he is, and I love him."

"Oh, I wasn't saying for a minute that you don't, you wouldn't. I'm sure he's a lovely lad."

"Are you? Are you really?" Her voice was rising. "Sure? Because he isn't always. That you've seen for yourself."

Ned began to wonder if his hurriedly offered suggestion had been a wise one. It seemed to have sprung more from an electric moment between himself and this unknown woman than from any desire to provide extra-curricular learning opportunities to some fourteen-year-old with a handy habit with matches and a sarky mum. "OK. Well, I'll leave it with you to think about." He turned, this time, to walk away. She reached out a hand and grabbed his arm.

"I'm sorry. You just get a bit defensive. It's a lovely offer. Can he come Saturday afternoons, after football?"

Which was how Ben was in today's work detail with permission to be off school on 'work experience'. Ben's mum had been delighted. "All they seem to do at that school of his is make toast and play shop. This would give him an insight into the real world. Maybe he could even get a landscaping job in the future. Maybe he could even…" Her voice trailed off and Ned look away non-committally.

"What shall we do, Ned?" An assorted group stand in front of him, those that have no real group to ally themselves to, being neither a doughty lady or one of the Sunday Supremoes. Bob the Elder, with his crooked stoop and arthritic knees. The tall chap from Byzantium Cottage who had had him in once to tackle the moss problem in his lawn and then taken six months to pay. Doreen from the post office. Ned wonders if between them they have the reach and articulation to cut up random bits of fencing and greenery for the skip.

"Give it a go, anyway, and see how you get on."

Ned looks up to the blue sky and sighs. It has taken about an hour to get all the volunteers organised but they are all beavering away now. It is a warm June morning. The sweet, lemony smell of elderflower fills his nose. Shame to cut back a flowering shrub but orders are orders. The noxious tang of hot oil and the rising and falling cadence of the chainsaw also fill the field. A couple of walkers observe from the other side of the river, their spaniel advancing and retreating, barking at full pitch.

He'll let them work for ten more minutes and then call a tea break.

If he were at all a sentimental soul, he would almost admit to this being a perfect moment, almost medieval. Everyone around bent to a common purpose; everyone engaged in their own perfect moments. None of the jobs in themselves were particularly elevating – quite the opposite, really. Who would, by choice, really want to crook their backs into picking up rubble, scratch their arms and faces on thorns, scuff their boots with a poorly aimed edger, breathe in petrol fumes and thick smoke from the bonfire? Who, on reflection, would really want to give up a day for the transient benefit of others and the longer-term benefit of someone vastly more privileged than themselves? It's not as if Major Welding is the most popular resident, and Chris Eveans seems to have angered or irritated just about everyone in the village. A couple of the Sunday lot are whistling a jaunty air.

It had all seemed very different the night before. "What's up with you?" Mandy had asked, finding Ned at the kitchen table with his head in his hands.

"Pyramid coercion, that's what it is. Nobody wants to do it but nobody wants to be seen to be the missing brick in the wall, the ha'porth of tar. I'd bloody say no, if I had half a mind."

"Well, you haven't and you won't."

"What if nobody does turn up? What if I have to do all the work myself – for free. Buckshee? What's the point of it all? Just to give muggins here a hard time of it? Don't expect Major Welding or that flash git will turn up to lend a hand tomorrow."

But Mandy wasn't listening. She already had her back turned to him, chopping potatoes for chips. What did she care? The peelings were soaking into the newspaper, turning it darker and greyer. She turned the peeler to twist out an eye. He felt a momentary pain in his own eye. Still he stared at her back; she hadn't even bothered to take off her coat. How long had she had that coat? It had lost its plush redness in its exposure to the elements, stitches in the quilting were coming undone so the diamond shapes ran into each other, giving the coat a weird, bumpy appearance. She must have highlighted her hair for Christmas. By now the red had turned a sludgy brown colour and was an unappealing foil to the tracts of grey. He was poised between tenderness and repulsion.

Mandy turned to him and gave him a long look. Their blank eyes locked. Neither spoke.

"What time's tea?" were the only words he could summon to break the moment.

Even Ned has to acknowledge, despite yesterday's gloom, the day is turning out better than he'd expected. Enough volunteers to see the job through in one day. Barring any disasters, they'll all be home for an early bath by four o'clock.

Oh Christ! What is that lad up to now? "Ben. No!"

Ned runs towards the burning heap of brambles and branches as Ben raises his arm, about to throw a black plastic container onto the flames. "Stop!"

Jim swiftly turns and grapples the container from Ben's hands until Ned arrives, panting. "Don't put that on the fire."

"Why not?"

"Well, plastic doesn't burn well, so it would make a lot of thick, bad-smelling smoke."

Ben's eyes light up.

"And you don't know what's inside. Could be petrol or anything."

"Mum said no petrol."

Ned sighs with inward relief that Ben seems to have got the message. It isn't always easy to get through to the lad. He looks at the world through a different lens than everyone else, one that refracts certain images to a crystal and imperative clarity and completely removes from sight others that are as plain as day to anyone else.

"Where did you find it, anyway?"

Ben points to a small rise in the ground in a far corner of the field. "OK. Well anything else you find, put it in the skip. Do you understand?"

Ben nods forlornly. Oh for goodness' sake, Ben, Ned pleads with him mutely. Don't cry. How would I explain that to your mother? "There's a good lad." He pats him on his meagre back. "Off you go." As Ben collects his barrow to resume his rounds, Ned and Jim exchange a glance and shake their heads.

"Right, everyone. Tea break," Ned shouts.

"It's alright, mate. We'll carry on, if that's OK with you." Already the Sunday Supremoes have cleared a wide swathe of land between the field's edge and the river bank. The ground is bare except for a sprinkling of dried leaves, the stumps all level with the ground. Another couple of hours' work and a good raking, that entire edge will be complete.

"Sure. Well done, lads."

Ned seeks out the Doughty Ladies. Last he saw of them, they were organising themselves pretty well following on behind the Rubble Diggers, filling in the holes with earth collected from molehills or tussocks of grass levered away by the enthusiastic path-edging team. The paths are inching their way across the face of the field, like the route of an advancing army, despite a skirmish that had broken out between the younger members, hurling newly liberated divots at each other.

"Tea break," he shouts again to the workers, having spotted the Doughty Ladies, fine respecters of their own comfort, already sitting on their upturned buckets and tucking into something steamy and, no doubt, tasty. His stomach surges, with nothing more than a few crumbled Weetabix to satisfy him at breakfast. Another conversation with Mandy is possibly upcoming, along the lines of the division of domestic duties. That old chestnut again. Perhaps the happiest lionesses haul the tastier carcasses back to the homestead; the unhappy ones just bring back bones.

If he wanders up to the little group sitting on their tuffets, one of them might take pity on him and offer him a doughnut. A cry, "Watch out!" goes up. The ladies scatter like startled hens as a flying divot knocks over a thermos and particles of earth splatter into a mug. "Just you bloody behave you." Ned turns away, disappointed.

He wanders towards the Rubble Rabble, amused to see that Cecily has tipped her barrow on its nose and is sitting in it. Disappointingly she seems to have just polished off a sausage roll; he can still see the drippings of brown sauce on the white serviette she scrunches up, calling over to him, "Not shirking, just having a sit down." He is about to playfully remonstrate when he finds himself obliged to rearrange his features in time for Marcus to take a photograph of 'Our Good Leader', as he is later to be flagged on the Facebook page.

"Right, everyone, don't get too comfortable." Ned claps his hands and flaps his arms as if moving a flock of recalcitrant sheep. "You know what will happen. If you sit down too long, you won't get up again."

A good-natured groan goes up but people stir and stow away their wrappers and containers for the short interval till lunchtime. Lunch! He can't bear to think of lunch. Even last night's chips had been a disaster. Raw on the inside, fatty on the outside. His stomach lurches painfully again.

Nonetheless, the calorie intake has imbued the group with renewed purpose and vitality. The landscape is changing before his very eyes. A good portion of the field is now flattened; the paths are stretching straight and true to the opposing corners; the river is running freer without its overhanging branches.

For the next couple of hours, warmed by the emerging sun, serenaded by the birdsong, comforted by the rising smells of burning wood, warming loam and released blossom, even Ned feels moderately content.

Again, it is the Doughty Ladies who call time on the morning. Lunch is an even more sumptuous affair, pulled from baskets and wicker hampers. A couple of the Sunday lot slink out of the field to seek refreshment in the Red Lion. Others pull packets wrapped in greaseproof paper or silver foil from pockets of coats or duffel bags slung on rampant spades.

Ben, who has applied himself usefully all morning, lopes towards Ned. "Alright, Ben. We're stopping now for a bite to eat. Have you got anything?" Ned is aware that even this simple enquiry into Ben's wellbeing has a plaintive twang to it.

"No, Mum said she was going to bring me dinner. Here she is. Mum! Over here!"

Ned turns to watch Ben's mum make her unsteady way across the field. She is carrying a grocer's cardboard box. "Looks like she's brought you twenty cabbages, Ben."

"'Ope not. Hate bleedin' cabbage."

"Only joking. Let's go and give your mum a hand there."

The two of them set off towards Ben's mum, walking unrhythmically beside each other. Ned cannot take his eyes off her. The box threatens to unbalance her. He watches her feet taking tiny steps in her characteristically oversized boots. Today's are black with more buckles and studs than are purely functional. Her slender, black-clad legs remind him of a crane or a heron. Perhaps, if she flew high in the sky, she would hook one ankle over the other as she trailed her legs behind her. He is familiar with her waxed jacket. It is the one she always wears to bring Ben to the nursery and to collect him again. He usually studies the innermost hole in the belt, the unfinished, ragged one that looks like it was made with a sharp point; a compass, perhaps, through which the pin is inserted. More and more he finds recently he cannot not raise his eyes to her face.

"Hi, Ben. Hello, Mr Gallagher," she calls.

Ben runs towards her, reaching for the box. "Mr Gallagher said you'd brought cabbages for my lunch. I told him I don't like cabbages."

Ben's mum laughs. "Don't be a numpty. I'm sure Mr Gallagher was just teasing." She holds the box flat while Ben rummages within. "Careful, Ben." Ben pulls out a packet of sandwiches.

"Are these ham?"

"Of course."

"Cheers, Mum." Ben, with quick steps and then slow steps, takes his bounty off to lean against a nearby wall.

"Would you like some? There's plenty." Ned can barely restrain his grateful enthusiasm and wishes he could rummage in the box as Ben had.

"Are you sure?"

"Can't seem to cater for small portions, certainly not for small appetites. Hang on a minute." She balances the box on one hand and lifts items for Ned's choice and approval. "Sandwiches. Cheese. Cheese and pickle. Plain ham. Jam. Various cartons of juice. Crisps. Battenburg. Chocolate Fingers." She looks up at him. "Goodness. You look starved.

142

Here, you. Put your hands out." She drops the box at her feet and loads up his outstretched arms, naming each item, as if he couldn't already taste them and relish them inside his mouth. "Finally, a piece of kitchen roll and an apple. Dah dah." She steps back and laughs.

"I can't take all this."

"Don't be daft. After everything you've done for Ben."

He tips his cache onto the floor in front of him and, spreading out his coat as a rug, settles down for a feast. "Will you join me?"

"I'll go and sit with Ben. Think he'd prefer that."

Picking up the box, still not empty, she makes her way to her son. They lean together against the wall, Ben peering into the various packets she opens for him and either adding them to the growing pile beside him or rejecting them. Ned watches her bite into an apple.

Oh dear, he thinks to himself. Oh dear. Oh dear.

Within half an hour, all have eaten well and several look as if they might fall asleep in the yellow sunshine. He doubts whether the shore party will return from the pub but it doesn't matter, there are still enough people to finish the job. He walks over to where Ben and his mum are playing noughts and crosses with twigs and pebbles. He fingers a stone he found earlier and placed in his pocket. "Thanks for lunch. A life saver."

"I'll call for Ben at four o'clock, if that's alright. He's got Chess Club later."

Ned's attention is snagged by a shout. "Before you go, can I take your photo?" It is that new guy, Marcus, who has spent most of the morning taking irksome shots as people work. "Come on then, budge up. Get in close."

Ben stands in the middle, Ned and his mum on either side. Her arm rests lightly on his behind Ben's back. The shutter closes before Ned could look to camera. "Fabulous."

Mid-afternoon and the pace of work is definitely slowing. Despite the morning's golden glory, the weather is changing. A sickly green light fills the newly created spaces. The sky thickens. A few drops of rain pattern the stone wall.

At quarter to four, those hardy souls who have stayed the course are gathered around Ned, hair tangled, faces smudged. "I can't thank you enough." He won't mention that he is fairly sure he saw Major Welding drive past in his gas-guzzling four-by-four and, although he couldn't swear to it, somebody remarkably like Chris Eveans was in the passenger seat. Doubtless they will be along later for an inspection. "Hurry home, everyone, before the rain starts. Again, many thanks for a sterling effort."

The crowd disperses, patting each other on the back, turning back to look at the results of their handiwork. As Ned makes his way to his trailer, he drops the stone from his pocket into the nearly empty lunch box that Ben's mum brought. Other bits and pieces have found their way there, he assumes, from Ben's forays with the barrow.

Where is Ben? There had been a couple of occasions during the day when he'd turned to look for Ben and just couldn't quite see him. A few moments later, he'd look up again and see Ben trundling his barrow across the field, sometimes in one direction, sometimes in the other. Whatever momentary panic he felt abated until the next time he disappeared. Somehow, though, Ben always just slid into view before outright alarm set in.

A rough breeze lifts and shakes the alder branches arching over the river. There is a definite change in the air. If Ben's mum doesn't hurry up, he and Ben will have to shelter in the van against the oncoming rain. Where is the woman? He should be annoyed. What does she think he is, some kind of unofficial babysitter? But his level of annoyance is low, almost non-existent. Goodness knows she has a time of it with this lad of hers.

"Come on, Ben. Give us a hand getting the last of these bits and pieces into the van."

"Righto, Mister Ned."

The lad is willing enough. Clumsy but dogged. Has a habit of wandering off. Loves his mum, that much is obvious. But that love is sometimes inappropriately expressed. There is sometimes a haunted look in her eye.

"Mum's here. Am off now. Ta-ra."

Ned waves to Ben's mum, standing over by the gate as Ben crane-walks over the near-perfect pitch. She waves back. He wants to tell her that her son pulled an absolute blinder today but she is already pulling her collar up about her ears, urging Ben to hurry up before the rains come.

11

Ned

By four thirty, the rain starts to fall in earnest. The fat splots that earlier fell percussively on the steel barrows and turned the piles of pebbles into ore, give way to sharper, more spiteful points of rain.

The field is now empty save for a few scuds of litter. The grass will quickly grow back over the bare patches where molehills were flattened and squirrel diggings and rabbit and rodent holes were filled in. The brutal flaying of the overgrown hedges will soon temper in colour. The ash from the still-smouldering bonfires will lift into the air and blow away in due course.

It is doubtful the Sunday Supremoes would ever call upon his services, all being of the 'Well How Hard Can It Be?' school of tricky undertakings. It is possible one or two Doughty Ladies might call him at some time but, to a woman, they all seemed eminently practical and capable, reducing their gardens down to a few herb pots and the odd hanging arrangement once the putative male of the house had shuffled off in his carpet slippers to the greater golf course/betting shop/bird hide in the sky.

The paths are neat and clearly marked, the widest one linking the gate to the rise in the bottom left corner of the now open field, with lesser paths branching off towards the river bank or continuing to a dead end in the hawthorn hedge. Maybe, at one time, there had been a bridge across Black Brook linking this field to Abbeyclere, the former religious house, now just a vast mound hunkering under agricultural land otherwise stretched flat and taut as far as Ned's eye can see, the tumble of stone blocks softened by centuries' accumulations of turf.

Several crows lift themselves into the freshening air from the copse in the next field. Alders and willows follow the river as it meanders off towards the low horizon. A line of poplar trees stands sentry against the sky. He'd heard the village legend that the trees were an unclaimed dowry, the bride-to-be preferring to hang herself than marry her prospective husband.

Ned drives out onto the road and jumps down to drag the warped and misshapen gate into place, securing it behind him. All in all, not a bad day.

Marcus

Walking back from the Town Field through the village, Marcus feels slightly harried after a day of working in the open, as if the cascade of roofs, the small unseeing windows, the miscellany of doors are a jostling crowd pushing into him; as if the houses, the workshops, the garretts, like the people who occupied this village over generations, are clamouring for his attention.

He passes the wide, generous door to Cecily's house. A bare light bulb is visible in the half-moon glass. He wonders if one day he could just knock.

What would he say? Would he ask if she can hear the voices too? The shouts of the warriors, the well-drivers, shoemakers, tailors, saddlers, grocers, blacksmiths, wheelwrights, carpenters, corn millers, farmers, ministers, publicans, glovers, fullers and lavanders, combers, tenterers, weavers, dyers, revenue men, potters, poets, painters, composers, horse-men, brick makers, shepherds, flint flakers and knappers, thatchers, millers, government commissioners, colourists, swedebashers, navvies, pilgrims, fashioners of gold and bronze, lime burners, saints, swordsmen, ship builders, ritualists, doctors, ploughmen, conquerors, dialectologists, martyrs, wherrymen, airmen, barons, bishops, masons, carpenters, pil-ferers, staithesmen, bell casters, stone pickers, toad catchers, Pharisees, witch finders, dissenters, drovers, sail makers, labourers, shearers, breeders, stockmen, high stewards, brewers, soap boilers, abbots, bishops, merchant adventurers, poulterers, drapers, mercers, spicers, tanners, skinners and ironmongers, cheesemongers, whitening makers, sextons, basket makers, beggars and swains, clock makers, yeoman, cottagers, squatters, maltsters, farriers, hurdle-makers?

Where are they all now?

He walks stiffly up the flight of stairs to his flat, emitting small groans with each rise. The chill that heralded the rain must have got in under his precautionary thermals and made straight for his knees. Although, maybe it is his lower back that is on the point of imminent seizure? He grabs the hand rail and pulls himself up the remaining steps, leaning against the archway into the kitchen while he catches his breath.

Rain patters against the kitchen window. He flicks a switch on the boiler. The surging flame seems to match a surge in his heart. Not arrhythmia, heaven forfend, but a feeling of fellowship, community, purpose. He'd felt nothing like it, really, since, well, he didn't know; maybe it was that time of the power outage on the Underground when the entire carriage had joined in with the charismatic West Indian vicar in singing hymns line by line. But that had only been for about fifteen minutes, the experience slightly marred by the French girl opposite him who seemed to be suffering from an attack of the vapours or at least a high degree of agitation.

Marcus hums to himself as he moves around his space, putting on the kettle, powering up his laptop, pulling the curtains tightly shut should the night become increasingly wild. No time like the present. He would eschew the pub tonight – bound to be some tins in the cupboard – and spend the evening uploading today's photographs.

Ned

Ned bumps his van down the track leading to the farm watched by Jasper the donkey in the middle of the paddock, chewing lugubriously on a pile of thistles, tenderly removing the spiky leaves and discarding the stalks like a trail of pick-up sticks. Ned parks the van and walks over to the fence, removing from his pocket the apple that Ben's mum had given him earlier. "Here you are, lad. Saved it for you." Jasper looks up from his pile, still chewing, considering his now augmented options. "Come on. Apple." His brown fringed ears swivel semi-independently at the sound of Ned's voice and he half walks, half runs towards the fruit balanced on Ned's outstretched hand. The donkey lifts his front lip to reveal brown scored teeth before biting into the apple. Juice and pulp spray with each chewing motion. Ned turns the apple round in his grip, the squelch and the crunch magnified by the creature's long muzzle. "Good boy." Jasper rears his head away from Ned's touch and returns to chewing and plain considering until he has finished the core. He smells of warm hay.

The farmhouse looms large in the near dusk. No lights on. Geoff would still be tending the fields or whatever Geoff does and Kate would still be at the bookshop. As he opens the door to the barn that he rents as a secure lock-up, dogs start barking in the conservatory, a Doberman licking rapaciously at the white smear of dried spittle left from his attempts to get at the previous intruder whilst a mottled shape that is the Jack Russell pogoes itself into a frenzy, like a night at the Wigan Casino.

Within half an hour, he has dismantled, cleaned, sharpened and stowed his kit. Time to go home. He returns down the track, the lights from the van hokey-cokey through the dusk as it bumps into and out of the potholes past Jasper, standing there with the patience of time and the poise of youth. Where did those spades go? Did some bugger pinch them?

Marcus

The kitchen warms as the tomato soup on a slow heat heaves and, expelling a large bubble, falls back in on itself. Marcus cuts bread and smears it with butter. Licking his fingers he tilts his laptop this way and that to find the – port, was it? – to attach his camera.

The images of the day flash onto his screen. He'd felt like a reporter going round with his pad and pen, writing down people's names. Have to get it right. Don't want to upset anybody by spelling their name wrongly or giving them the wrong name altogether.

Cecily had shown him how to 'tag', match up people's faces with their names if they were already members of the site. It was rather like playing happy families. A feeling of panic comes over him, similar to the confusion he felt while pinioned by Madge on the hard chair in the post office, awaiting Mr Edge, on his first day in Bullenden. Not all are recognisable from their names alone, some choosing to identify themselves by a picture of what, he supposed, to be their avatar.

Thereby Jacquetta from the crystals shop is identified by a winged horse; Mrs Turpin by a fat spotted teapot; Cecily by a black-and-white picture of three young girls, her sisters perhaps. Possibly Major Welding thought it rather beneath his dignity to take part in such a democratic, people-centric, vulgarian movement as social networking, but then again he hadn't deigned to attend today either so would not be appearing in the Grand Clear-Up Album. Nor, Marcus muses, had Mr Eveans, although, as self-appointed czar of the Village Fete, if indeed one could be a czar to such a thing, one might have expected him to put in an appearance.

What is the etiquette in this event? Should he ask people's permission to post their pictures? Not to do so is, surely, rather invasive, rather cavalier, but Paul had just said, "Just upload them, Dad. Everyone does it." Mob diktat had never been Marcus's modus operandi but then again, so much is new these days. About time he caught up. If anyone objects, they can remove themselves. Can't they?

He slurps his soup from an oversized mug, dunking in the bread and butter, dividing his attention between the globules of butterfat spreading over the surface of his red, velvety soup and the images posting themselves one by one onto the site. One or two make him laugh. A duck put to flight by a well-aimed apple core. Someone, arms crossed, ankles crossed, asleep under a cricket umpire's hat. One or two are rather artistic, even a little risqué. The row of stout posteriors lined up on the stone wall. Nice one of Cecily, head thrown back in laughter.

Ned

The house is empty and cold. The breakfast things, such as they were, are still on the kitchen table. He stacks them besides the other pots waiting to go into the dishwasher and wipes the table free of crumbs before setting up his laptop. He'll work in the kitchen before Mandy comes home and then decamp up to the spare bedroom that acts as his office. The kitchen is warmer. The storm is picking up.

It is all rather irrelevant how many times this recession has dipped. The outcome is undeniable. He'd had to let go three workers over the past two years, including Irene, who did the wages and the accounts. Back in the days when he had wages and accounts.

Ned spreads out receipts on the kitchen table, for petrol and chainsaw oil. "If you let me have a total for the consumables, we'll see what we can do," that patronising bastard Chris Eveans had said, when he'd asked about out-of-pocket expenses. Would he notice that some of the receipts are dated before the work was even commissioned? What does it matter to that slimy toad anyway? Oh, what the heck! Ned crumples up the out-of-date receipts and lobs them into the far corner of the kitchen towards the swing bin. Defrauding is far too big a word for it but, even if it fit, he'd only be defrauding the village fund. And how could he do that when everyone had so willingly given their time. Sad cretins, all of them.

Ned's phone beeps. He barely hears it and chooses to ignore it anyway.

He enters his expenses figures onto the spreadsheet. £15.37. Hardly worth the paper. Hardly worth the shame of asking. Sod it.

His phone beeps again. It'll be Mandy wanting him to go to the chippy. She could go herself. He isn't going to go out again in a night like this. Fat cow. She'd come to no harm spending a day working with him rather than painting nails in that old people's home.

Marcus

A congratulatory whisky might be in order tonight. What had Ned said? A good job well done. That's exactly what it was. Marcus watches in satisfaction as people 'Like' the photos, some actually posting shots and comments of their own. Even Cecily, somewhere in the house opposite, is online. The web is twitching all around him.

Ned

Didn't look like any fatted calf was going to be slaughtered on his behalf tonight. A can of lager would dull the ache.

Where *is* Mandy?

He flips his phone open. Two text messages. Both from Ben's mum. He puts down the can, unopened, and presses the first message. "Sorry to bother you. Ben's found something." He cracks open the ring-pull with his fingernail. Bubbles froth at the opening. The sharp, metal smell of alcohol whets his senses. He squints at the second message with the can to his mouth. "Wouldn't try and contact you unless important. Are you there?"

Should he text back? Or phone even? They have never spoken this way. He only has her number in case of any emergency with Ben. Cradling her voice in the palm of his hand at his own kitchen table just seems too impossibly intimate. "Whats up?" he replies. Within seconds the reply comes back. "Ben found cave and kitten!!!!"

Well, at least he hadn't found needles or a weapon while supposedly in Ned's care. Ben's mum's reply is cryptic. What does it mean? She asks for help only very rarely. He should make himself available. That he could not do if Mandy was to walk through the door at any moment. "Do U want me 2 come over?" Ned grabs his coat and van keys. If nothing else, he can park up somewhere and sit in the van while the mystery unfurls, ready to be there at a moment's notice, should the situation warrant it. And Mandy would be none the wiser.

The front door whips out of his hands and pulls back hard on the hinges. Clouds spin like a fairground carousel around the high moon. The night is alive with a manic energy. He drives the van round the corner and checks his phone to see if she has replied. She hasn't. What is going on?

Now he is in the van, should he at least drive round to the house? He knows where it is, for he'd dropped Ben off several times after a late shift. He'd usually shout a few pleasantries through the open passenger window while his mum waved from the doorstep, Ben running as if on a zip-wire between them. Occasionally he had come to the front door, if further explanation was required. He'd never been inside.

As he approaches the junction, he sees Mandy's car come up the road behind him and swing into their drive. She won't have seen him in this dark part of the street.

He parks in a corner of the pub car park, waiting for her to reply. He is an unlikely rescuer, he knows that. It might all be some kind of weird joke. A prank. Who else might get access to her phone? Did someone want to shake things up a bit and see what fell out? What had the boy found? A cave and a kitten. They seemed like trophies in some kind of a fantasy game. How is he supposed to reply to that? I've found an armadillo and a suit of armour? The whole thing is ridiculous. He will count to sixty and then head back home.

151

His phone beeps again. Heart racing, he looks at the screen. Special offer, two pizzas for the price of one. Dammit. He texts a row of question marks to Ben's mum. Rain falls on the van roof, an irritating noise that marks time on his indecision and impatience. He'll set off again and make a decision at the junction past the church.

Within five minutes, he is standing at the front door, pressing the bell until the porch light comes on. A collection of objects form an irregular heap by the door, objects that Ben had found that day – the black plastic container; some sodden, orange-speckled logs; a shoe; some shards of glass and, pushing aside a flattened football with the toe of his boot, he could see the heart-shaped stone he'd dropped into the lunch box.

The door opens. Ben's mum stands in the light. "Those are Ben's finds from today. There's more. Come in." She is wearing thick woolly socks, two tiny pompoms on the heel swinging crazily from side to side as she walks into the living room.

Ben is arranged on the sofa. "Get up, Ben. Mr Gallagher is here."

"Hello, Mr Gallagher."

The lights are low. A game show plays itself out silently on the TV in the corner. The gas fire bubbles quietly. There are no obvious signs of disaster or catastrophe. What on earth is going on? He turns to look at Ben's mum, now even shorter than usual. She looks flustered, pulling her fingers through her hair, snagging them on the big gripper comb. She twists a strand round and round, pulling her head to one side. There is silence, until Ben starts to speak. "Look what I found, Mr Gallagher." Ben uncups his hands to reveal a small ball of grey fluff. It looks like what came out from under the bed during one of Mandy's annual spring cleans. Ned approaches, remembering the text about a cave and kittens.

Whilst it is undoubtedly a charming scene, did it really warrant calling him out on a stormy night, even if it did provide a hither-to unaccorded entrée into the house? He feels far too big for the cluttered room. The air is too warm and stuffy, hard to suck down.

"So what's the deal, Ben?"

"It's a kitten, Mr Gallagher."

"Yes, I can see that." This is getting a little exasperating.

"The thing is, this kitten is far too young to be away from its mother. It's only a couple of weeks old. We need to return it." Ben kicks the sofa with his heel while his mum talks.

"And..?"

"And…Ben said he found the kitten in the cave in the field where you were working today. You've got the key to the gate, right? Also, I don't really want to go down there on our own."

"What cave?" There isn't a cave."

"Ben said there is."

"There is, Mr Gallagher, honest."

Whatever inducement there might have been for stepping over a line tacitly drawn between himself and Ben's mum, random incidents like these were sufficient reason to restate the line and restate one's rightful position relative to the line. The fear of becoming sucked into a different world where normal rules just don't apply is rising within him. Give the boy a good talking to and send him to his room would be Ned's response. Children, these days, seem to have a far greater gravitational pull on the adults around them than had ever been allowed in his day. But maybe he'll just have to go along with this farrago till it sorts itself out. That is clearly what is expected of him. And what does he know about kids anyway?

"OK. So, we need to go back to the field. Find this so-called cave. Return this…kitten. Go home." Ben's mum looks pained at the brevity of his tone; Ben, on the other hand, is nodding enthusiastically in agreement.

"Mum says we can't keep the kitten. It's sad and it's missing its mum."

Oh, the good Lord preserve us. "Right. Everyone. In the van. Let's go."

Marcus

The pale, oaky malt glows in the low light. Marcus, in his armchair, allows himself a rare feeling of contentment. A few minutes longer and he'll close up for the night. Just a few moments more.

Ned

Driving through the estate and past his house, he can see that Mandy must have gone straight upstairs; the bedroom light is on. She hadn't bothered to text him to find out where he was. Is that a good thing? Or not? Should he care? Or not? Oddly, there's an uneven row of spades against the garden wall that he hadn't seen before. Oh, yes, he remembers now.

The wind is easing though it still barges and jostles the van down the High Street. He parks in front of the field gate. "Come on. Let's get this over and done with." Ben's mum had sat immobile and silent on the short journey, Ben had chattered all the way.

By the light of a torch, they make their way along the main path towards the bottom corner of the field where the ground rises and hummocks slightly. Ben, who had been playing stepping stones as the torch spotlit the ground, jumps down into a gully running alongside the hedge. The gusty wind plays an eerie note on some nearby telegraph wires. But for objects caught in the yellow light of the torch, everywhere is monochrome. Ned jumps down the few feet into darkness after him, leaving Ben's mum silhouetted against the sky. They squeeze their way through brambles and tall grasses. This corner of the field had not been part of the clear-up. "In here, Mr Gallagher."

Ned shines the torch in Ben's wake. His voice, previously muted by the night air, now acquires a slight echoing tone. He follows the boy to the mouth of what looks like a giant burrow. Would the White Rabbit come hurrying past? "You have to jump down, Mr Gallagher."

"Ben. Don't go any further. You don't know if it's safe."

"It's alright, Mum. I'm fine."

"No, Ben, your mum's right. Stay here."

Ned moves Ben onto a patch where the greenery had been trampled flat, mashed into a glutinous, shiny, acidic mess, presumably by Ben earlier in the day. The burrow reveals itself in the spotlight. It isn't a cave. But it is like a cave. No more than three strides long and two strides wide, the stone walls and floor are undoubtedly manmade; each block is hand cut and hewn to shape. The ceiling is rounded, lower than a grown man's height. Even leaning in from the low arched entrance, his hand on the keystone, he can tell the air inside is still and cold and musty. A rustling sound and a guttural warning issue from a pile of leaves in the far corner. "Give me the kitten, Ben." Ned takes the warm, brittle creature in his hands and places it as close to the leaves as he dares. The warning grows in pitch and intensity from the dark corner. "OK, Ben. Well. Wow! What a find!"

"Can somebody help me down? I want to see." Ned and Ben offer their hands up for Ben's mum to swing down into the gully. Three abreast, they gather at the opening, peering in, silently gazing as the yellow beam picks out the chamfered edges of the stone blocks, the centuries' slow seep of minerals, the empty clutches of slender tree roots.

After a few minutes, by silent consent, they make their way along the ditch to where the field edge slopes down slightly, stepping back onto level ground. Tree branches lift and shimmer in the moonlight. It feels as if they have peered into a different dimension. Maybe he had been right and the kitten and the cave were some tokens in an otherworldly game.

Back at the house, Ned ruffles Ben's hair and places a steadying hand on his mum's shoulder. "I'll ring you in the morning, after I've spoken to Major Welding."

Marcus

Marcus minutely adjusts his aching joints in his sleep. Although he doesn't know it yet, tomorrow is going to be his Big Day.

Ned

It is gone ten o'clock by the time he returns home. Parking the van, he checks his mobile to see if Mandy has texted. No text. Where would she think he'd been? Better to play to her assumptions than add fuel to any unwelcome suspicions. He'd tell her that Geoff and Kate had a problem up at the farm. He'd say the wind had blown some metal sheeting off of a barn roof which he needed to make secure.

He closes the front door quietly after himself. The bright lights in the hall and kitchen are dazzling. Pulling his coat off as he walks into the kitchen, he doesn't see Mandy straight away. She is sitting at the kitchen table, a bluish light from his laptop reflecting in the lenses of her glasses. "Alright, love?" he asks, hanging his coat on the back of a kitchen chair. Was it a sense of guilt that made him add the term of endearment? Something about the set of her jaw tells him she isn't exactly alright. "What's up?"

Mandy stares at the screen, her arms folded, nodding slowly and repeatedly. "So, that's her name is it?"

"What?"

"Bernadette."

"Eh?"

"Bern-a-bloody-dette."

"What you going on about?"

"There." She points at the screen. "There, for all the world to see."

Ned comes cautiously round the table.

On the screen, a magnified photograph. His eyes flicker over the scene. It had undoubtedly been taken today at the field clearance. What was there that was causing Mandy so much stress? A wisp of smoke rises into the air from a tangle of cut branches. A pile of coats lies on the floor with a Jack Russell asleep on top. There seems no real focus to the picture, more like one of those busy paintings where the main action takes place in some inconsequential corner, life going on all around, oblivious to the man with melted wings falling out of the sky. There seems to be an impromptu game of cricket going on. Marcus, or whatever his name is, is taking photographs.

Then he sees it.

Between the camera that took this shot and Marcus taking his, the three of them, from the back. Marcus is directing them to stand a bit closer. Ben is standing between his Mum and Ned, their fingers tightly interlaced behind the boy.

12

Marcus

A private message awaited Marcus on his laptop along with the early morning market reports and weather forecast for the area of his former home. Would he, please, make his way immediately to the Town Field where Major Welding's representative wishes to consult with him. On no account is he to mention his mission or destination to anyone.

Torn between disdain for what is obviously a silly little PR wheeze conjured up by grown men who should know better, and a spirit of adventure buoyed along by a slightly increased heart rate, Marcus now finds himself at the duly appointed spot at the duly appointed time. A crowd of twenty school children fills the lay-by opposite, joshing and chewing and chatting and spitting. He has the suspicion that proximity makes him an automatic paedophile. He turns his back to them, resting his forearms on the rickety old wooden gate, and whistles a tune into the field. A blackbird responds.

As the yellow school bus draws away, a new-plated Bentley with blacked-out windows and razor-fin radiator glides silently into the vacated space. Marcus flashes back to every spy thriller he has ever watched. Is he going to be kidnapped? Who would possibly pay a ransom? Certainly not Velda. His kids? Not on their wages. He glances over his left shoulder and then over his right. Can he make a getaway? Hail down one of those delivery Johnnies whizzing by?

There seems to be a stand-off. No movement from the car. Should he approach? Slowly, after an anxious minute or two, the darkened window lowers. In place of a rifle barrel, the glossy, impossibly smooth face of

157

Major Welding's oppo appears. "Be with you in a minute," he shouts over the road, waving a mobile phone in his hand.

Relieved to see a face he recognises, but still intriguingly none the wiser as to what this is all about, Marcus waits while Chris Eveans struggles into his outdoor attire. "Got something to show you. Follow me." Mr Eveans's boots seem far too large an impediment for him as he struggles over the gate. Marcus doesn't know whether to offer to heave him over or let him get on with his unsteady progress. He decides, as every Englishman would, to leave well alone.

They set off at a diagonal over the field, Chris Eveans talking unintelligibly into his mobile all the way. Marcus follows Eveans as he jumps down into a gully and effetely bushwhacks his way towards the very corner of the field. Marcus can't remember being in this part of the field the day before and begins to feel an uneasy concern that he might be about to be reprimanded or nobbled.

"Had a phone call last night from a chappie in the village. Says he found a buried chamber. Thought you'd be the man to take a squizzle at it. Tell us if it's somehow important, like."

Marcus ducks his head down and peers into the cavern.

Marcus had always had a feel for history. He assumed it was inherited from his school teacher parents and born of endless holidays spent exploring the steam heritage of the Isle of Man, trundling over sturdy Victorian viaducts in locomotives and flying the flag on the castles of the Welsh borders. There is security in history; it has a known end. It doesn't matter who won the wars, all truly was well in the end. Maybe his love for History at school came from the fact that the history books had the best pictures; History as well as RE. He couldn't quite believe in the balls of fire rolling down the mountainside, the slender basket plucked from the reeds by an almond-eyed maiden. But he could believe in the glint of the sword raised in the new dawn; he could believe in the long march to the edge of civilisation; he could believe in unlocking the bonds of treachery. He'd seen the evidence. There was the blood on the altar steps. There was the peace treaty, repeal and abolition, the Magna Carta. There was the clipped coin. Put against algebra, algorithms, ohms, amo, amas, amat, his heart would always skip a beat when a king took a new queen, when the balance of power shifted between supporters of the crown and supporters of the commonwealth, when the rose changed colour, for he knew there would be bravery, honour, derring-do, tests of strength and endurance, as well as duplicity and intrigue and bargaining.

"So, what do you think?"

"Well, I'm not too sure really."

The structure, as far as Marcus can see, is strangely positioned, in the corner of a field, facing due east, surrounded by more and more fields. Why had it been buried, albeit within the purlieus of the village but yet hardly at hand's reach? It is possible, he contemplates, that its use or purpose could be linked to structures long since disappeared. A gaol perhaps, although it would have been a long walk from the village for a gaoler to attend to his charge. And what is the point of incarceration if, by being at one remove from civilisation, you can't see the fruits that lack of freedom denies you?

Marcus peers at the rim of the opening for any tell-tale holes where posts or metalwork might have been inserted, might have formed some type of barrier. He can find none.

"It just seems stuffed in this odd corner." Marcus's eye takes in the gully and the hedge-line. It will be interesting to look into the village records to see if any mention is made of a cell. "Ah, now, there's a thought. Perhaps it was a hermit's cell." Eveans looks at him blankly. "Where a monk would go to live in isolation to pray and ponder his God."

"Ah."

That might well be an explanation. Hadn't he read of Abbeyclere, the nearby buried ruins of a monastic church with its cloisters and ranges of domestic buildings – kitchens, piggeries, sluice rooms – surrounded by a high wall and gateway? In this case, removal of self from the fruits of freedom would be a desired outcome. Although, from what he recalls, hermits tended to be bricked in, food and drink brought by conscientious supporters. Bit of a risk of being forgotten about, out here.

"What about an ice house?" Eveans offers.

"Mmmm. Interesting proposition but they tended to belong to grand houses and, as far as I know, there wasn't one in the immediate vicinity. Also, I don't think this is submerged enough, and they tended to be of brick construction and of a more conical shape."

A look of weariness flickers across Eveans's face. "Listen, mate, I gave up tramping across the countryside when Shep was a lad. If this is just a mouldering heap of nothing much in particular, let's get out of here. I've got more important things to do."

A low-throated threat issues from the deep recess and the two men turn on their heels to leave the nursing feline alone.

Making their way back across the field, Eveans tells Marcus that he wants a clear judgement on the find. Is it significant? If it is significant, then in what way? What is its unique selling point? Marcus rather wonders if historical artefacts have no USP other than their own intrinsic beauty but presumes that all things within Major Welding's keep have to serve a purpose. Nothing unnecessary or deleterious will be harboured.

Marcus, now back at his desk in front of the sitting room window, ponders on the curious relationship between Major Welding and his olea-cious sidekick. He has the sense of Mr Eveans as a frontman, interpreter and mouthpiece. Very few people have been privileged enough to see the Major, let alone meet him. He is a shadow figure, a puppet-master concealed behind an impenetrable blackout. A man of influence but not presence. Why is he so disconnected from the community but sufficiently engaged to send Eveans to mastermind the summer fair? If Eveans is a public relations bod, what is there about the Major that requires a PR makeover? Could this historical find be part of this reinvention?

He had agreed to conduct some research and to report back on his findings as quickly as possible. Time is pressing. Needless to say, he was sworn to secrecy.

"By the way," he'd asked Eveans as they made their way back across the newly shorn field, "what made you ask me? I'm not a local. I don't have any local knowledge."

"Precisely. You're not going to give us any horse shit about dragons' lairs and fairy dells."

Marcus thought back to his brief encounters with Eveans. Perhaps it was his impromptu discourse on the significance of the swan in heraldic imagery that he'd offered the swiftly thinning crowds one night at the Red (previously known as the Duke of Wellington, incidentally, at the 1820 Census) after one of those committee meetings. His eyes had alighted on a wooden carving recessed into the wall. Cecily's eyes had followed his.

"It's a chained swan, rumoured to have been scavenged from Abbeyclere," she'd offered.

"Ah, well, that's interesting, because I do know a little bit about this." He'd fidgeted in his seat. This was going to be a far more positive line of intercourse than any of the previous conversational gambits he had tried. So far he had failed to find out very much at all about this enigmatic lady, Cecily. Possibly he could interest her in what he knew of the Mortimer family and their claim to the Plantagenet throne.

As he gathered his facts and his courage, a familiar voice vibrated in his ear. "Oh, get over yourself," Velda scoffed. But he hadn't been able to stop himself. "My knowledge of this is rather sketchy but it is a rather interesting tale of late fourteenth, early fifteenth-century dynastic rivalries, rebellions and plots by the landed nobility for control of the throne occupied by Richard II. Although it is not entirely clear why Henry IV's badge, this chained and crowned swan, would appear in local architecture, for it was Henry who kept the heir presumptive – Mortimer – within gilded imprisonment in various castles up and down the country, yet the connection with Mortimer to this part of the world is very clear, given that he endowed the religious college and is buried therein."

He had paused to gauge Cecily's reaction. How could he possibly convey some of his supreme excitement at the tale of civil wars, ransoms, allegiances, conspiracies and beheadings? Did she thrill at the heady names of Hotspur, Percy, Holland, Glyndwr? Was it possible that she was stifling a yawn? Yet, she did seem fairly absorbed by his tale of monarchical misdemeanours. And even Chris Eveans looked vaguely impressed. Or was he simply bemused? Distracted? Biding his time till he could clock off?

It was that unrehearsed, ad hoc five minutes that had undoubtedly earned himself this commission as historical sleuth to find out what he could about this unexpected find in the Town Field.

The Village

By midday the following day, a contractor's van pulls up in the lay-by opposite the Town Field entrance. Two yellow-clad men are sitting in the cab, staring fixedly ahead. They'd caused a stir in the post office moments earlier by asking for the Town Field. Madge assumed they had been charged with setting up a Lions Treasure Hunt, one of those crazy escapades where people drive madly round the countryside screeching to a halt to jump over brooks or shimmy up road signs looking for clues. Sort of thing that her estranged and his new squeeze were into.

She persuaded them to leave with a packet of mini sausage rolls, sell-by date covertly covered by her thumb, a packet of Eccles cakes that were reverting to their original flakiness and three black bananas. "Better for you when they're like this. Slow-release sugars and all that."

"Aw, bloody hell," one of the workmen exclaims as, unzipping an overripe banana to find that it has lost any tensile strength, it releases itself slowly into his lap. "What are we waiting for, anyway?"

"Mister Wilding, I think his name is. Said he'd meet us here."

A car beeps behind them. The two workmen jump down as a man emerges from a Bentley. They both look at his burgundy snakeskin shoes, his skinny burgundy trousers leaving an expanse of un-socked ankle on show and tweed puffer jacket. They had worked as a gang of two for long enough to know precisely what the other is thinking without needing to exchange a glance. "Good afternoon, gentlemen. Chris Eveans. Pleased to meet you." They both shake the proffered hand – cautiously. "I represent Major Welding."

"Jacko."

"Wacko. Pleased to meet you, mate."

They wait while Eveans pops up the boot of his car and takes out a boot bag, fussing with oversocks before putting on a pair of pristine wellies. "This way."

By late afternoon, the entrance to the Town Field, normally served by a simple, rickety wooden five-bar gate, is protected by a seven-foot wire-mesh gate with chains and padlocks. Similar ironmongery protects the entrance to the newly found excavations.

"What's that all about, Madge?" visitors to the post office enquire. It grieves Madge not to be able to provide an answer, so she feigns a knowing mien, saying that all will be revealed in due course.

Cecily

"I can't help but feel that Major Welding is making a mountain over what is, admittedly, quite a substantial molehill." She had bumped into Marcus as they were both stocking up on provisions at the deli. They stand outside on the warm July street, reviewing the events of the last couple of days.

"Well, it is quite a significant find."

"I know. I know," Cecily hurriedly cuts in, anxious not to offend Marcus who is, now, a bit of a local hero. "And it's great what's been discovered and what you've found out. Changes the whole village really. It's just that, oh, I don't know. Something about Chris Eveans that sits uncomfortably with me. That ghastly piece that he put on YouTube! Have you seen it?"

Marcus pulls a face to suggest that a history buff with a special interest in fifteenth-century heraldry is not likely to be watching web videos.

"I know what you mean. It's as if the whole thing is being managed like the launch of a major new product. First it's only hush-hush, under wraps. Nobody's allowed access. Then bit by bit, we find out more. There's reporters, local TV. Even somebody from that Sunday farming programme's supposed to be interested.

"I just get the feeling that there's a bit more than the unearthing of a medieval relic at stake here."

"We-ell." Marcus lowers his voice and lowers his head towards Cecily's. She feels herself immediately torn between being given privileged access to some restricted information and a reluctance to come too closely within Marcus's purlieus. "I have found something out," he whispers conspiratorially.

"But you're under embargo not to reveal anything?"

"Yes. To do with the find. But, there's more. About the Major."

Cecily questions internally whether she is that interested. Really, the whole thing has gone on far too long. Is anyone *that* interested? It seems that the whole discovery is being manipulated. History as celebrity. Shouldn't it just be sealed up and left to moulder in peace? Instead, Major Welding and his PR agents appear to be gifting something that didn't belong to them back to the village, which doesn't really know what to do with it, and to the nation, who couldn't give a monkey's stuff.

"I did sort of wonder whether it would turn out that the land didn't even belong to the Major in the first place."

"There is that. All property being theft and that. No, that's not what I mean. Something altogether a bit more sinister. It's not for general release, you understand?" Marcus whispers *sotto voce*.

Is Marcus getting drawn into the whole charade of back stories, press releases, sequels, expert opinions, media, intrigue? Is he making a giant leap over half a millennium into the twenty-first century?

"Do I understand it's not something you can discuss on the street?"

"Exactly!" Cecily's fears are confirmed. Is this a pretence, a pretext? The last time Marcus had just 'popped round', it had been bloody difficult to get rid of him, to shift him off the doormat.

"Pub?"

"Too public. Give me a couple of minutes to get my laptop. On your way home, aren't you? I'll pop round in a few minutes."

Cecily turns homewards with an anguished sigh. No, she hadn't been on her way home. But now it seems she is.

Ned

Mandy has gone, technically missing again. This time in broad daylight. It is of course perfectly reasonable for a person in full control of their faculties to steer themselves as they see fit through the maelstrom of a day. But Mandy isn't in full control.

Ned had come home to another farewell note. He had quite a collection of them in his sock drawer. All along the 'gone to get a life' theme. Goodness knows why he keeps them. Maybe, at the final reckoning, he could stand there with them bunched up in his fist, shaking it at whichever figure of justice he comes up against, just to prove that he wasn't such a bad guy after all. That he did have stickability. That he was married for life. That there might be an answer as to why he'd got saddled with this wretched creature for the remainder of his adult life.

Sometimes she only got as far as the bypass. He'd heard about her encounter with this Jerry fellow. Look how unhappy that had made her. He knows he has his shortcomings. Business not so good, but it will get better. It always does. So why, oh why, does she just have to run out on him like this?

But, hey, he knows why she's run away. Stock answer to an unresolvable problem. She'd seen that photo of him and Bernadette and Ben. He couldn't explain it away, not without sounding mealy-mouthed and pathetic. He'd tried, though, saying, "That's what you do, isn't it, when you stand next to someone for a photo. You put your arm round them." Their fingers must have just got accidentally dovetailed just at the moment some dickhead had taken the photo.

No, he knew it didn't sound plausible. When you're fat and you live in the same faded red coat and the guy you marry to shelter you from the harsh realities of the world turns out to be a pathetic waster who can't even run a business mowing a few lawns and potting up a few begonias without putting it all in jeopardy, then you just don't believe any old con. You're past having any dreams, past believing in any fairy tales.

He sighs heavily. What should he do? Experience tells him that the swifter he runs after her, the harder and further she goes. Sometimes it is better just to let her off the leash, let her run her course and be around to pick her up when she runs out of steam. But this time is different. It is so, so different. Looks like she isn't just going down. Looks like she is going to take Bernadette down with her.

He hadn't told Bernadette about the row after the day of the field clearance. They'd just carried on as usual. She'd drop Ben off on a Saturday for a shift in the nursery. They'd exchange cordialities when she picked him up or when he dropped Ben off. Why involve Bernadette in the mash-up that is his marriage?

Anyway, what is there to tell? My wife, who is nuts anyway, thinks we are having an affair. He imagined her looking at him, her head on one side, laughing discreetly at the absurdity of the very idea. He felt his heart shrivel. Bad enough being an object of scorn and disdain from a woman such as Mandy. A very different matter if Bernadette got the giggles.

Of course Ben had badgered him every Saturday to go and see the kittens in the cave. He told him, perhaps unfairly, that the mother would eat them if she were disturbed. That seemed to hush him up. Until the next time.

Cecily

Cecily opens the back door to let Trueman out. He lugubriously lifts first one paw over the threshold and then, slowly and considerately, follows that with the other paws. He seems weighed by the heat. Picking his way like a camel through the desert, he ambles to the shade of a tree in the orchard and lets himself down with a grunt. His chin descends to his outstretched paws and his eyes, after a quick check left and right, close gratefully.

"Dear heart," Cecily murmurs. His tail thumps twice in agreement. "Right," she says, to no one in particular, "better get the kettle on," although by far her greater wish would be to swing in the hammock and doze off to the busy hum of the insects. Whatever Marcus has to tell her about Major Welding and Chris Eveans had better be important.

The kettle boils and switches itself off but no Marcus. She pulls a kitchen chair into a rectangle of sunlight shining through the opened back door and wiggles her bare toes, arching her back, arms behind her head. Recumbent yoga, perhaps? The future? Two Cabbage Whites lift from the vegetable bed and dance frenziedly around each other. Is this love or war?

Only a few days now to the summer fair. Thank goodness, only one more meeting to finalise arrangements then they can all just get on with what they are supposed to be doing, turn up on the day, raise a packet of money, put all the bunting and trestles away and then spend six months arguing how they are going to spend the proceeds. Is the effort truly worth the reward?

While she is waiting for Marcus, she might as well make an action plan for the cake stall.

What is keeping him?

Drawing a large pad of paper towards her, she begins to write up lists of who had promised cakes and buns and biscuits. She will borrow some white linen tablecloths. These she'd weigh down with cobbles, tying some bunting round the edge of the table for effect. Maybe she could ask people to bring bunches of flowers from their gardens. On a parallel list, she writes down what she will need to shop for: paper plates, brown luggage labels, plastic forks, napkins, italic pens, cake boxes, plastic bags.

She'll have to ask people to lend cool boxes to keep the confectionery out of the hoped-for sun.

Should she check the forecast? What if it rains? A tightness bands her heart, making it beat insistently. What if rain comes down on the butterfly cakes, the princess cakes, the flapjacks, the tortes, the tarts? The hot summer's air feels too thick to breathe. The whole blessed thing is a stupid idea from start to finish. Her hands tremble and her fingers lose their grip on the pen, which falls to the floor with a clatter. Doomed to fail. And where is that bloody Marcus anyway? She kicks the pen towards the back door.

Calm yourself, woman, she admonishes herself, taking a deep breath. If it rains, they'll just find a way. It isn't all down to her to make a success of it. It is a joint effort. Just play your part. What was it Mummy used to say? "Over prepare, and then go with the flow." Maybe next year she could excuse herself. Maybe next year she will be off somewhere having a fabulous adventure. Maybe. Maybe. Maybe.

The panic goes but leaves a heavy numbness within her body. This is the problem with a half-empty life. It gets filled with other people's projects, edging out her own potential.

At the end of her shopping list, she boxes off a big empty square. If only she knew what to put in it. Something that would change her life. Something that is hers. Hers alone. Something that justifies Cecily Marchant still being on this planet.

Suddenly there is a noise at the front door. Her head shoots up in alarm. It isn't Marcus, surely, because he would ring the bell. Panic twists viperously in her gut, again. Someone is trying to gain entry. Burglars? Trueman, alerted to the sound of a key scraping in the lock, hurries to her side, the hairs raised in a ridge on his back. Who could possibly be coming through the front door? She stands in readiness, scraping the chair back on the stone floor behind her.

"Who's there?"

The rasping sound stops but the door doesn't move. Perhaps the intruder has the wrong key, the wrong house – but how likely is that?

Cecily and Trueman advance cautiously down the hallway. "I've got a dog," Cecily shouts, although all too aware that Trueman's killer instinct is set, as it always is, to nil. Through the outer door and the glazed inner door comes the reply, "I know."

"Amelia!"

Cecily flies down the hall. Trueman, stirred by an access of relief into manly bravery, throws himself into a paroxysm of barking. "Oh, shut up, you stupid dog!"

Amelia steps over the threshold, heaving an enormous rucksack off her shoulder and onto the stone floor. The two sisters stand, fingertips touching, allowing their gaze to travel over each other. Cecily mouths voicelessly, "Oh. My. God." Amelia grins and shrugs her palms upwards. "I don't know what to say! I, we, I thought you were an intruder! Oh my god!"

"How about, 'Come in. Sit down. Cup of tea?'"

"Yes, yes, of course, come in, sit down, have some tea, oh my god."

"I know you don't like surprises..."

"I'll make an exception at this one."

"Thanks. I'm sorry, sis. I'll explain."

"Amelia. This is the best surprise *ever*."

"Sure?"

"Of course. What are you talking about? I just don't know what to say. I've suddenly got a million questions buzzing round my head and I don't know which one to pick first."

"Let's say no questions until we've had a cup of tea. OK?"

"Right."

Cecily grabs the rucksack by one of the straps and grapples it to the bottom of the stairs. "This is so heavy."

"Half a lifetime in there."

"Does that mean you're..."

"No questions. Embargo. Remember?"

"Sure. Sit down here and I'll put the kettle on." The water is still warm but Cecily pours it away and draws fresh. Marcus will just have to wait. Slowly the questions marshal themselves in her mind. Was there a hint that Amelia is home to stay? What happened to Enzo? Does Tilly know? How is she? Is she ill? Why has she come here?

Amelia places a key on the table in front of her. Cecily picks it up and turns it over and over in her hands. The key fob is a plastic globe. "I remember this. This was your key. From school days." The channel running the length of the key has worn smooth, the teeth look blunted, the metal is matt and scratched. "You've kept it all this time."

Amelia grins, nods and reaches for a packet of cigarettes. Cecily watches her light up and consciously draws in a few clean breaths before the smoke hits her, quelling the scratchy little commentary about people obviously doing things differently on the Continent. Amelia pulls another chair towards her for her feet and blows a turbulent column of smoke towards the ceiling. "God I could really go for a cup of tea." Cecily jumps to, in honour of Amelia's status of esteemed visitor.

Moving the paperwork out of the way, Cecily begins to load the kitchen table with food. Amelia looks so skinny. What can she tempt her with? What does she like to eat? There is no chatter as Cecily empties crisps into a bowl, cheese sticks into a glass, finding some fancies that she'd bought from the post office a few days ago but which curiously are already past their sell-by date, fruit, thick chocolate biscuits. "Have you got any sugar?" She hadn't remembered that either, that Amelia took sugar in tea. Amelia loads three heaped spoons into her mug and stirs noisily and distractedly. Cecily puts her hand over hers to stay it, proffering up plate after plate, all of which Amelia refuses with a shake of her head.

"Go on. You need to eat something."

"I'm fine. Fine." Cecily feels herself slightly admonished by Melly's sharp tone and stays her own hand. "You always were a feeder!"

"OK. You're right. It's too hot to eat." She picks a few plump grapes from the fruit bowl and nibbles round the skin, watching Amelia light her second cigarette. Why is it, within two minutes of her long-absent sister coming home, they are having a go at each other? They need Tilly to alkalise the mix, get them all smiling and laughing. "Does Tilly know you're here?"

"No."

Amelia turns the cigarette packet over and over on the table. She is looking distracted, worried, unkempt. A thought strikes Cecily. "Does Enzo know you're here?"

"No."

Offers of food and conversation rejected, Cecily decides to take a different tack. "Right then. Drink your tea. I'm going to get your room ready and run you a bath. Come up when you're ready."

Amelia nods. As Cecily leaves the kitchen to go upstairs, she looks back. Her sister, her darling sister, sits immobile at the table, her head slightly bent. Her shoulder blades jut out above her camisole top, each vertebrae moulded by sallow skin. Too much structure and not enough form. Her hair is parted into two ragged plaits, a few stray strands exposing the vulnerability of her slender neck. She seems oblivious to her surroundings. Trueman, bless his dear heart, is sitting on her feet, an agent perhaps of comfort and warmth.

Marcus

Marcus snatches a moment to himself to fire off a hasty text to Cecily. "Velda's here! Unexpected. Sorry. Chat soonest."

Cecily

The water is still in the bath when she goes upstairs half an hour later to check on Amelia. A couple of towels lie crumpled on the floor. A gentle evening breeze wafts through the open window, lifting the white linen blind. The room smells of lemon verbena.

She pushes open the door to Amelia's room. She is lying on her side, back to the door. Despite the vividness of the light outside, it is like dusk in the warm bedroom. A few items spill out of the top of the rucksack as if released from their inner press. Amelia breathes slowly and deeply, the ends of her hair lying in a damp curl on the pillow. Cecily stands and watches, arrested by the impossibly exquisite intimacy of seeing her sister asleep.

The Village

That same day, the following article appears in the local press and online.

> Local landowner, Major St John Welding, was delighted to find what may be an entire medieval chapel buried in the corner of a field in the village of Bullenden. As residents clear the field in preparation for their summer fair, an underground opening was unearthed. Local historian, Marcus Blatt, believes it could be either

a chapel or a hermit's cell dating back to the eighth or ninth century. Research shows that a substantial abbey called Abbeyclere stood on this land, probably on land belonging to Sir Roger de Familham. This was reputed to have been razed to the ground during civil riots and certain artefacts associated with the religious house have turned up in local buildings.

Whilst it is still too early to say exactly what the structure is, the Long Belford Historical and Archaeological Project are undertaking further research.

Major Welding tells the Daily Post that he is delighted to have made such a significant historical find on his land and hopes that it will be enjoyed by current residents and many future generations to come. Discussions are under way how best to preserve and exhibit this exciting find.

All members of the local community are invited to the forthcoming summer fair at the Town Field, Bullenden on July 18th. There will be rides, entertainments, refreshments, competitions, something for all the family.

13

The Village

Madge has her feet up after yesterday's rush. She'd never seen so many people. Amazing what a bit of TV coverage does for a place. They'd never shifted so much ice cream. Trust Tony to have a go, but it is hard enough to make a living these days. Who gives a fudge for Trade Descriptions? If they want to come out on a busy Sunday in the middle of the rush for cold refreshments, well let them. If not, then they can hold their peace, and so can Tony.

"Naff ice cream at premium prices. You're selling a lie." She'd not bothered to dignify his sarcasm with a reply but kept her head down filling the small tubs. "It's just chemical gloop. How can you say it's 'farmhouse ice cream, fresh from the churn'?" While he made his first of three trips to the cash and carry, twelve and a half miles each way, she'd printed some labels off the Internet of a cartoon cow with a large flower in its mouth and hand-coloured the flowers appropriate to the supposed flavour – red for raspberry, yellow for vanilla, blue for mint.

"Well, I didn't have a green pen, did I?" Hand-coloured, so it had to be authentic stuff; stands to reason. For the raspberry, she grated some white chocolate and stuck a frozen raspberry on top before sealing the lid. Vanilla got a splodge of syrup mixed with synthetic vanilla essence and a coffee bean while for the Mint, she smeared the lid with a dab of toothpaste and chopped in some crushed Polos and some green stuff from the garden which might well have been spearmint.

"And have you even weighed them?"

"Oh naff off yourself."

To his credit, Tony had stayed all afternoon, handing over packages in posh white paper bags with string handles and taking the money, shooting her a hostile glance while she ran the spiel about artisan, hand-crafted, rural products being the lifeblood of a place like this.

Her feet throb. Let that lazy mare Doreen run things for a while. Anyway, there are packages of sweets to be made up, some for the Lucky Dip and some to sell. She'd made sure that Chris Eveans, no easy man to negotiate with, knew what her percentage was. She is still narked with him for not giving her the food concession. Why would outside caterers do any better a job? Keep it local, why wouldn't you? The fair is only a few days away and if she is going to make the most of it, then she needs to get busy.

"Ton-ee! Door-eeen!"

Marcus

Well, that had been a shock! The last person he'd expected to see was Velda. Had the kids put her up to it? Apparently not, although she did hint that she'd been prompted to visit after watching the video on YouTube. "Thought I'd call in while I was here. Bit disappointing that it's all locked up though." Marcus muted the thought that she'd never shown an iota of interest in medieval architecture at any point in their married life. So why now? Funny how it all came back. He'd felt himself adopt the kind of latent good humour that, he supposed, had served him well during his years of cohabitation with this woman. It seemed to work. She'd even looked at him from under one arched eyebrow and said, "You've changed, you know."

"So have you," he replied. He knew she wanted him to ask in what way he'd changed, but to be frank, he really didn't want to be told that he'd lost weight, gone greyer, got coarser in his domestic habits, was missing the Tidy Fairy, had all the freedom in the world now to put his feet on the coffee table. He really didn't want to get led down the path of listening to how she now felt empowered, more truly herself than she'd ever been, indebted to the sisterhood for their support, except for somebody who shall remain nameless who'd do well to examine her own motives before she started criticising someone else's; how she'd found serenity; how sometimes you needed to lose love to find love. He didn't want to – but he had.

Two hours after she'd arrived and four cups of tea later, he stands up. "Well, it's been nice to see you. Got to get on. Need to put together some fact sheets on our buried chapel and organise a nature trail for the kids. Fair's next weekend." Velda rises too, looking somewhat astonished.

"Do you want me to go?"

"Well, you've got a long drive ahead of you. It's been lovely to catch up."

He feels slightly cruel. It is obvious that there was some hidden pretext for Velda's visit. Visiting a 'mouldering old ruin', which would have been her previous verdict, is clearly not her top priority today. At any point up until six months ago, he would probably have worked hard to find the right words to give her the opportunity to voice her concerns. But, she is right, he has changed. He, quite frankly, can no longer be arsed. He is about to disappoint her. At least there is some consistency in that.

Showing her to the door, he makes no attempt to offer to meet up again. He issues no invitation to come again and for longer next time. He pays no compliment or pulls a mournful moue at her departure. But it is hard to break a habit of thirty years. He can't let her leave with nothing. Velda is there on the doorstep. She seems reluctant to go. Heavens, it even seems as if her eyes are misting up slightly. "No kiss?" she asks.

He bends down to brush his lips against her powdery cheek. In a clumsy yet fluid move, Velda drops her handbag and flings her arms around him. He feels trapped within her poncho, his face pressed hard into the scratchy, unforgiving wool. "Oh, Marcus. You silly, silly man," she moans plangently. He wants desperately to right himself. His back is bent at a most unnatural angle, and who knows who is looking. Oh, Christ, what if Cecily can see them?

Marcus pulls himself free gently but emphatically. It seems more appropriate to pat her on the head than to kiss her. "Righto. Well, safe journey and all that." Velda looks up at him, her eyes pleading with him. A remarkable turn-up for the books. She is giving him a chance, a chance to put what she might call this 'silly nonsense' behind them and begin afresh. But he has begun afresh. With a jolt, he realises that this new life in Bullenden – uncertain, unpredictable, even lonely at times – is just what he wanted. He has stopped playing the fool.

Bending to the step, he picks up Velda's handbag and hangs it on her shoulder. "Goodbye, old fruit," he says and closes the door. From his sitting room window, he watches as she fumbles with her car keys, sitting for a moment at the wheel before inching her way out into the traffic. "Watch out, woman!" he calls out as Ned's battered white van comes to a tyre tearing halt just before it collides with her. Ned is evidently in even more of a hurry than usual.

Velda, however, is oblivious and drives off, trailing a plume of black smoke. He'll have to message Paul and get him to check the oil.

Still, today is another day. Carpe diem and all that. It is now time to go and speak to Cecily.

Cecily

Midday and Amelia is still asleep. She has been asleep for nearly twenty-four hours. Breakfast time, Cecily had taken a cup of tea and placed it by the bedside. Amelia's face was squashed into the pillow, her body seemingly flung on the bed, abandoned, surplus, her sleeping breath guttural and slow. When Cecily had checked later, the tea had been partially drunk, leaving a brown line of fatty milk around the inside of the cup. On she sleeps, as if drugged. Cecily looks down at her, waiting for a glimmer of awareness, as if Amelia might coolly lift an eyelid and say, "Gotcha." She represses a childish urge to pull the duvet off the bed, catching Amelia out, bouncing her into quickly snatching the upper edge and holding on. But she looks so fragile, so vulnerable, that she tiptoes out of the room; this is no place for a practical joke. Even as she leaves, she half expects Amelia to call out something, to let her know she'd been had. The hairs stand up on the back of her neck with a giggling, tingling anticipation. She turns at the door. Still Amelia dozes on, sleeping a narcotic sleep.

Of course, there is so much she wants to ask Amelia. Curiosity burns dyspeptically inside her. What is the significance of the overstuffed rucksack? Where is Enzo? Does Amelia plan to stay? Is this a stopping-off

175

place before her next adventure? Is she hurt? Heart-broken? Does she have news of some import to tell? All will have to wait.

It is strange having Amelia in the house, even though she is virtually motionless, soundless. It feels like a pressing weight, an unaccustomed responsibility, as if Cecily herself is bound to the same lack of movement and voice as Melly.

It is a time for waiting, standing at windows, staring out.

The Village

With just over a week to go to the summer fair, the village has an air of self-important bustle. Perhaps spurred on by the rippling media interest in the recently discovered sunken chapel and the by now maniacal excitement of Chris Eveans, a Bunting Committee had been formed. The boy scouts had leafleted every household in the village notifying everyone of the Twenty-Four-Hour Bun-ting-a-ling taking place in the Scout Hut from Friday night to Saturday night. Everyone was invited to bring sewing materials, cardboard, string, scissors, strong coffee.

Bleary-eyed and pricked-about, a handful of stalwarts emerge from the hut at the end of the day and night-long stint. "Five kilometres of bunting" chirrups the Facebook page, together with pictures of the sewing bee looked on by groups of bemused-looking families each holding garishly coloured tubs of ice cream in their hands.

Cecily watches from her window as three men in a hired cherry picker move from lamppost to lamppost festooning the street at height with zigzags of fluttering triangles. Ben unfurls ropes of the stuff from black plastic bags placed at intervals along the pavement.

"Jesus Christ. Be careful," Cecily shouts onto the window pane as Ned's van comes careering down the street, narrowly avoiding a large lady in a little white Fiat pulling out of the car park opposite the deli. Ned swerves and ricochets down the street exploding a black bin bag with the wheel of his van. A multi-coloured bundle of bunting quickly whips itself up into the underside of the rear mud guard and lodges there. Ben runs down the road for a short distance, shouting, "Mr Gallagher. Mr Gallagher!" The van is soon out of sight.

Ned

"Oh for Christ's sake! Get out of the way you stupid bloody woman!" Ned lifts his hand to strike the horn but feels the van buck and shimmy so quickly grabs the steering wheel again. Cretinous Sunday drivers in their little white pudding basins should bloody well look before they pull out.

He is getting too old to go chasing round the countryside; one day, one day, one day he'll call her bluff and just let her get on with it.

She'd barely spoken to him since that evening with the kitten and the photo and the hellish accusations. To his shame, he'd coloured up as soon as she showed him the picture on the screen with him and Ben's mum, their hands interlocked behind Ben. But there was nothing to be guilty about. It was the force of Mandy's anger and certainty that had made his blood rise. They'd stood either side of the boy, a proud mum and a benevolent mentor; that's all they were. Ben's mum was a fantastic lady who worked all hours to give her son a decent upbringing. Where did Mandy get off making false accusations and stirring up trouble?

He'd thought about having a quiet word with somebody to get that photo taken down. But to do so would be tantamount to admitting there was something to feel ashamed about. And it would mean a whole lot of explanation about something that was delicate and, actually, nobody's business. He didn't want it known to all and sundry that his wife had a bit of a jealousy issue. He was just grateful that she hadn't posted any spiteful comments.

The note on the table this morning told him that she had gone round to 'sort that woman out'. He couldn't let Mandy do that to her. "Bitch. Bitch. Why can't you just be fucking normal?" He bangs the steering wheel with the heel of his hand. The faster you want to go, the longer it takes.

He turns into the familiar street. No sign of anyone. So what if he has got it wrong? What will Bernadette say if he rocks up at the house and, as far as she's concerned, it is just like any other ordinary day? He'd be a fool. And he'd probably expose himself for being the lovestruck fool that he now, truly, knows himself to be.

But what if Mandy's threats are real? What if she is about to say some of the things that she'd mouthed off at home? Doesn't bear thinking about.

Ben's mum comes to the door. Her face is pale. He wants to smooth out the two parallel frown lines with his thumb. "Come in. Mandy's here." His heart sinks. He tries to grab her arm as she walks down the hallway, to stop her, to wordlessly apologise, but she is out of reach.

"Darling!" Ned cringes. Mandy waggles her phone. "I knew you'd come. I so need a lift. Thank you for the cup of tea, Mrs Nolan. So lovely to meet you. Ned's so pleased with Ben. Talks of little else."

A buzzing goes off in Ned's head. This is all so false, so bloody false.

"Come on. Let's go." Mandy offers her hand, which Ned grabs, lifting her brusquely off the chair and pushing her, her hand at an awkward angle behind her, down the hallway and into the van. He hears the front door close quietly behind them. Mandy slides into the cab. As he walks round the back, he notices a pile of grimy, oily rags caught under the back wheel. He tries to work it free, but it is wound fast round the axle. Sod it. He'll sort it out later.

Mandy is po-faced all the way home. It was either going to be that or a ranting tirade. He prefers the silence. Even before the van stops, she slides out of the passenger side and, leaving the door open, disappears into the house. He should go into the house to hear her out. A long trail of what looks like kite string has unfurled itself from the rear of the van. Little triangles of oily, grimy fabric lift and flutter inches off the road. What kind of a fucking joke is this? He just wants to cry.

Cecily

Marcus emerges from the alleyway. He has bundles of papers and appears to be heading her way. She ducks out of sight for to be seen standing idly at a window would admit to being listless, feckless. Which was a bit daft, because wasn't that what windows were for? But she has no wish to start a teleological discussion with herself or to appear anything other than purposeful and in command. Besides, he might think she was watching out for him, especially after he failed to turn up yesterday, and that definitely wouldn't do.

Cecily's view of Marcus is suddenly blocked by a vehicle bumping up on the kerb directly outside the window. It pops and spews as the driver turns off the ignition. The mud sprays and the decals could only mean one person. Tilly. She should have phoned Tilly to tell her of Amelia's arrival. Of course she was going to, but was there any point before Amelia woke up? So, is Tilly here on a completely spontaneous visit, or does she know? It might look like she had been hoarding Amelia for the last twenty-four hours, keeping her to herself, excluding Tilly. Which, of course, wasn't her plan at all. Was it?

Tilly bounds up the steps, coming to a juddering halt at the front door, immutably closed and locked in front of her. "Just a minute," Cecily calls from inside.

"Sorry. Old habits. Just expect it to be open. Hope you don't think I was barging in."

"Not at all." The sisters hug briefly in the lobby.

Tilly is electric with excitement. "Where is she?"

She obviously knows of Amelia's arrival.

Cecily tamps down her first thought – how did she know? – and speaks while drawing Tilly down the hall. "She's still asleep. Looked in on her a few minutes ago. She's absolutely flat out. Drank a cup of tea, that's all, since she got here yesterday. Was going to call you, obviously, but thought it was best to wait till she woke up. No idea she'd sleep for this long."

"Come on. Let's go and wake her up."

Cecily's slower canter up the stairs behind Tilly is halted by a knock on the front door. "You go. I'll see who this is."

She turns carefully on the stairs and makes her way down the hallway again. The sound of excited shrieks ricochet off the hard surfaces above her. Tilly had obviously just bounded into Amelia's room. Was that what Amelia was waiting for? Why couldn't Cecily have done that?

Marcus is standing on the threshold, also evidently jerked by some inner excitement. Cecily stands back as he bullets his way down the hallway, heading straight for the kitchen, talking as he goes. She follows him into the kitchen. Trueman, released from his confines, speeds past and up the stairs. She can hear the delight in the raised voices as the sisters invite him to 'hup, hup' onto the bed. She pictures the scene of chaos and joy upstairs. But where would she be in that little scenario? Jumping on the bed, or pulling the corners tidy? Squeezing herself into the middle of

179

the harum scarum, or leaning against the door jamb? Even the blinking dog has deserted her, preferring the easy laughs upstairs to the quieter, studied, earnest feel of the kitchen.

Marcus seems oblivious to it all. A feeling of almost overwhelming frustration wells up as she tunes into Marcus's flow of words.

"I've been following two very interesting strands of enquiry. One that you know about. The other that you possibly don't, but which I think I should make you aware of."

Cecily turns her back on him to fill the kettle, working her jaw silently around the words 'pompous ass' over and over.

"Are you alright?"

"Yes, yes, fine."

"Only, it's...I thought..."

"No. No. Tea?"

Marcus doesn't reply but continues to spread papers from his briefcase over the table. She wants to shout at him, to tell him to have the grace to acknowledge a simple offer of tea. She knows that he obviously has very important things to tell her, things that he is proud of, that elevate him by their discovery, that reflect well on his skills of enquiry, that very possibly allow all the world to see, shining deep inside him, that single crystal of worth and value that makes his life entirely worthwhile – while she can only stand back and observe and offer the creative genius tea. Tea that, once proffered, gets ignored. Ignored. Ignored, while Tilly and Amelia upstairs tumble over each other, finger locks of each other's hair, smile with radiance, laugh and chatter. Always on the edge. Always on the margins.

"Oh dear, you seem to have broken a cup." Marcus looks up briefly at Cecily standing with a raw-edged handle in her hand. "Anyway, as I was saying... Have you got company by the way?" Marcus's head shoots up as he glances at the ceiling.

"My sisters," she tells him abruptly. She places a steaming cup on the table, holding hers gingerly by the rim in the absence of its handle. The other two can come and make tea when they are good and ready.

"Right. Well. I hardly know where to begin. It's all great stuff. As you know, I've been looking into the origins of our sunken hideout.

And I think I'm getting close. But..." here Marcus nods slowly and portentously, "there...is...more."

Cecily puts her face to the steam. She feels droplets form on the tender skin beneath her eyes. The sharp scent of bergamot jags inside her nose. Closing her wet eyelashes, she urges herself to be nice, to play the role of palimpsest.

"Oh. How wonderful. Do tell."

The mercury bubble inside her settles and she sits back to listen graciously and calmly to what he has to say.

With a ringmaster's flourish, Marcus places a photocopied newspaper cutting in front of her.

"Why, that's Major Welding."

Marcus looks gratified.

Cecily peers closer at the photograph. A three-man head shot. Major Welding in the foreground, head slightly bent, eyes downcast. Flanking him and towering above him, two uniformed men. One, stern-faced, insignia above the peak of his baseball cap, seems to sweep the view to the left. The other, eyes obscured by sunglasses, looks straight to camera, out of focus save for the gold law-enforcement badge on his chest. The man in the middle, Welding, sparse grey hair swept back into coiffured curls on the crisp white collar of his shirt, would appear to be walking into an unknown future.

"Read the headline, and the caption. That should give you the bones of the story."

Cecily reads them out loud. "Stop! Police!" She glances up at Marcus, disbelieving her eyes. Marcus nods to her to continue. "Bernard Gorman – scapegoat or genuine investor?"

"I shall read you the first paragraph." Cecily hands back the page. "Within the closed world of high finance, it is rare for a global investor to be pushed out into the cold. However, these are extraordinary times. Bernard Gorman, director of one of the sixty or so failed financial institutions to be found in the landlocked republican enclave of Northern Italy, claims that he is being made a scapegoat following investigations by Bank Italia."

"You've lost me."

"Well, it seems that our Major Welding has been somewhat of a naughty boy when it comes to paying his taxes and those of his old boy network. It's a bit of a long and complicated story, which I won't bore you with, but it goes something like this."

As Marcus pauses for wind, Cecily fights a rush of rising pique at the suggestion she would be easily bored or uncomprehending. She also listens for signs of life upstairs. All is quiet, except for the sound of Trueman bumping his way down the stairs. Letting out air as he positions himself under Cecily's seat, she feels inordinately grateful to the hound for returning to her after his brief, disloyal foray upstairs.

"It seems our man, on leaving the army, gets himself voted onto the board of various financial institutions in both France and Switzerland where he introduces certain of his associates to the joys of offshore investments. By a process of creep and gravity, funds make their way to a certain banking house in San Marino. Gorman, as he's known, sidles these funds into high-earning, non-tax-paying accounts set up in fictitious names. Nobody's too bothered. Nobody asks too many embarrassing questions. Dividends are good. Tax liability minimal to zero. He's everyone's friend.

"Then comes the perfect storm. Along with the global crash in credit, a certain whistle-blower in Switzerland and the Italian government undergoing *una crisi di coscienza*, Gorman's name pops up on a top secret list that gets circulated by confidential degrees around Europe. This list, by the way, has well over twenty thousand names on it. It's perhaps just a bit unfortunate that Gorman's is the one that catches someone's eye.

"He fits the bill perfectly. He's not a major player. He has no direct links with the Mexican drug cartels, the quartermasters to various Russian separatist outfits, who benefit the most from the no-questions-asked loans and other financial services offered by Gorman's company. So, there will be little come-back if the authorities make an example of him and hang him out to dry in public view. He gets escorted to the international airport by members of the Polizia Civile and the Guardia di Rocca in the full glare of the world's media and told never to darken the financial fortress again.

"Now, happily, everyone can say they take very seriously the task of combatting money laundering and tax evasion – witness his extradition – while they quietly get on with what they're good at – running funds through intermediary companies at multiple levels to wash any stain off the filthy lucre. Gorman's safe, happy again, as there is no fear that the UK tax authority has any intention of prosecuting any of its citizens named on the whistleblower's list.

"Gorman returns to the UK, a bit battered and bruised. Vows never to mix in the world of high finance again and picks up the life of a Suffolk gent."

"Well, well, well." Trueman is moved to lift his head off the kitchen floor and wag his tail to the rhythm of Cecily's astonishment. "Are we sure it's Major Welding though? The bit you've just told me concerns somebody with a different name entirely."

"Totally sure. We've got the picture here. There's no doubting this is our Major Welding. So I did a bit more digging around and found that the Welding family have quite a presence in this county, and not all of it quite laudatory. He adopted the name 'Gorman' from a distant aunt on his mother's side while playing the money game. When that didn't work out, he took his CV off in a different direction, reverting back to his post-Army persona."

Cecily sits for a moment to take it all in. The upstairs loo flushes.

"As Major Welding, he moves into Haughton Hall, no doubt financed by a certain amount of hush money from his cronies. No one would be any the wiser, except that he happens to own the Town Field and a compulsive hankering for the limelight."

"I see." She can hear Amelia and Tilly come down the stairs, one's footfall a regular beat, the other's irregular. They appear at the kitchen door; Amelia has her arm round Tilly's shoulder. Just like when Tilly broke her leg at gymkhana and hobbled round the house for six weeks with a pot on her leg and the temper of an irascible bear. Cecily remembers having to blank out with felt-tip pen what Mother would call 'unsavoury comments' written by Tilly's classmates before they came to the attention of any grown-up.

Marcus continues talking, oblivious apparently to the two women standing behind him.

"Sorry, Marcus. Just a minute."

Cecily rises and approaches her sisters. She gives Amelia a tender kiss on the top of her head. Despite yesterday's bath, she still has about her all the smells of travel, of cheap food, of exhaustion, of other times. Marcus is forced to stop, look up at the new arrivals. Cecily is amused to see his eyes skip from face to face to face, as if scalded.

Amelia rescues the strap of her cami top from its falling place off her shoulder. She is not wearing a bra and Marcus's eyes zip to her prone nipples. Amelia lowers herself into a chair and folds her knees and long thin arms in front, like a cricket ready to flee. "Who's this?"

Marcus doesn't reply. Cecily relates a little of Marcus's investigations. Amelia listens while propelling smoke towards the ceiling. This seems to smudge Marcus's earlier fascination as he gathers the pages towards him, preparing to leave. Cecily is amused to see him hold his breath, so as not to ingest any smoke, as he lifts his posterior off the chair to reach for the furthest sheaves. Tilly and Cecily share a look as Marcus, trapped by the sight of Amelia reaching revealingly for the sugar bowl, colours a culpable red.

"I can see you're busy," he says in one quick exhalation of precious air.

"I'll see you to the door."

"Well, it's a shame that we didn't have time to...er...that... Anyway. There's more I want to tell you." Marcus puts his hand on the false door knob in the centre panel of the front door. "I've found out a bit about our omnipresent Mr Eveans too. Turns out he's from a PR company that specialises in the rescue of dented reputations."

Cecily opens the door for him. Marcus turns at the top of the steps. "By the way, Velda called in yesterday. That was why I couldn't come over before."

She isn't too sure what response is required to this so just nods.

"Well," Marcus shrugs. "That's that."

"Indeed."

She closes the door once he has scuffed his way down the steps to street level and turned right towards the pub. A smell of warm olive oil and the spitting of frying eggs fill the passageway. The house is warming up again.

SUMMER

In the quiet centuries that follow, the Angul-Seaxan spread from their landing places. Danes, Norwegians, Saxons. Before them fall the Old English trees and the Old English men. Falling to the ground, lined like bundles of brushwood, the new-bared land scored by articulating talons into ridges and furrows. Water – streams, lakes, rivers – bring life to new crops. Villages, with an east field and a west field, a north field or a south field, two or three acres each.

By the time of the Domesday book, nearly every non-industrial village has been hacked and drained and elevated by axe, mattock, billhook, hoe. Livestock working in tandem with the new drive for settlement, grinding away the bark and shoots of the competing scrubland. But still a man could shout into the waste and not be heard by another or only receive back a faint echoing shout.

With a new millennium, a new order. One of castles, charters, villeins and taxes. The village becomes the feudal centre of a number of manors, ruled from the baron's castle. There is a market, meadowland, swine roaming in the wood; vineyards and sheep support over 100 households. The French have come.

It is the soft tissue of life that disappears first, the orchards, fishponds, water mill, vineyard, kennels, dovecot and swannery. Then go the forges, potteries, studios, brewhouses and bakeries. Again, four hundred years and all that flourished is gone.

M. Blatt

14

The Village

It is the day before the summer fair. For a brief moment, before the events of the day unfold, nature reforms itself after the stormy night. In the cottage gardens, the red poppies, wounded by the previous night's downpour, hang out their battle-torn petals like drying flags. Waxy rose petals hold onto beads of moisture as if to slake a thirst, while lupins and hollyhocks rattle themselves dry in the gentle, lifting breeze. Bees drone above the open canopies of elderberry, flies strafe the thick, heat-laden air. Over the horizon step high-banked clouds like a line of white-frilled chorus girls in a slow-motion rehearsal. "Looks like we should be lucky with the weather tomorrow," predict the few to venture out early.

Madge

"Well, never mind, dearie. I'm sure you'll be alright. Anything I can get you? Got plasters at 67p – they're not waterproof, but it doesn't look like that should trouble you too much." Sitting on an imperfectly balanced wooden chair inside the post office is what she can only describe as a 'rather disreputable-looking young gentleman'. He'd staggered into her shop only a few minutes earlier with a cut above his left eye. Madge scrutinises him coolly from behind the counter, trying to assess whether the dirt ingrained into every micropore was caused by the injury or whether it might itself offer an explanation for the injury. She takes in the dreadlocks, the patchwork jacket and nose ring and decides that he is not likely to be a high spender. She toggles the under-counter switch that causes the closed circuit camera to whirr and shift ostentatiously, just to make sure he fully understands that he is being watched. Ever since the fairground has come to town, you cannot be too careful.

"I couldn't have a cup of tea, could I? It's just that I've had a bit of a shock. The van's gone off the road and into the hedge."

A quick mental calculation leads Madge shrewdly to the conclusion that it is going to be easier to make this indigent ne'er-do-well a cup of tea than to try and sort his camper van out, which is, on his account, balanced precariously, nose down, arse up, among the spiny branches of a hawthorn hedge somewhere.

"You haven't got any soya milk, have you, by any chance?"

"No, I bleedin' haven't." Madge stomps off into the back of the shop to put the kettle on, giving the toggle a purposeful wiggle as she goes.

"Tony! Tony!" she whispers urgently into her mobile under cover of the whistling kettle. "There's one of them druids in the shop." The silly old duffer tells her to speak up. Best thing, she decides, is to give the lad a cup of tea and send him on his merry way.

"Sugar, too, if you've got any," comes the shout from the shop front.

"I'll sugar you, dearie," mutters Madge, hoicking a squashed brown tea bag out of the recycled waste bin.

The Village

In the early dawn, the Town Field lies quiet and open. A family of swifts cling to the tight telegraph wire while, beneath, a few blackbirds mine for worms, heckled by a clutch of crows in the higher branches of the border oaks. New growth now smudges the rawness of the cut-about look of the field after the big clear-up. Young, green blackberries, sloes and hips hint forward to harvest time. Tilly's flock of Blue-Faced Framlinghams contentedly tear up the lush grass. Moving with a collective mind they chomp their way selectively around the field, leaving the tall clumps of bitter buttercup, thistle and dock. Later that day, Tilly and sheepdog Pip will corral them between woven willow hurdles, polish their cloven hooves, clip out their woolly moss and display a board with rosettes from various agricultural shows. Three of the ewes have lambs – almost as full-grown and broad-backed as their mothers but with a whiter, tighter fleece and trusting eyes.

In the damp shade of three alder trees loom two shipping containers craned in during the previous week. Inside are tables, chairs, bales of straw, decking, a stage, lighting, public address system, generators and gazebos. Bishy Barnabee's (Eastern Counties) Est. 1932 had arrived on Wednesday and were setting up a Tipping Roulette, a Hungry Caterpillar, a Bouncy Castle and Montgolfier's Centrifugalarium in preparation for tomorrow.

Rather incongruously, the flat-fronted, stumpy nose of a 1970s Dodge Commer van looks in on the proceedings from two fields away, like an inquisitive old milker. No one is sure if it belongs to the fair people or if it is one of Chris Eveans's latest wheezes, a self-referencing art installation. As such, it is largely ignored.

For now, all is going according to plan.

At nine thirty, dads and lads from the local rugby team, the Bullenden Bulls, arrive to erect the beer tent, establish power lines and set up wooden trestles in preparation for the brewer's dray arriving at two thirty to deliver and install twenty barrels of Summer Lightning, Badger's Frenzy and Holy Cow. Two of their number, Daniel Holland and Martyn Harris, loose-head prop and fly half respectively for the Under 18s, have volunteered to camp out to ensure the beer's safety over the coming night.

The local GP, Dr Carmichael, and other members of the Vintage and Veteran Car Club are to spend the day prepping and polishing in readiness for the procession down the High Street, escorting the May Queen, Phillipa Grayson. There had been some uproar concerning the majorettes twirling their batons within a fifty-yard radius of such rare and precious bodywork but Ariadne Montague, high-pitched and irrepressible, had given her 'personal guarantee' that none of her girls had ever, *ever* dropped a baton while on public display. The old boys had been persuaded to take her at her word.

Marcus

Marcus is planning his address to the villagers that evening, on his investigations into the sunken chapel, hoping to lend each and every one of them a lens through which to see their own multi-layered, complex world, a world that had, in the last few days, tilted and reassembled slightly. It is rumoured that Major Welding has put some money behind the bar for afters. He would call his piece 'Smacking the Rump of England'.

He stares at the pile of books and handwritten pages scattered about his desk. Trouble is, the more he needs to place his finger on the pulse of this handmade world, the more the pulse jumps and shifts.

Would anyone in the audience really be that bothered? For most, surely, the things that stand prone upon the surface of the earth are what matter. Should they care that the church has a tower or a spire? For most, church is a place of hard wooden pews, views of the nativity encumbered by stone pillars, a brief flash of coloured light upon a grey slab. An arena for funerals.

Talking to Cecily, he knew how some villagers, including her husband, had been lowered into the rich earth of the county, to slowly lose their grip on their human form and seep into matter. Yet in the next village, the church abuts right onto the road, denied burial rights by the avaricious rector of this church. Fascinating stuff but only if you could, like Marcus, smell the ink on the petition, see the powder fall softly to the ground, the blow of the petitioner within his cheek, the roll and dispatch of the parchment.

Nothing exemplifies more the abrupt, random, haphazard nature of history than the view from his window. In contrast to the uniformity and built-for-purpose architecture of London's suburbs, each blink of an eye in his passage along Bullenden's streets seems to offer up a magic lantern view. The colours are at their best this time in the morning, he observes, with the sun gathering herself up from the horizon. The lemons and pinks of the painted render. The black and tan of the stovepipe chimneys. Glassy-eyed flint and friable brick. The black-as-tar wooden boards. The duck-egg blue of the bookshop. The fuchsia pink of the hardware store. Long spires of rosebay, tumbling tendrils of wild rose.

The streets please him for their lack of uniformity. Taken as a complete view, it is as if someone had slid a door here, a window there, raked a roof, lowered a dormer, stretched and elided features to deliberately confound, to snatch and snag the viewer's attention, let it not slide carelessly away on a smooth vista. Buildings turn their shoulders to the road. Small lead-lined lookout windows, lukums, set in a roof line, pop like eyes. An old mother's hovel abuts a white brick gentleman's residence.

He stands in front of the mirror hanging on a chain above the bulbous, glazed fireplace. He can just about see the top of his head but not his shaking hands.

"Ladies and gentlemen. Thank you for coming out this evening. I know we all have a busy day tomorrow, so I shall be brief." [Pause for murmurs of appreciation.]

"As you know, our 'chapel' [grip papers to execute the floating quotation marks sign] has been something of a discovery for us – for Major Welding on whose field it is located, and for the entire village, prompting as it has some interest from local TV and the press, due in no small part to the auspices of Mr Eveans." [Pause again for perhaps more muted appreciation this time as the media glare has not been to everyone's liking.]

"Those of you who have watched the piece on *Look East* and have read the piece in *Eastern Life*, will know that there has been some uncertainty regarding the origins and, thereby, purpose of this space.

"Damn." Marcus leans to pause the recording on his phone and answer the incoming call. Caller ID unknown. No-one there. Third time in as many days.

"Ahem." He coughs to bring his voice down an octave. Bit alarming these unexplained phone calls. Has he been rumbled? Any chance that his discreet enquiries concerning the origins and purpose of the Major and his oleaginous sidekick have been found out? But how is that possible? And…and…and…well, the information is out there, in the public domain, isn't it? Would they put a gagging order on him? Get out an injunction? His throat tightens at the thought of gagging. Water. Need a glass of water. Pressing Stop on the recording app on his phone, Marcus places his pages – by now a little damp and crumpled – on the coffee table and goes into the kitchen for something to soothe and moisten his throat.

Madge

He'd thanked her, very politely, for the cup of tea and placed the mug on the counter. She'd given brief consideration to his request for work – "Any sort, window cleaning, painting…" – but decided she couldn't keep an eye on him and the stock at the same time so sent him on his way. Not a bad sort of lad all in all. She'd asked him where he was headed to. He told her he was on his way to a festival in the next county. Didn't matter, had a day or two to get there. Apparently he'd been in touch with his mates and they were on their way to sort out the van. Maybe she should have got him to rod the drains while he was waiting. Too late now. He'd promised to fix the hedge, so no harm done, eh?

Marcus

"Right. Where was I? I am delighted to be able to present to you my initial findings." Here he would signal to whoever was operating the PowerPoint to move to the first slide: a shot he'd taken by jumping into the gully and pressing his back firmly into the hedge. "Cut into the exposed flank of the grassy knoll, you can clearly see an arched opening. By scraping away some of the sub soil, there are the flat roof tiles, probably baked clay. And if we look further down, there you can see the stone walls and buttresses."

Gwyddno

The cup of tea had been disgusting. An insult really. It left a metallic taste in his mouth, like someone had applied electrodes to his fillings. It will be a few hours before the others get to this backwater of a place. The sun is warm so he might walk down the High Street. Doubtless Tanya would think it was all a bit bourgeois, but he likes the place. OK, maybe they weren't so into sullying their own back yard – he'd seen quite a few signs up: No to the Wind Farm. No to Pylons. No to the Prison. No to the Incinerator. No to Fracking. Yes to the Bypass.

It had the feel of the children's adventure books his mum used to read. Wide, dusty roads. Cheery postmen. Somebody always ready with a sixpence for an ice cream. Sticklebacks in a jar. He wouldn't be surprised if they went round saying things like "Gosh" and "Up the wooden hill to Bedfordshire."

But he should have got the number plate of that geezer in a white van that came careering round the corner on the wrong side of the road and knocked him flying over the ditch and straight into the hedge. Christ knows what Wylff will say when he sees his precious green and cream van perpendicular to the hawthorn hedge. Mind you, if the brakes hadn't have been so dodgy, he would have stopped in time. As it is, he never liked the van anyway. He has a very vague memory of going to see Mum's nan in a place where you had to walk down echoing corridors that smelled of bleach and piss. The colours of the tiles on the walls had been the same colours as the van.

He'll find a quiet spot and have one of those flapjacks he'd helped himself to from the post office.

Cecily

Amelia worked alongside, quiet and efficient. By midday they had zested and juiced ten dozen lemons. The tiny spritzes of lemon released by the grater had settled on the backs of their hands, on the table top, drying to a sticky white film. Tiny, translucent juice sacs stuck to the inside of the glass measuring jugs. The sight of them set her front teeth on edge. Lemon husks were piled up on the black granite worktop as they gently simmered small batches with sugar to make a syrup. Five bluebottles buzzed and bumped round the kitchen ceiling.

Has Amelia said much to Tilly? She certainly hadn't said much in their times together. Throwing her arms wide and saying, in a long drawn-out way, "So…" had produced zilch by way of explanation. "The more you push her, the more she'll clam up," Tilly had said. And it is true. It is almost as if Amelia is as insubstantial as she was hundreds of miles away, a kind of phantasmagorical being that shades in and out of existence at whim. She'll just have to wait, Cecily tells herself.

Once the syrup had cooled, they would bottle it and serve it tomorrow over ice and white mint leaves with a good splash of chilled mineral water. One pound fifty a shot.

"Weather looks like it might hold for tomorrow." Amelia nods but offers no reply.

Marcus

He would then show a series of photographs from inside the space. The long, thin, rectangular stones, rough cut and held fast by age and compression. The gently barrelled ceiling that seems to taper off behind the vertical walls, suggesting more than just soil and rubble behind. Maybe at one point the elegantly arching roof had reached right down to the floor and these were load-bearing walls added later, maybe after some collapse or destruction. A close-up of the microscopic lichen softening the hard edges of the infill. Plucky Hart's Tongue clinging halfway up the walls.

How can he convey a sense of the place to his audience tonight? How can he instil in them the sense of awe that this small and undoubtedly sacred space conjures in him? To describe it literally only diminishes it. Or is he just being far too pretentious? Would they just think he was being a pompous twit and fidget and squirm until they could get to the bar and their free pint?

Amelia

Since she'd been home, Enzo had left twenty-seven text messages and eight voicemail messages. His tone had varied between angry and conciliatory; blaming her and then blaming himself and covering his own head in ashes. He loved her. He hated her. How dare she humiliate him like this in front of everyone? No one knew; he'd keep it their little secret, just say she had to fly home on family business. Hadn't he shown her nothing but love and consideration? Come back, cara, nobody loves him like she loves him. Who does she think she is? He understands completely where she is coming from.

If only Cecily would stop looking at her with that wide-eyed, expectant tilt to her head. Not asking her outright but tactfully giving her space to open up, if she needs to. It fucking does her head in.

Just leave me alone.

Marcus

"And so for the big reveal!" No, possibly he wouldn't say that. Makes him sound like one of those awful prize-givers on TV who preface each announcement with a carefully calibrated thirty seconds of silence.

Besides, this place has far too much mystery and dignity to be messed about with. Wouldn't it be better, anyway, to just block it up again? For all he knows, come back in a few months' time and there'd be graffiti on the wall and litter and other detritus in the corners. In which case, it would have been better never discovered.

"The way I look at it is this…" That's better; tone more suited to his status as an amateur sleuthing historian. Not as if he is Tony Robinson, ha ha! But, whichever way you look at it, the facts seem to suggest that "…what we have here is, indeed, a sunken chapel, as it's been described. But my guess is that it's an extremely primitive space, possibly on a site of specific sacred or pagan significance, one that has subsequently been taken over and appropriated as a Christian site."

Nod here to operator to move to next slide, showing a square indent in the floor, an uneven notch about two inches in diameter. Torch holder? Altar? Post hole for some internal feature?

Who will he be talking to tonight anyway? Could be mouthing off into an empty room for all he knows.

"The reason I believe this to be an early, primitive site is in the clues around. Look at the floor. What do you see? It's not earth, it's not tiled, it's bare rock. Not rock that's been hewed and hefted here, but bedrock. Bed-rock."

Another slide. "This time taken from inside the chapel. Ladies and gentlemen, look at where the step is in relation to ground level. A good two feet of earth and rubble and pebbles are clearly visible, forcing you to step *up* when leaving. Such has been the build-up of loam and hummus over centuries, millennia even."

For goodness' sake. Listen to yourself. Do you even imagine anyone would be interested? Velda's voice is mild yet mocking. Even she, the imaginary Velda, seems to be demonstrating some small pity for his fruitless efforts to get across the sheer awesomeness of stepping into this ancient arena.

That day, several weeks ago, when Chris Eveans had brought him to the site, had been one of the most memorable of his life. He knew, he just knew, that this was an ancient primitive site, invested with so much mystery. It was almost like an antechamber between two worlds. This stone had absorbed miasmas of breath exhaled in worship, fear, exhaustion. It had held fast against flood, tectonic movement, collapse. Like the sleeping princess, time had smudged away all markers, stopped up its opening, covered and softened its shape so it became just another overlooked, unexplained mound. Even the workmen who had dug the gully a mere yard in front of its entrance had failed to discover it. It had taken a peculiar combination of erosion, clearance, Ben's zealous application to a single task and a pregnant feline to release this particular jewel from the clasp of time.

Smugglers' den. Hermit's cave. Shrine. Refuge. It had been all of these. It had sheltered people, inspired people, imprisoned people, implicated people. A tiny, tiny space; of huge significance to possibly legions of people, its simple beauty earthed up for generations, its rare beauty now opened up for all to see.

"Looking at the floor, in this slide, you can see that it is bone dry. Yet there is a marked fissure in the floor. This is another clue to it being a primitive site of worship. We are not far from a tributary of the Orrell, a tidal river. Water would have risen and fallen between this fissure, before being taken away out to sea beyond whatever that wall conceals. Water was extremely important, a symbol and supporter of life. Nowadays, due to intensive agriculture and modern housing, the water table is so much lower and water is channelled more, so we no longer have the rise and flush and ebb, the magic of water appearing up through the floor, the symbolism of water as a gift, a cleansing agent. Water as a carrier.

"Moving forward to Roman times, if we look at this map [nod], we can see how our village is directly on the route the Roman army would have taken from Colchester, now their principle city in Britannia, to quell the Iceni tribe in the North. It is quite feasible, in my mind, that a small shrine, previously dedicated to the goddess Freyja would now undergo a conversion to Minerva to bring good fortune to the fighting army.

"In the six hundreds, St Felix comes to Dunwich in East Anglia. As his influence spreads, so over the centuries can we see that the expression of Christian worship flows back the other way as Dunwich becomes an important embarkation point for Saint James de Compostela. Pilgrims would have marched this route, possibly stopping off here to rest, give thanks, pray at the now defunct abbey.

"Evidence points to the abbey being virtually by this spot. So it's reasonable to assume that the monks will have appropriated this site, rebuilt the stone structure we see today and operated it as some kind of place of worship, place of safety, a place of alms, or, for the wealthier, a place for extracting tolls.

"And, allowing myself a small point of reflection here, this is what I find absolutely fascinating. Twelve hundred years ago, an early Christian religious house stood in these fields. It is now completely gone. Invading forces, starting with the Danes, have destroyed and dismantled it piece by piece. This small shelter is all that remains. By a quirk of fate, it has been allowed to descend further and further into the earth, almost as if the earth has thrown itself as a mantle over it. As the axes of modern life change, we have turned our gaze elsewhere. This corner of a domestic field has remained forever ancient."

Gwyddno

Where are they? If they don't hurry up, he'll go plum crazy in this place. Hicksville. But quaint for all that. Ten minutes, tops. That's how long it takes to walk from end to end. Probably a bit longer for the old ones. Strange sort of place. The old bint in the post office was a piece of work although she had given him a pork pie, which he had eaten with all the speed of guilt and fear of discovery. What Tanya didn't know, Tanya needn't fret about. He breathes into his hands. Would she smell the meat on his breath? His stomach turns flipside and a greasy, sulphurous bubble rises in his mouth. Kate in the bookshop was alright though. They'd had a good old chat about stuff. She'd been at Greenham. He wondered if she had met his mum at all.

His bum is getting numb sitting on the kerb. His back aches too with leaning forward away from the spiny hawthorn hedge. Two dog walkers are the only people he's seen. Neither had offered much help or reassurance. One of the dogs had growled at him. Wylff, when he'd finally got through on the phone, had told him to wait by the van, "AND DO NOT BUDGE." It remains to be seen what Wylff's reaction is going to be when he sees his precious van stuck in a hedge. Odds on, it isn't going to be a good one.

God his head is itchy. A corona of flies buzzes round him. Finally, absorbed in the challenge of balancing more than four pieces of gravel on top of each other, he hears a familiar throaty mechanical roar. "Where've you been? Been waiting effin' ages." Wylff and Tanya tip out of the front of the bright orange, suped-up Discovery. "Where's Alice?"

"Asleep in there." Wylff nods to the caravan. Tanya comes and stands close to him. Smoke from her rollie wreathes up his nose. She is holding a plastic stemmed glass in the other hand, its contents sloshing onto his shoes as she shucks up to him, "Alright, hun?" There seems to be dried vomit on the lapel of her waxed jacket.

"Mmm, suppose so."

"Jesus, Gwy, how have you done *that*?" Wylff stands looking at the campervan astride the ditch, breasting the hedge.

"Well, this guy in a big white van just came out of nowhere..."

"OK. Listen, I don't really want to know. If you've scratched the paintwork, you'll bloody pay for it."

The look of exhaustion on Wylff's face stops Gwyddno from voicing his observation that none of the assembled vehicles are in particularly mint condition. The suspension springs on the Discovery are rusted to buggery, the passenger door is green, and the oil-choked fumes from the vertical exhaust are enough to wipe out an entire sub-species, let alone any unwitting occupant of the caravan behind that, in turn, looks like it would fold like a wet cardboard box at any moment. Jesus, this travelling lark is hard work. Roll on the autumn and he can get back to Cardiff and student life again. He can feel the eczema in the creases around his eyes flare again. He can't scratch it because it might look like he is crying.

"Give us a hand unhitching the caravan and we'll winch you back on the road. Did nobody offer to help?" He points to the groups of people standing around in the field in the distance. "What about them?"

Gwyddno shrugged. "Setting up for a fair tomorrow, I heard. Nobody else has been down here all day. Except for a couple of dog walkers."

"You're such an arse."

Gwyddno shrugs again, noncommittally.

"Shall I get Alice out the caravan?" Wylff gives him a look that suggests that not only is he an arse, but he is a total, complete and utter arse. Trouble is, that doesn't really answer the question for him. He is none the wiser what Wylff expects him to do, still in a state of pant-wetting quandary. In fact, he'd already decided. Balance four bits of gravel on top of each other and he'll stay with the gang. Balance five bits and he'll go. It was cast. He has now officially gone as far as he wants, ever, to go again in search of himself. Life on the road as an indigent holds no glamour, no purpose for him whatsoever now. All he wants to go in search of is a hot shower, a roast dinner and the comfort and certainty of timetables and obligations and routines.

The atmosphere in the caravan is gloomy and fusty. From the thin light filtering through the ethic prints strung across the windows, he can just make out Alice under a pile of coats and unsheathed, stained duvets. She is wearing a woolly hat with knitted strings, harem pants and odd boots. "Come on, old girl." He drapes her arm over his shoulder and half drags, half escorts her towards the door. Turning sideways to negotiate the narrow exit and the step down, she falls on top of him, laughing hysterically. Christ, this woman is nearly three times his age. Shouldn't she get a grip or something?

Hitched together, Wylff reverses slowly down the track. Gwyddno stands close by. Wylff told him to 'supervise'. So why is he now shouting, "Get out the way. You'll have it on top of you." He jumps back as the front of the van slides out of the hedge and jerks down into the shallow grassy ditch. He hopes Wylff can't hear the banshee-like shriek as the hawthorn spines graffiti a farewell message on the front mudguard, but he seems intent on his manoeuvrings. Spit and a rub with his cuff should sort that out.

In a billow of noxious smoke and the smell of hot engine parts, they reverse down to the lay-by where the caravan is parked, listing, Alice and Tanya sitting waiting for them.

Marcus

It is approaching four o'clock when Marcus walks into the Garden Room of the pub. Chris Eveans is already setting up the presentation equipment. He watches as Eveans struggles to unfurl a six-foot rolling projector screen. "Couldn't give us a hand here, mate, could you? The spring on this thing is savage." Before Marcus can cross the room, the screen snaps itself back into its case with a loud and extended kerfuffle. Eveans curses, placing both feet on the casing and, with a yawl, extends the screen upwards as far as his arms can go. "Oi, mate! Over here!"

"Oh, yes, sorry." Marcus hurries to the overstretched Eveans and lifts the screen the last few inches to hook it in place. Eveans backs out from under Marcus's arms, his hair awry and a look of discomfort on his face.

"Got the memory stick, then?"

As Eveans loads Marcus's images on to a laptop, Marcus asks if Major Welding will be coming. "Don't think so, mate. In fact, I know so. Important dinner in *tahn*. He'll be back later tonight."

Marcus is somewhat relieved that the Major will not be attending tonight. Hard enough to undertake the task in hand, to hopefully convey a little bit of his enthusiasm at the find to the villagers before it disappears, possibly, into obscurity again without having images of the handcuffed Major being escorted to the border flashing in front of his eyes.

He sets to and puts a printed timeline of the chapel out on the tables.

Village

Daniel Holland and Martyn Harris have finished setting up the beer tent. Twenty wooden casks are supported on frames at the back of the tent; the beers are each draped with damp tea towels and ice packs to keep them cool overnight. There are soft drinks, plastic glasses, bungs, hammers, straws, scratchings, wine coolers, bottles and cans, bottle openers, plastic bags, all arranged on trestles. The generator is out back, ready to be charged up tomorrow. The marquee sides are tied down. All is quiet except for an occasional crow call and a gentle, rhythmic knock knock knock as Holland and Harris persuade themselves that it would really not do much harm to tap a keg and sample some unsettled beer. As they move about, a disc of light from the torch dances a mazurka across the stretched white walls of the marquee.

The beer is black. A thick line of carbonated bubbles rings the inside of the plastic glass. It tastes of Dandelion and Burdock and grass cuttings and is delicious. Too delicious.

Marcus

Well. That didn't go too badly. One couldn't possibly hope for too big a turnout on the night before the fair but seven plus the three friends of the dreadlocked young man he'd got into conversation with, who knew a surprising amount about Napoleonic British Light Dragoons, wasn't a bad number. He'd done his bit. One could only hope that the chapel would be allowed to continue unmolested, a pinpoint in an ever-changing world, a signpost pointing back through the centuries. It would just remain to be seen.

Gwyddno

There is a smattering of polite applause. A small group of people exit the Garden Room with empty glasses in their hand and make for the bar. Gwyddno, Wylff, Alice and Tanya weave their way back into the room with their free drinks. Alice sits at a separate table, one by the open window, and lights up a cigarette. For nine days more, only nine days, does he have to swallow down his law-abiding instincts. Definitely those five pieces of gravel hovered in place long enough to indicate that he should be gone, before they came tumbling down into the road again, like runes. He'll see the festival through and then tell them he's off. He picks up Marcus's printed sheet of A4 paper from one of the tables and reads it, ignoring the acrid smoke from Alice's dubious cigarette making its way into the room.

Village

By closing time, both boys are fast asleep, unwary of the perils of drinking lively beer.

The torch light that once danced inside the canvas is now a fixed, unblinking eye on the night.

Lights go out, one by one, throughout the town.

From inside the chapel come the sound of drumming and the smell of burning sage.

15

Chris Eveans

Crying shame the Major wanted the Bentley back. This poxy little hire car is barely one-up from a Robin Reliant. Hadn't been cleaned too well either since the last occupant chose to decorate the underside of the driver's seat with some nose art. He'll have to have a word with Rebekkah or whoever the MD's latest dolly intern is when he gets back to London tonight.

Glory be! Today's the last day being the Major's major-domo. This has got to be one of the craziest projects he's been on. To be frank, finding that freakin' hole in the ground had been the best stroke of luck when it came to restyling the Major as an all-round good egg, smiling benevolently down on the labouring serfs. Still, mission accomplished. Or at least nearly accomplished, after today's little shindig. He can shine with all the glory reflected from the family pewter and silver, even if it has made its way here in a container over the China Seas. And, more to the good, he can put his dodgy financial dealings behind him. Bye bye, Bernard Gorman, and the whiff of tainted money and the Italian clink. All hail Major Welding, paternalistic squire and benefactor.

Eveans slides the bolt on the high mesh gates installed to keep the hoi polloi from tampering with the goods and drags them open, stepping tentatively over some emerging nettles. The weather is great too. Really, it couldn't have turned out better.

Village

By eight o'clock, the sun is already high in a clear blue sky. Those on early detail are making their way to the Town Field. Cars and vans are arriving,

204

scouts, volunteers, kids, tipping out to set up stalls, tables, amusements, entertainments.

Chris Eveans is spotted parked up under a long-limbed beech tree, steam from a large corrugated cup of coffee misting up a patch on the windscreen. "Don't think his remit actually includes getting out and helping, do you?" someone observes tersely. Eveans' head does not rise from whatever is occupying his attention below sight level.

Chris Eveans

Email to Major, reminding him of Grand Opening at 2pm today. Copy of report sent to MD, proposing MW might like to think about presenting the field and the chapel to the good people of Bullenden and endowing a kiddies' play area. Get the chapel listed on one of those 150 Best Kept Secrets websites. Stick a plaque up somewhere. Get Rebekkah to organise the celebratory drinks party and Press because it is time he got himself out of this time warp.

Ned

"Ben. Why are you painted like a tiger?"

"Me mum's doing the face painting. Rooo-aaa-rrr."

"Don't, Ben. Don't do that."

"Scared ya?"

"Not exactly. Just don't do it again. OK?"

"Say so."

"Right. Get in the van. We need to go and fence off that den you found so nobody wanders in today and hurts themselves."

Ned drives the short distance from Ben's house to the Town Field through the village, Ben roaring at passers-by. He'd been told to get there for ten o'clock as the vicar wants to do a short service in the chapel before it is closed up. Ben bumps exaggeratedly over every hummock, roaring and snarling with each uplift. God, he would swing for the boy one day.

A knot of people are standing around at the bottom corner. They must be the bucolic worshippers. He'll wait for the valediction, scoot them all out and then fence off the area good and proper. With any luck, by the time they've finished, Ben's mum will be here with her face-painting kit and can take Ben off his hands.

Typically, Mandy hasn't told him yet whether she is coming to the fair or not. Last thing he wants is a major blow-out.

Gwyddno

He had woken to find Alice's outflung arm cutting off his windpipe. He wriggled out from under her and went to look out, one foot raised up on the step. The space between the opening and the hedgerow is still dark, a fresh herby smell rising from the dew-speckled, trampled grass. Between the hawthorn stems he can see the flat farmland stretched out, dipping smoothly away.

He could really go for a cigarette right now. Not one of Wylff's that skyrocket you onto Planet Numbskull in twenty seconds. No, a proper cigarette, a working man's cigarette, like his dad used to smoke. He fills his lungs with the scent of lush grass and fertiliser instead. It feels good to be here. Well, almost. Perhaps he should do some kind of obeisance to the something god in thankfulness for something. But he really can't be arsed. More Tanya's sort of thing.

More than anything, he wants food. How can the others drink in lieu of eating? They'd had a few at the pub last night, taking it in turns to visit the toilets to have a wash. Alice must have washed her hair from the soap dispenser; she had come out of the ladies smelling of chemically loaded cranberries. She didn't look so scary with fluffy hair. His stomach rumbles with hunger.

Jumping down into the gully, he looks for a spot to pee. Almost seems a shame to offload when he is so ravenous. When they're not drinking, the others just seem to live off air. Maybe Wylff would reward him with breakfast for having found them this cave. "Look, why don't we crash here tonight?" he'd offered, showing them one of the leaflets scudding around the Garden Room in the pub the night before.

"Cool," Tanya had said. "Too hot in the 'van." Might just have a bit more leg room, had been Gwyddno's thought. Also, he'd heard the speaker enthuse about it being an ancient space, a monument to the ages. He'd agreed with Tanya; it would be cool to sleep there. Anarchic enough to earn him some brownie points, safe and warm and dry enough to keep Wylff from banging on about the scratches on his precious van.

It had been a bit surreal wandering through the field after closing time. Somebody had erected massive gates at the entrance, chained and padlocked. No match for Tanya: "They called me mum Breaker Beryl. Nowhere she couldn't get into or out of." Giggling and shushing, they'd let themselves into the field and locked up again behind them. They'd made their procession past the dark trapezoid tents in the field, stepping over guy ropes, hurdles and wires in an exaggerated cameo of robbers in the night.

"Look!" Tanya whispered theatrically as she gripped his arm. "Look!" She dragged him towards the beam of light issuing through the canvas wall of a marquee. Someone had left a torch on. He had no option but to go along with her. "Hello, ickle ickle spi-dah." A small spider crossed the lit circle which she tried unsuccessfully to track with her finger, her arm flailing wildly under the effects of six pints of ale.

"Come on, Tans." He gently pulled her away to follow the others across the field. This was the closest he'd come to her all summer without her snarling at him or asking him what the feck he was looking at. He hoped the anaesthetic of the alcohol wouldn't wear off too quickly. "Guys! Guys! Wait for us." This had been way more responsibility than he was comfortable with. Being in charge of Tanya felt as scary as when he'd taken the school pet home and his mates convinced him that the tarantula could unscrew the lid from *inside* the jar and would crawl over his bedclothes in the middle of the night.

He aims his stream of piss onto a few blackberry leaves, making the tendril bob and sway. Doh. Fah. So. Doh. Each leaf a different note. For once, this small act of urinating outdoors seems a glorious, musical joy. He is happy. "Doh. Doh. Laaaah." Funny how when you pee outdoors, it smells of apple sauce. His stomach growls again as he briefly catches sight in his mind's eye of a sugar-coated pastry case, flowing golden chunks of steaming apple punctuated by swollen cloves, a big jug of thick custard. "Oh, God, don't." Torture.

He has no idea what time it is. Possibly the sun shines only rarely in this sheltered place although, looking down the dark and dank gully, it is definitely daylight elsewhere. He'll risk peering round the side of the mound.

"Guys. Guys. Think you'd better wake up. Guys. Need to get up. Now!" The field they had made their way through last night now looks like a film set for Wonder Land. Tables are placed randomly about; some dressed in white cloths, others bare. Fairground rides cluster in one corner, coloured bulbs winking silently. A tousled head emerges from the spider's tent and then withdraws, groaning. People are walking in through the field gate, which now stands wide open, with arms full of boxes. A white van slaloms its way across the field and appears to be heading straight towards them.

Besides, he is staring right up into the eyes of a vicar.

Chris Eveans

Christ, he'd forgotten about the vicar. She'd messaged him and asked if it would be OK to have a little service in the chapel before the fair. Would have been impolite to say no. For pity's sake, how long is this shenanigans going to take? Is he ever going to get out of here?

Gwyddno

"I'll go and get...get somebody," he offers in a manner that he hopes is friendly and co-operative, before scuttling back into the chapel. "Er. Guys. You have to wake up."

Tanya stirs at his feet. "Who says?"

"Somebody's here. We need to clear out."

Wylff jumps to his feet. "I'll take care of this." He walks over to the woman but the sight of her collar arrests even his swagger. "Oh. Right."

She peers down into the chapel, taking in the djembes, the sleeping bags, the two prone girls and all the debris that accompanies them wherever they go, before signalling Wylff and Gwyddno to the side of the grassy dome. She twists coils of her long, golden hair round her finger. Individual strands shine like celestial harp strings. Gwyddno guiltily lowers his gaze to make sure she isn't standing in his puddle. Maybe she takes this for contrition because when he looks up again, she is smiling, albeit in a steely sort of a way.

"I'll just go and tidy up." Gwyddno makes to hurriedly scoop up their belongings and wake the others. Wylff stays his arm.

Wylff speaks, jutting out his chin: "Who says we can't be here?"

Gwyddno doesn't like his tone, feeling that he might be called upon at any moment to make a choice between Wylff and a higher authority. It could be an uncomfortably close call; his guts twist in panic.

"Let me introduce myself." Pulling a Bible closer to her pink blouse, she extends her right hand. "Reverend Bethel. Sue Bethel." Wylff doesn't extend his. Oh crumbs, swallows Gwyddno, this is high mutiny indeed. He is relieved that Tanya and Alice both emerge from the doorway, yawning and scratching their heads. They seem disinclined to observe the formalities too. In an access of sheer bravery, Gwyddno reaches forward and gives the vicar's arm a hearty shake.

"Gwyddno. Well, that's my Celtic name. I'm really James Timms, student, not of this parish." He twists his lips at this little ecclesiastical joke which seems lost on those around him. "I'm from South Wales, actually. Student. Environmental Sciences. Third year. Been travelling this summer. Visiting historical sites, well, Glastonbury, Stonehenge, that sort of thing." He is aware that he is babbling but something drives him to prove he is more of the conventional world than of one he has been subsumed into for the past few months. It feels like he is one of those kidnap victims who have three seconds to prove their hostage status or risk being shot as a terrorist. His throat goes rather dry.

"Pleased to meet you, James." She turns to the others but they remain steadfast in their anonymity. "Well, as you can see, we are getting ready for our summer fair, and we are holding a little service in thanksgiving for the rediscovery of our medieval chapel and to pray for God's blessing today. You are welcome to join us but I would ask you to clear up your belongings first."

Gwyddno watches in wonder as the six legs of a fairground ride stretch themselves out behind her, gold light bulbs winking silently, turning her into a kind of English Goddess Durga. At the same time, a feeling of enormous gratitude overtakes him. Simple, bite size instructions. Put the milk bottles out. Give little Jacob his cornflakes. Express y as the coefficient of x. Pack up your belongings. He can understand all that. This whole business of letting free his inhibitions, aligning his chakras, inviting in his spirit guides just freaks him. At last, he has been rescued.

He isn't sure if vicars exactly constitute God's representatives on earth but they are close enough. Fate has seen fit to intervene on his behalf. Fate has sent Reverend Bethel who, alone and unintimidated by the force of their personalities, gives instructions to Wylff, Tanya and, less crucially, Alice. The bonds of slavery have been broken. His shackles burst open. By her intercession, he is now free. Hallelujah! He'll phone Mum and tell her he'll be home by dinner time.

"Hang on a minute." Alice grabs a sheet of paper. "It says on here that this place of worship predates any Christian site."

He recognises the notes left from the meeting in the pub last night. Oh dear. If Alice is about to kick off, then it is definitely time to leave. But he can't. He is rooted to the spot.

"So, by rights, seeing as we are pagans, we have first dibs."

"But, if I may remind you of John chapter one verses one to five, 'Before anything else existed, there was Christ, with God. He has always been alive, and is himself God.'"

Gwyddno looks at her as she speaks these words. This is just like Sunday School. Words spoken simply and in faith.

"He created everything there is," she continues. "Nothing exists that he didn't make."

A feeling of surety comes over him. What he'd been looking for wasn't out on the road with this raggle-taggle trio. What beauty there was yet to find, and certainty and quiet kind, dah dah dah-daaaah, something something something where the church clock stands at ten to three and there was honey still for tea. That's where it is at for him. The universe is far too random and unpredictable. Give him, any day, the eagle-back pulpit, the mouse-damaged hassock, the hand-worn sallies. A church peopled with types like the guy who had spoken about the chapel last night. He'd have liked to have listened to that but Tanya told him to stop being a twat.

A voice interrupts his reverie. "So, what the vicar is saying is, we got here first, basically," comes a voice from behind Reverend Bethel's shoulder.

"I don't think we can quite look at it like that, but thank you, Mr Gallagher for your input."

That is it. He'll tell Wylff that he'll send money to get the van resprayed. One of the girls can drive it down to the festival in Dorset. They don't need him. He never fitted in anyway. They just kept him on as a mildly entertaining pet. Taking bets amongst themselves how long it would be before he spewed his guts up, lost the plot or went crying back home to Mummy. Nonetheless, and his initial euphoria abates slightly at this thought, he still has the problem of how to get out of this bind – stuck in a ditch between three crazies and an implacable vicar.

Ned

"Look, Vicar, do you think we could wrap this up? I've got to get this area fenced off before the fair starts." Ned points to the trailer at the back of the van loaded with stakes and livestock wiring. "Besides, Ben's getting bored," and that never did bode well.

Thankfully she seems to understand. "Right." She speaks with quiet authority. "Ben. If you would be kind enough to come with me back to the vicarage," she looks to Ned who nods his agreement, "we can have a quick game on the XBox for half an hour. I'm sure that will give everyone time to pack up their belongings and leave the space nice and tidy for our worship."

Gwyddno, or is it James?

Somehow the vicar electrifies everyone into action. Wylff, Alice and Tanya obediently return to the space and begin to gather their belongings. As he stuffs his Spice into his sleeping bag, words from Sunday school pop into his head: "There's nothing unseen that shall not be seen." Oops. He kind of envies that young lad with the tiger painted face. He wouldn't have minded a quick game of Minecraft with the vicar.

Never mind. Time for his farewells. Time to go back to being James. He might even call into Grantchester on the way home.

Chris Eveans

Brain wave. Text the Major. Get him to attend little service of thanksgiving. Half an hour. Picture in the papers. Community spirited *and* godly! A media triumph.

Madge

She follows the caterer's van onto the field. What are they going to do that she can't do? Slap a few burgers on a hot plate and charge a fortune for the favour. She can fry onions as well as the next person. That Chris Eveans bloke. Probably gave the contract to one of his cronies. How much is she going to make today selling a few jelly beans and wine gums? Hardly worth her time.

What is going on at the bottom corner of the field? Sounds like the bleeding Zulus are coming. She'd already seen the vicar stomp off up the field with that Bernadette's boy in tow. Looked to be in high dudgeon. There was that hobo hippy chap who came into the shop yesterday looking sorry for himself. And more of them! At least eight! All drumming. Drumming! What are they trying to do? Make it rain? Summon up more of their kind?

Time for pre-emptive action. Time for honest shopkeepers to strike back! Before all the flapjacks and pork pies disappear. Place is overrun with them. She has a phone call to make.

Ned

One left first, carrying his sleeping bag over his shoulder like a swag bag. He'd turned to shake hands with each of the others and they all ignored him in turn. He just grinned slightly and picked up his kit and strode out across the field. Oh, the freedom of the young.

The other three might be more of a problem, looking quite disinclined to pick up their belongings and go. Instead, they sit cross-legged on the mound beating out a rhythm on their drums. One of the girls, her head back, is singing a clear-throated chant. Her voice lifts to the skies, powered by the quiet, insistent rhythm, carrying with it, it seems, all his hopes and fears.

Chris Eveans

Great. Welding's replied. He's on his way. Let's get this pikey scum shifted. Enough of this Kum Ba Yah nonsense.

"Right, everyone. Let's get a move on. Busy day. Lots to do. I'm sure we've all got things we need to attend to."

Village

The atmosphere changes abruptly. The song ends midstream. Eveans tries to grab one of the girls to force her to stand up. A scrum develops, a tight knot of people shouting and shoving. Ned catches one of the girls in his arms as she comes skittering down the slope, out of control, flung out by some centrifugal force. She curses him.

Out of the blue, there is a police car driving across the field, lights flashing. Two police officers get out, adjusting their hats. The brouhaha stops as suddenly as it started. Within a few moments it is all sorted.

The three travellers are put in the back of the squad car and driven to where they left their vehicles. They wave to the vicar who is returning to the field with Ben.

The Major, red-faced and livid, storms back across the field towards his car with his little PR chappie running behind.

Madge is leaning against a lurid sweet cart, arms crossed, a smug expression on her face, snapping away on her phone.

The vicar and attendants step into the chapel. Along the east wall, at least twenty candles burn brightly, their flames dancing and guttering in the movement of air. Accompanying each candle is a tiny posy of field poppy and feverfew tied together with barley stalks.

The Cat

It would seem that Fate has given this cat a wandering, nomadic, gypsy star under which to be born. She finds herself and her three offspring, by now several weeks old and nearly weaned, lifted gently and placed within a rucksack, its cotton soft black lining absorbing the few rays of sunlight that penetrate its eyeholes. She curls herself around the kittens who are calmed by her presence. Motion. Smooth. Then bumpy. Then smooth again as the bag is lowered gently to the floor and the opening held wide. For now she will stay where she is, despite the encouragement to 'Come out, Kitty.' Later she'll explore her new surroundings, the rags and debris and litter that cover the floor of this strange new vehicle.

16

Amelia

There is no one about. She moves slowly from her bedroom across the wide landing to the top of the stairs, her bare feet warmed by patches of sunlight on the carpet. The house seems to be holding her close. Yet, at the same time, it seems to be surveying her, measuring her, comparing her against the young woman who left all those years ago.

The house isn't quite as she remembered it but, in essence, beneath the changes, it is the same. Home. So different from the concrete flat she shares sporadically with Enzo. Images of home used to flash randomly into her mind during her long years away. For no apparent reason she might recall the shape of something, the sound of something, the feel of something, the memory fading as quickly as it arrived. Other times, usually low times, she would hug a treasured memory close to her breast – of her sisters, of her younger self.

There is comfort in being on her own here. A strange feeling of privilege, of being the sole trustee of a rare gift, overtakes her. When was she ever in this house alone? Probably never. She stands at the top of the stairs and reaches out into the quiet depths.

Although colours have changed, the light is the same; although objects have moved or been replaced, the sense of solidity, of holding a stake in the life of this house remains. And the house holds a stake in Amelia's life too, as if it whispers to her, I know you; I know the real you; I have watched you grow up; no one else knows you better. Come home.

Amelia slides her heels, tah-dum, tah-dum, tah-dum, down a few steps. "Don't bump down the stairs. Come down properly." as if Mother is still in the kitchen scraping carrots, stirring sauce.

Amelia, cautiously and less defiantly, reaches the bottom step. A familiar band of steel begins to coil around her chest. Is it the evocation of Mother's voice? Is it the crushing familiarity of the place? Is it, actually, true that she is her most perfect self when here, or is that an outright lie? Is she more the Amelia she wants to be when cut loose, wandering, on the move?

After all, look what's happened to Cecily. Bored, lacklustre, unoccupied. One foot in the past, too tentative to take the next step. For Cecily, this house has become a sentimental trap.

The thought of being trapped – anywhere – pulls the band tighter round her chest. Inevitably a house can do nothing other than outlast its occupants as it hurtles through time, callously leaving those who loved it and cared for it behind.

"Oh shit." Amelia stands at the door to the kitchen. "Forgot," she speaks aloud. Cecily had asked her the night before to lend a hand with finishing the cakes for the fair and taking them down to the field. She will be mad that Amelia hadn't helped.

Empty, streaky mixing bowls are stacked precariously on the kitchen table, dive-bombed by spatulas and scrapers, the sticky buttercream parted by a probing tongue. That would be Tilly. She always popped up like an opportunistic terrier whenever there were treats, fully and knowingly exploiting her status as the youngest to get the best leavings. Rounds of greaseproof paper stiffened by baking and cake parings. Floury glasses. Raw pastry rolled and folded in upon itself like a bloodless lifeform. A black fly makes its way around the top edge of a creamy bowl, each leg waving in turn to its audience. Others hang in the air by the back door as if waiting for an invitation to come in.

"Cigarette first." Amelia sits down at the table, running a dry finger round a bowl of chocolate cake mix. It tastes bitter.

An ancient reflex sends her free hand beneath the table top. Her mind elsewhere, blowing smoke towards the window pane, her nail flicks against consecutive edges of tightly folded paper. A note! Isn't that just what they did as sisters, so many, many years ago? Write each other covert notes and stuff them between the planks of the underside of the kitchen table. She bends double under the table to pull it out. "Hi sis. Knew you'd find it. Left you sleeping. Again! See you later xxx".

A tidal wave of emotion washes over her. She has not been part of this for so long. That basic tribal feeling of being where one's inside colours match one's outside colours, of being made of the same clay as the earth one stands on. Anxiety and displacement leave her in great gouts; relief is sucked up in great mouthfuls.

Nothing more tribal than three sisters.

It's not what you know. It's the things you don't know you know.

It is a beguiling prospect. If she came home again – surely Cecily would let her stay – then she could swing through life again with all the ease of a de Mare sister.

Amelia pulls her phone out of the back pocket of her jeans to text Cecily to say she'd found the note and to ask whether she would earn more Brownie points cleaning up the kitchen or coming over to the field to help set up. As she switches it on beep follows beep. After the message from the service provider welcoming her, again, to the United Kingdom, text after text from Enzo fills the screen. Why hadn't she made it clear that she was going somewhere? Why hadn't she filled in the holiday rota in the staff room? Why didn't she let him drive her to the airport, *mi cara*? Didn't she know she was the most precious thing to him? Had he done anything to offend? All he wanted to know was that she had arrived safely. How is he to know where she is if she doesn't contact him? What kind of game is she playing? Does she want to mess with his head? How can he concentrate on anything if she doesn't speak to him? It's been forty-eight hours now. Darling? Hey, you bitch. What is this? The massive brush-off? Is this how you treat someone who has been more than good to you? Fuck off.

She groans. What a mess. She can hear his voice as he scrolls through the cadences of surprise, amusement, indignation, self-pity, anger. There is one more stage to go. Their rows always finished on a tone of petulance, a kind of cute-boy moue that might work with Mama but which fails to cut much ice with Amelia any more.

She'll text him later. No, she had better do it now. Get it over with. "Arrived safely. Sorry. Phone broken. Just got replacement. Chat soon."

She knows it will do nothing to placate him – more likely rake over the coals of his resentment. Best to keep it short.

He will either reply immediately or make her wait several hours before revealing the tenor of his response. She counts to ten and sharply switches the phone off.

"Damn." She'd forgotten to text Cecily for instructions.

She'll tidy up, have a shower and get down to the field in time for the start of the fair. Give Cecily time to simmer down.

Village

The bunting that zigzags above the street flutters sharply in the early afternoon breeze marking the route of the procession from the church to the Town Field. In the fore, a brass band, ten or twelve musicians from the sugar factory in royal purple uniforms, beat and blow their way down the street. Cars and people bump up on the verges to watch them pass. The band marches in step, except the boy bugler who runs and halts and scurries, a mouse compelled to follow the feet of a slow-moving elephant. Members of the crowd laugh as his prompts flutter out of their clip. "Melt down your instrument for buttons," someone remarks too loudly.

Next comes the May Queen sitting sullen and ignored atop a flat bed trailer, her three attendants giggling into a mobile phone. The tractor jolts its impeded way through the market square. A small child throws sweets into the crowd with deadly force and accuracy.

Bringing up the rear of the parade, anyone with an interest to promote and a banner. The WI, the Catholic Mothers, the Great Yarmouth Corporation Tramways Appreciation Society, Gay Marriage and Rock Against Racism.

Amelia

Amelia pulls the front door closed behind her and stands on the steps looking down onto the passing parade.

"Hey, Amelia. Heard you were back."

She looks to see who is calling her, blinded and confused by the busy melee.

"Amelia! Over here!" spoken in a soft, Suffolk burr. Such a long time since she'd heard her name uttered thus, in anything other than the emphatic, punchy, commanding Sicilian way. The crowds move past her as she steps down into the road. A man pushing a buggy catches the back of her heels. "Sorry, love." His companion, presumably the baby's mother, stares at her malevolently. The musical strands of the band unravel themselves the further down the street they go so that, by now, the steady one-two-three notes on the euphonium are gobbling up the reedy, vulnerable notes of the cornets.

"Here. Hop in!"

The long snout of an open-topped vintage car advances into view, its burgundy paintwork gleaming in the sunlight. Her eyes sweep from the mascot to the driver holding the wide, slender steering wheel in one hand and opening the passenger door with the other.

"Quick. Get in before I run anyone over."

The car thrums and jiggles and then stalls. "Blast this damned thing." Bob, dressed in blue button-down overalls and a Formula One racing cap, lets go of the door's strap to slide levers on the wheel and pump a pedal on the wooden floor.

Amelia tentatively grasps the chrome door handle and, stepping up onto the running board, lets herself down onto the smooth, scuffed, overstuffed black leather bench seat. The seat is hot against the back of her bare legs.

"Cursed thing. Never idled well."

She sits there, looking fixedly ahead, bemused by her state of capture, watching the last of the town process towards the fairground, leaving her, the car and Bob behind.

The moment explodes into a thousand different impressions, questions, flashbacks. Which should she chase after first?

Seconds pass as the car fails to respond to Bob's pugilistic efforts to get it started. He leans back in his seat, removing his cap. "Give it a few minutes and try again. How are you? Been ages."

She can see his features now. "Good thanks. You?"

Shards, confetti, fall about them, each piece glinting with snatches of memory. Bob at sixteen, playing his heart out on the football field to impress Amelia, standing for him on the sidelines. Smoking behind the cage with the gas tanks at the garage. A kiss. A thousand kisses. Hanging out on the church wall into the dusky summer nights, watching the bats above their heads against a darkening sky. Waiting at the bus stop outside school. The death of his mother. Watching his life fall apart. Saying goodbye at Bremen station. Hating his father, Old Bob, for his breakdown. They were going to see the world together. They promised they would come home. Just give them a year. Two years max. Then Bob would help his dad out in the garage and Amelia would run the shop, do the accounts, probably a few kids by the time they were both thirty. Dad could have done what he wanted.

"Well," Amelia laughs, looking around at the empty street. A drinks can rolls towards the gutter. The bunting flutters in the breeze. "Here we are again. What do we do now?"

"It'll be alright in a minute."

The hot metal engine clicks as Amelia counts their seconds together.

"Listen. I was really sorry to hear about your mum. And your dad."

"That's OK. It was…" but she can't remember how long ago it was and, anyway, what was she saying? Fine? They were old? Didn't need them in her life anyway? Or is it his sympathy that she doesn't need?

"And Cecily's husband, Henry."

"Of course. Yes. Thanks. Not been easy." More platitudes. But a conversational lull of over thirty years has to stop somewhere. "What about you? What's happened in your life?"

"Oh, you know." Bob shrugs. "The usual. Married. Two kids." Why doesn't he look at her?

"I'm pleased for you." But her response is drowned out by the roar of the engine coaxed back into life.

A few minutes later, thin tyres slipping on the coconut matting between the gateposts, they head down the flattened grass tracks to join the rest of the local car club. There is a screech as the music on the PA stops mid-track and someone coughs loudly and repeatedly into the microphone prior to welcoming everyone to the start of the Twenty-Ninth Annual Bullenden Fair.

"Thanks for the lift."

"Any time."

"See ya."

"See ya."

Marcus

After the kerfuffle with the druids or Celts or pagans or however they styled themselves, Marcus positions himself at the entrance to the chapel. Someone had brought blue twisted rope from the church and strung it between knee-high posts. He could clip and unclip one end to allow entrance and exit. He feels rather like St Peter, although doubts that St Peter would have need of a clipboard to record visitor numbers. That vicar was quite impressive. He liked the way she handled the interlopers.

A pile of his factsheets flutter in the faint breeze under a weighty stone. He hopes that nobody will ask anything too complicated or erudite. After all, he is only the amateur historian, even if he has acquired minor celebrity status after his piece to camera on local TV a few nights ago.

A small group of people dislodge themselves from the slow-moving current around the stalls and make their way towards him. "Just give them a quick story," Chris Eveans had briefed him. "Something to take away with them. They're not bothered if it's 3rd century BC or 34th century intergalactica time. Tell them about the pilgrims' bandaged feet. Give them a few beheadings and throw in something about ghostly monks walking abroad under a moonlit night. Give them a burning bush story if you've got any godly types. Just get them in and get them out again. Got it?"

Marcus nodded, his throat suddenly as dry as sand.

"Good afternoon. This way to our newly discovered sunken chapel. Can I take a few minutes of your time to tell you about St Winifrede, a local devout woman and her talking cat..."

Bob

Well, that was a turn-up for the books. Seeing Amelia again, after all these years. Since Bremen. Over twenty years ago.

She had been scrupulous in dividing up the money. He'd wanted her to keep it all with just enough to get him home, but she didn't want it. He'd escorted her out of the train station to pick up a taxi. She'd turned to him, kissed his cheek and told him she'd be back.

That was the last he saw of her, in the two-dimensional, dim light of pre-dawn as she strode up the pavement away from him. She opened the door of a taxi idling a few hundred yards up the hill. The overhead light came on; she leant in to speak to the driver. After a brief exchange, the car drove off. He waited and waited, breathing the acrid fumes of the car's exhaust, long after the brake lights had disappeared from view.

Bob pulls his attention back to the here and now. The guys are standing around their cars, polishing, drinking tea, sharing sandwiches and a joke. Bit of a farce being here at the fair, but it might raise the profile of the garage and the restoration business. Dad does most of the chat. He loves these days. Loves having his son beside him. Dad doesn't have a single worry in the whole world.

Amelia

There were times in Sicily she felt like one of those pine trees that grow in the scrubby sandy margin between the town and the sea. A displaced native. Shallow roots. Standing stock still while all activity flows around. Kids playing, the onshore breeze, sleeping tramps, a foil for others' energy, taking the knocks, sighing softly, pushing back.

Cecily

Quite frankly, Amelia is being less than useless. She casts her eye over her sister slumped into the folding chair at the edge of the shade cast by an oak tree. Tilly is walking towards the stall, the Strong Man's hammer in her hand, a little boy running after her. "Miss. Miss. Can we have the hammer back please, miss." Tilly turns and graciously returns the overlooked item to him.

Marcus beckons from the corner of the field, miming that his throat has been cut. "Listen, Tils, be a love and take Marcus a drink would you?"

"You go. I'll mind the stall."

"Sure?" She was reluctant to leave her sisters in charge of the cake stall, one looking as if she's getting by on 500 calories and 40 fags a day, the other sweaty and flushed from an hour's sheep-shearing demonstration. "OK. Well, just don't touch anything. That's all."

"Oh, Cecily. Stop it!"

Marcus

Mercifully Cecily is walking towards him with two large bottles of water. "How's it going?" His throat is so dry he has almost lost the reflex to swallow. His hand round the cool, blue, moist bottle feels hot and oafish. Is this the effect of the heat or of Cecily standing so close to him in her short bright skirt, crinkled top and garish sandals? Doesn't she have big feet! A strand of her piled-up hair keeps catching at the side of her mouth. As she speaks to him, she pushes it abstractedly away. Each time she releases hold, a sprite of nature, a sylph perhaps, disarmingly places it back in the crease at the side of her mouth.

"Had many visitors?"

The water slides down his throat. It feels like a benediction. "Yes, quite a few. Most people haven't got a clue what they are looking at." He coughs. "Excuse me." He takes another long draught, aware that Cecily is standing close and watching him. She swallows in unison. "Want some?"

She shakes her head.

"Some have got what it's about. Others have just looked in, made some comment about the walls not being straight, and pulled their heads out again."

Cecily laughs, "Probably the same people who ask if my cakes are selling like…hot cakes."

"Like Marley's doornail."

"Mm?"

"Well, Dickens said that he would have thought that a coffin nail was the deadest piece of ironmongery but the 'wisdom of our ancestors is in the simile', so doornail it shall be."

"And cakes of the hot variety."

Marcus, mid-slug, spots something down the length of his water bottle. A movement in the distance, a disturbance. He slowly lowers the bottle to take a better look. "I'm not sure, but…"

Cecily looks to where Marcus is pointing across the field.

"Seems like some of the sheep have got out." He watches her quick retreat until the crowds swallow her up.

Cecily

"Tilly! Tilly!" Tilly and Amelia are both deeply intent upon something between them and oblivious to the fact that the willow hurdles have collapsed and Tilly's ten Framlinghams are nonchalantly strolling amongst the crowds. Fly, Tilly's best working dog, is asleep beneath the cake table, only her black nose visible under the white cloth, apparently off duty.

Cecily rushes towards them, out of breath. "Tilly. The sheep have got out!"

"Oh, they're alright. Not doing any harm."

Well, yes, concedes Cecily, that is true - in the strictest sense. They are merely nibbling at the grass between the stalls that hasn't been trampled in the day's activities. "So long as no one causes a stampede, we'll be alright, I guess." Maybe she should stop shepherding her sisters. "What are you two doing?"

"Sssh. Melly's talking to Enzo on her phone. He phoned her. They're having an argument. Can't understand a word they're saying."

Cecily and Tilly creep closer, close enough to ring fence Amelia from enquiring ears, close enough to bolster her in what is, evidently, a heated conversation.

"How long's this being going on?" Cecily whispers.

"Oh, about five minutes. She said she was just switching her phone on to check it had charged, and he was there. He doesn't seem too happy."

"Well, nor does Melly." They look at their sister hunched in the folding chair, one elbow on her knee, the phone pressed to her ear. The other hand twirls and twists a lock of hair. "Listen. Are you sure your sheep are OK?"

"Oh, they're fine. Can't leave her, can I?"

"Suppose not. Well, just keep an eye on them."

"Yes, Cecily. I will," Tilly assures her in a weary tone.

Cecily divides her watchful gaze between Amelia and the wandering sheep fanning out amongst the fairgoers. The creatures have lost their bouffant fleeces and are looking altogether less appealing while overall more in proportion with their thin, jointed legs. Where Tilly's electric shears had cut the soft under-wool from the body, tram lines appear above the white flesh, flowing around the muscles. Their backs and bellies twitch in the unaccustomed coolness as, heads down, they tear and grind at the short-cut grass, wiggling their tails to dispense copious handfuls of round, glossy pellets. She watches as one wanders in through the open flap of the beer tent, appearing, at speed, at the other end, presumably propelled out by the bar staff. Toddlers in buggies stretch out to stroke them, one offering a lick of an ice cream before it is hastily removed by an adult hand. A speckle-faced sheep lowers herself mechanically first onto her front knees and then onto her back in the cool shade of a tree, chewing calmly while surveying the crowds.

Amelia's voice rises higher and higher in pitch and urgency. Tilly looks at Cecily and both shrug. "It's really kicking off now," Tilly whispers. Cecily feels uncomfortable at such an open display in full sight and sound of all around. Why can't Amelia just take herself off to a quieter spot?

Then, abruptly, it is all over. The shouting has stopped. The sisters look again at Amelia, still coiled in upon herself. For the briefest moment, all appears to stand still, until Amelia leaps to her feet, shouting at the phone, as if the object itself conveys all that is loathsome and contemptible about, what must be assumed to be, her former lover.

The defiled phone leaves Amelia's hand at speed, following a clear and perfect path into a strawberry pavlova, chinking against a jug of iced lemonade on its way. Amelia kicks at the corner of the table, shouting and swearing. Cecily watches in horror as the top of the trestle slides off its triangulated supports and, tipping to one side, ushers several cakes onto the grass.

"Amelia. Pull yourself together. This is ridiculous."

"Don't shout at her. Can't you see she's upset?" defends Tilly.

"Just fucking leave me alone," shouts Amelia as she strides off to the margins of the field.

"Amelia! Come back!"

"Oh. Bloody. Hell," voices Tilly, slowly and ominously.

The sheep, startled by the ruckus, have, indeed, started a stampede. Three raise themselves up on their hind hooves and, bucking and kicking, knock into fair goers, the PA system, buckets of sand, craft tables. Others pick up speed and run full pelt in all directions, taking with them tablecloths, bunting, electrical cables, cordons. Fly, alerted now to the emergency by the collapse of her impromptu shelter, sets off to round them up, barking and yapping in her efforts to bring order to chaos.

Other dogs both off and on leads join in the commotion. Men gamely adopt Maori poses to try and capture the marauding beasts who trot daintily past their outstretched fingertips. Children scream, climbing up their parents in a bid to be lifted above the commotion. Those dogs who had either slipped their leads or had freedom to roam, trot over to the mess in front of what was once the cake table, greedily and systematically making in-roads into the cake and cream and fruit, distracted only momentarily by Amelia's phone issuing the first few notes of 'Dancing Queen' before it capsizes irretrievably into confectionous oblivion.

Marcus

It is difficult to make out exactly what is going on. Whatever it is, it has a sort of impromptu, unplanned look about it. Sheep rustling? What should he do? Join the melee or stay in post and ensure no one enters the chapel unsupervised or riffles the leaflets? He opts to watch from a safe distance.

A moment or two later, bizarrely, one of the sheep breaks away from the churning crowd and runs towards him. What is he to do? He rattles the tin of sweets and calls out, quietly, "Sheepie. Sheepie," unhooking the guide rope. The lumpen creature walks right past his sentry position, drops down into the ditch and pokes its head curiously into the opening of the chapel. "Good sheepie. There's a good sheepie." A trembling baa alerts him to the arrival of the next sheep. Well, gadzooks, there is a queue of them, all following the lead sheep and making their way towards him.

He steps back, still rattling the tin, in the most inviting and non-threatening way he can muster, whispering almost, "Sheepie. There you are, good sheepies," until at least six have wandered in to have a look. Mercifully a ruddy fellow of the soil then comes along with a couple of hurdles and blocks them in.

Tilly insists on buying him a pint. "Here you are, lad. Get that down you."

He sort of likes Tilly. Very different to any creature he'd met on his commute into and out of London. Not many shepherdesses in Camden. Although, there might have been at one point. Mental note to pursue that line of enquiry. She stands directly in front of him offering up the glass of beer. Orange string tumbles from her pockets; white filling works its way out of the slits in her sleeves. Her hair part-flattened, part-spiky, follows no particular pattern, her blue eyes twinkle with mischief while her nose reddens in the sharp sunlight.

"Thank you. Although you didn't have to. Have you got them all rounded up?"

"Yes. They're all back. Some dozy bugger left the latch off." He stands with the glass in his hand, utterly discomforted. It doesn't seem right to be drinking while on duty.

"Are you not having a drink?"

"No, driving home later."

Marcus wishes he could summon up some arcane but nonetheless amusing sheep fact when she turns to look over her shoulder.

"Ah, Jeremiah! Hang on a minute." Marcus nods vigorously, his mouth now full of the taste of hops, his nose assaulted by bubbles. He'd taken too big a mouthful. How asinine. Like a fresher at the Student Union bar. All over again. An overwhelming but self-cancelling compulsion to either snort or swallow conflicts with the pleasing novelty of standing in a busy field on a warm summer's day with someone who appears to be as much at variance with the rest of society as he feels. Turning to Marcus she touches his arm, saying, "Got to go. Thanks again."

She waits a second for Marcus to reply. Mouth, throat and now nasal cavity awash, he can only pray for her to depart immediately. Each nod is nearly a swill too far. Mercifully Tilly turns on her heels, allowing him then the opportunity to draw breath and suck the beer down into his stomach, gurgling its plunging, vacuum-inducing way.

"You alright, mate?" one of the lads asks as he passes with a mallet in his hand.

"Yes. Yes," he rasps. "Fine."

"That's OK then. There's someone here says she knows you..."

Village

By six o'clock, Teddy Nesbitt, winner of the Strong Man Competition, had rung the bell a massive forty times and been declared the strongest six-year-old ever. Jasper the donkey had completed his 26th circuit and refused to go any further. The brass band had stowed their implements and got back on the bus for Ipswich. Unwanted bric-a-brac and raffle

226

prizes had shifted themselves one stop further on their unloved and lonely lives. Marcus helped Rev Bethel carry the blue rope back to the church. Tilly loaded up the sheep and the hurdles into the trailer and said she'd be back in a day or two. Tilly's daughter, Lizzie, and Amelia said a tender farewell.

The field was emptying gradually. A few diehards including a couple of members of the jazz band stayed on with the crew of the fair to see off the beer. Shadows were lengthening. Midges were rising from the ground. The doughty ladies joined the Scouts in picking up litter. Crows were taking possession of the air. Madge trundled the sweet trolley back to the post office. Amelia and Cecily carried plastic boxes and cake plates back to the house for washing. The vintage cars popped and bubbled their way home. Ned said he'd come back later to lock up. Thistle down floated in the cooling evening air.

17

Marcus

Marcus awakes the next morning. Daylight forms a sharply pointed lightning strike that pierces his left eyeball with the intensity of a laser beam. He has difficulty locating the other eyeball which is subject to a different kind of pain altogether. A pressing kind of pain. With the lucidity of the very confused, his mind decides that this is probably a good thing, a *very* good thing, given the explosions that are going off inside his head. If something is pressing into his eyeball, then that blocks off at least one expulsion route for his brains.

With each blink of his one functioning eye he tries to pull back into its rightful position the opposite wall, which, if left unattended, detaches itself and skitters pell-mell with all the other disconnected paraphernalia of his usually tidy bedroom.

Something about this movement brings a faint memory back to mind. The sensation of whirling round and round, his head flung back helplessly, unable to right itself and the unusual gargle that issued from his throat that was part laughter, part acrid beer.

Why is he thinking planets? Planets come into it somewhere.

A groan issues from the other side of his bed.

Oh, no! What he is apparently reliving is a throw-back to his student days. A monumental hangover. Although, Marcus decides, it is probably better not to focus too strongly on any concept with the word 'throw' in it. As in throw *up*. His stomach, in response to this thought, sets up a similar parabolic spin to the room, but on a completely different plane.

Ah. It is coming back to him. This thing about planets and spinning.

For some reason at about ten o'clock last night, just as the guys in the beer tent were switching off the generators and dousing the lights, he'd got into a discussion with a very earnest ten-year-old about cosmology. At the time, it seemed, planetary alignments could be best demonstrated by a spin on the teacups. The obliging lads had taken it upon themselves to restart the fairground ride and Marcus and the earnest youngster – what was the poor lad's name? Maximilian? – and some of the other boozers had jumped aboard and shouted out their various planetary affiliations. He'd been Phobos. Where the blazes is Phobos? Where the blazes were this lad's parents?

A shape shifts on the other side of the bed. The pain in his eyeball lessens and then increases exponentially.

But, do you know what, he thinks to himself, it had been a fab night out with the lads. With the lads! When had he ever had a night out 'with the lads'? Chess Club at uni had been about as riotous as it had got before his married days. Sure, he and Velda had had a social life, or at least in the beginning when they'd invited their neighbours on the new estate round for Trivial Pursuit and a curry.

Last night had been a blast.

Velda!

Another lightning crack goes off in his brain. The adrenalin rush induced by the sudden recall of Velda appearing at the fair yesterday has the benefit of at least slowing down the free flow of his bedroom walls and effects but brings with it a much weightier (*pace* Velda) issue. Where is she now?

Staring fixedly ahead at the fleeting wall, it is becoming dauntingly apparent that he is not alone in the bed. Oh my goodness. It isn't? Is it? He dares not turn his head to look.

Of course. She'd appeared, out of the blue. There'd been some bizarre story about how she'd become part of this, what was it? Some sort of peripatetic, para-sisters nonsense. Someone had posted on a forum a distress message. Whoever is in the vicinity, known or unknown, hops to and pours tea and sympathy while the defects, shortcomings and indiscretions of the common man are picked over with surgical precision. Apparently yesterday she'd picked up a call from this neck of the woods and galloped (galumphed more like) to the rescue.

Oh, please, please, no. If she was pouring balm on yet another unwitting victim of the unfair sex, what the blazes is she doing in the bed next to him?

He has absolutely no recall how they had both got there. None at all. She'd been quite amicable on the field but not in such a way as to suppose they might end up in bed together. After the sheep had been safely corralled and he'd finished the pint Tilly had bought him, she stood smiling by his side, even patted his arm and held on to it while he showed her round the sunken chapel.

Oh God. Quite another thought occurs to him. They hadn't...had they? Risking lowering his eyes from the opposite wall, tentatively and slowly in case it wound up its magic lantern spin again, he checks out his attire. Good. Intact. Well, all except for his tie. Socks. Slacks. Belt. Countryman shirt. Still tucked in. All present. Hail, most merciful heart of Jesus.

Had he given her a key? Had she joined in the carousing on the field? This was long after the day visitors had left. Only the guys from the microbrewery, Bishy Barnabee's fairground and the gardener chappie, Ned, who had come along at six o'clock to lock up and Marcus had remained. They'd all larked around until, as he explained to the wee lad, Maximilian, Pleiades had made its way into the third quartile of the summer sky. He couldn't remember Velda turning up again, after she'd trotted off on her rescue mission, but then again, there seems to be a fair amount he can't quite remember.

How had he got home? Probably braced between two strong shoulders, toes of his shoes scuffing along the ground, singing 'We'll Roll the Old Chariot Along' to the tune of 'Nelson's Blood', his favourite bar room chant.

And who on earth is that in the bathroom next door?

Are there now two stowaways in the flat?

Had Velda presumed to bring her latest waif to stay?

There's a knock on the bedroom door, brisk and businesslike. Should he invite them in? Assuming that Velda would wish her identity hidden, as it is beyond the bounds of all reasonableness that she would wish it known she had spent the night in her estranged husband's bed, he moves to pull the covers over the recumbent figure in the bed. So, it is not without some startlement that his eyes focus on his estranged wife pushing open the bedroom door with her ample behind, carrying a tea tray in her outstretched arms. It is suddenly even more imperative to hide the identity of the person who had made their way into his bed. He pulls the covers up tight, decorum momentarily winning out over curiosity.

Velda advances into the room. Marcus lies rigid, eyes popping. "Marcus."

"Velda."

A bare arm makes its way through the swaddling of the bedclothes. Marcus's eyes lock on to those of his wife in mute terror as the person in the bed next to him wriggles and shifts to a seated position.

"Cecily!"

"Cecily?"

"Marcus. Hello."

"Well, I'll go and get another cup, shall I?" offers Velda, somewhat archly.

"No. Please don't bother. I'm going. Right now." Velda leaves the bedroom door wide open and goes to clatter some crockery in the kitchen, turning her back on the bed containing the unusual and still unexplained combination of both Cecily and Marcus. In amongst his confusion and bewilderment at this most unexpected turn of events is also a gut-wrenching panic that Velda might find the green and cream plaster of Paris monstrosity, provenance unknown, in its beheaded state under the kitchen sink. That could possibly be all that is required to move this rather delicate situation into one of all-out warfare. And he really does not have the head for it this morning.

Neither Cecily nor Marcus wish to look too closely at the other nor ask the unaskable questions. Marcus makes to swing his legs out of the bed to allow Cecily room to exit, given that her side of the bed is close by the wall. Every movement sets off an ominous tolling in his head. Mutely, she straightens her clothing, also all accounted for and intact, before clambering rather inelegantly, given the encumbrance of the duvet and an ancient eiderdown, over Marcus's aching body. "Sorry."

"No. I'm sorry. Can you manage?"

"Yes, I think so." Cecily reaches the floor and, by the smallest degrees, stands upright, a vertebrae at a time. "Oooh, no, I'm not so good. Rotten head. What about you?"

"Punishing."

A timpani of drawer- and door-slamming filters through from the kitchen. "Ouch."

"Eeuuughhww."

"Are you going to be sick?"

"No, don't think so."

"Who's that in the kitchen?" Cecily whispers loudly.

"That's Velda. My ex."

"Oh my goodness. I'm so sorry. Have I interrupted…?" What is Cecily imagining? Swingers? A troika? Voyeurism? Revenge attack bunny boiler? Unrequited reconciliation?

"No. No. Nothing like that. She arrived yesterday. Had no idea she was coming."

"And I certainly wouldn't have bothered if I'd known what I was going to find," comes Velda's strident voice from the kitchen.

Cecily, on all fours, apparently searching for something, snorts loudly.

"You are going to be sick."

"No."

Marcus checks Cecily's condition. Clearly some vague post-matrimonial protocol has been seriously breached here even if technically he is at liberty to invite whomsoever he likes into his bed. If Cecily, however, were to be sick, then this would certainly take top billing in Velda's Dead Weight, Look What Depths/Company He Keeps, Glad I Got Out When I Did Ex-Husband scenario.

"Are you sure?" he asks with concern, for Cecily's shoulders are rocking and heaving. She is clearly challenged by something.

She snorts again, alarmingly.

"What's the matter?"

"Nothing," she gulps, rocking back on her heels. Tears are pouring down her cheeks. "Sorry, think I'm still a bit drunk." She collapses against the wardrobe with a resonant thud. "This is all just a bit…bizarre."

Marcus recalls the times that he'd been in close quarters with Cecily

– in the pub, in her kitchen, passing on the pavement. She'd always been pleasant, polite but apart, unwilling to keep herself anything other than contained, defined, irreproachable. Not one of those types who fill any social vacuum with themselves, selves, selves. So, the inescapable and hilarious fact that she is recumbent on his bedroom floor, with the wardrobe door creaking against her weight, snorting hilariously while his ex-wife is in the kitchen oozing disapproval suddenly hits him.

"Ha. Ha. Yes, I get it."

As he starts laughing, discreetly, he feels that yes, he *does* get it! Here he is, in the most absurd situation, not entirely sure how it had come about – that is for later – and it is just plain funny. For which he is enormously grateful. And buoyed up. And lifted. And just…oh, what the hell. It doesn't matter he can't find the right words to describe the irrepressible, tickling bubble rising up inside him right now. He hasn't laughed like this – with such abandon and joy – ever.

"Here. Let me help you up."

"I'm alright. I can manage." She staggers to her feet, upper torso rotating precariously.

"You sure?"

"Yup."

"Think Velda said something about a cup of tea."

"Really, no, don't bother. Must go."

"Let me see you out."

"No. Stay where you are. I'm alright."

Marcus lays his head back on the pillow. Through one part-raised eyelid he watches as Cecily ragdolls out of the bedroom. He can hear the brief conversation that takes place in the kitchen next door.

"Velda."

"Cecily."

"I'm sure you know your own way out."

He hears her unsteady footsteps down the stairs and the front door slam. Now, Velda permitting, he can go back to wallowing in his hangover. If he is lucky, the old girl might bring him a fresh brew. He stretches out his legs in the bed. What is that? Reaching under the disordered bedclothes he pulls out Cecily's sandal. Good lord, that woman really does have big feet.

233

Cecily

Oh fucking shitting bastard botheration. This is not good. This is so not good. Waking up in Marcus's bed with a sour-faced ex-wife staring down at the pair of them and no real idea how she'd got there in the first place. With any luck Amelia would still be in bed and so would not witness her ignominious return home. She'll go back for her shoe another time.

Luckily the front door key is in the geranium pot; she must have had the presence of mind to leave it there before she escorted Marcus back to his flat. She'd discovered him, or at least Trueman had, curled up under the camellia bush in the front garden somewhere around midnight. It would appear that 'the lads' had left him outside his place but he'd given his key to his Best Little Dumpling, now revealed by her presence in his flat to mean Velda. He must have wandered over the street to her house.

"Hello. Good boy. Are you hungry?" Trueman turns circles, his claws clattering on the tiled floor of the hallway. "Ssssh. You'll wake Amelia."

"I'm awake already. Where *have* you been?" Amelia stands at the top of the stairs looking down. "And where's your shoe?"

"Don't ask."

"Of course I'm asking."

In a reversal of the last couple of days, Amelia gently guides Cecily to the kitchen table and fills the kettle.

"Can you manage, Cecily? I was just on my way to have a shower."

Cecily sits quietly on a wooden chair and watches steam from the whistling kettle billow against the window.

Yesterday had been a crazy, crazy day. She'd been a bit piqued that Amelia hadn't come to help set up the cake stall. However, by two o'clock, everything was set. The cake makers, biscuit bakers and cupcake queens had excelled themselves. No flavours or regions were left unrepresented. Even usually abstemious Amelia had a wide-eyed, hungry look about her when she finally turned up. All around them were bric-a-brac stalls, a coconut shy, face painting, wet sponge stocks, guess the weight of the jar and the name of the piglet, donkey rides, raffles, home crafts, jewellery. Goal posts were set up. Plant sales, a sweet stall, candy floss. The smell of frying onions moved listlessly in the heavy air.

"Seems there's a bit of a mash-up at the gates," Tilly observed, a few minutes before two o'clock and the official opening.

"Carnage, more like," offered Cecily.

At the locked gates a melee of majorettes, the brass band (tooting loud enough to drown out the out-of-tune bugler), the vintage cars and the May Queen thronged colourfully, circulating like tropical fish in a whirlpool.

"Where's Major Welding? Thought he was supposed to be making a speech, declaring the fair open, cutting the ribbon, that sort of thing?"

"Last saw him a few hours ago driving off at high speed with his little pipsqueak chasing after him," Madge piped up. "Don't think he'll be back. Not good for his precious public image to be seen anywhere near any scuffles involving the police, an unwashed band of druids and a lady vicar with all and sundry clicking away on their phones."

"Let's just open the gates and get on with it then."

Ned pulled back the gates and the players and punters piled in, randomly, joyously, haphazardly, all except for the May Queen abandoned ingloriously on the trailer, her attendants having left to march with the trombone and the flugelhorn.

As the afternoon wore on, she had spotted Marcus and the vicar standing by the chapel, handing out leaflets to visitors, both talking rapturously about the new find. The brass band had finished their set with Joseph Haydn's 'Trumpet Concerto', her favourite piece. Scores of people stood around the beer tent or sat at café tables or on bales of straw. Painted children ran carefree, winding between the legs of the eight-foot juggling stilt man. The headmaster of St Anthony's was getting a soaking in the stocks. The jazz band was playing all the standards.

Everything was held fast in the warm summer air. Undoubtedly everyone was loaded with e numbers, sugar and a false sense of arcadia, but it didn't matter. It was about as perfect as it could get.

Until Amelia rowed with Enzo and kicked over the table and the sheep escaped and half the neighbourhood dogs had vomited on coconut, cream, jam, cherries, pastry, chocolate, cake, marzipan, icing.

But it had all righted itself. No harm done.

Amelia's row with Enzo on the phone had cleared the air. Tilly's daughter, Lizzie, appeared at the stall holding a helium balloon and some fuzzy candyfloss in one hand and a lead in the other. "Hi, Mum. I'm just going to enter Fly in the dog agility. Can I have some more cake?"

"Hang on, I'll come with you." Amelia peeled off her apron and, arm round her niece's shoulder, they walked off in a mock three-legged fashion.

"They both look so much happier."

Tilly agreed. "But they've both eaten half our cake stall! Never seen the girl eat so much."

"They take after each other I think. Neither of them misery eaters. Carb me happy!"

It had been a crazy, crazy day yesterday. All these lives, all this activity, all this effort had come together to create a near perfect afternoon. And now – what? A quiet, familiar gloom settles around Cecily's shoulders.

Marcus

When he wakes again to find the duvet and eiderdown has been straightened, he has a vague memory of a disappearing dream. A TV crew in his bedroom. He had been wearing women's shoes. A train carriage load of people sang 'For He's a Jolly Good Fellow'. Then it had gone.

Outside has the quietness of Sunday afternoon about it.

His mouth is parched and his teeth do not feel like his own, but at least the cleaver has been removed from his head. Thinking of which, is Velda still around, or has she melted away too like his dream?

He tries to call out for her but his voice cracks like a branch struck by lightning. He'd better get up anyway. Urgent call of nature.

Supported by the furniture, he makes his way into the living room. There she is. She'd nodded off in the armchair, head back, chin high. He tries to tiptoe past. "Afternoon, Marcus. You're up, I see." He nods, fearing to speak lest his vocal chords twang their last. He points downstairs from which she gets his meaning. "I'll put the kettle on." He nods again, slowly but gratefully. On his way through the kitchen, he spots Cecily's cup of tea from the morning, undrunk and pointedly left with a teaspoon and bowl of sugar cubes. This is not going to be easy.

After splashing water on his face and climbing hand over hand up the stairs again, he drops himself onto the sofa. "You'll be alright by four o'clock, Paul always says." Mercy. There are still two hours to go.

She takes to fettling in the kitchen. What is she doing in there? Living on his own, he'd grown unaccustomed to the domestic sounds of someone else going about their business in his living space. She chatters away to him, leaning backwards from the worktop to check if he is still listening. "Yes. Uh-huh. Mmm." He'd not lost the knack of proactively zoning out.

"Here you are. I've made you some sandwiches."

"Thank you."

"I suppose it's alright to eat them in here as you don't seem to have a dining room." His mouth is full of liver sausage. He can't reply. Velda sits back in the armchair, to which she now appears to have some sort of proprietorial claim, and watches him while he eats. He half expects her to get out her knitting or pick up her crossword book. "I could only find a black banana in the fruit bowl. Don't think that would be too good for you right now."

"Righto, dear."

The sandwich is like cotton wool in his mouth but the tea is superb – hot, steamy, just the right colour and it sluices his desiccated insides better than anything imaginable. He leans back and sighs with emerging contentment. He is beginning to feel better. Miraculously.

"Well then, Marcus." He turns a raised eyebrow in her direction. Might she want to have one of her little chats? "How are things?"

"Good. Good."

"Cecily?"

"Oh no, no, no. No, no." Is he rather overdoing the denial? "Actually, I've been thinking." He stops. A small smile comes to her lips. "I've made some decisions."

"Right." Her face is open, her eyes twinkling. She shuffles slightly in her seat as if at the start of an exciting bedtime story.

"I'm going to buy a house. I'm going to settle here. You might think it's a bit of a backwater around here but it suits me." He isn't looking to her for approval but he cannot help noticing that, while her mouth is still wide, her eyes look shadowed, disappointed. "I've some ideas of what I'd like to do. There's a wealth of stories and history and fable in this part of the world. Thought I might blog. Blatt's Blog. Possibly."

She lowers her head and puts down her metaphorical knitting; her hands remain folded in her lap as he tells her how he's signed up for a digital media course at the college. It is going to be interesting. He knows he is only an enthusiastic amateur but putting things on the Web would help focus his interest. She could follow him, if she wants. Velda raises her head sharply. "On the Web, I mean."

"Well, that's all very nice, Marcus. I'm glad for you. Anyway, must be getting off." The brief, and borrowed, sense of community vanishes with Velda's expressed desire to leave.

"Good to see you and all that."

"You too."

In no time at all, she is out of the building and driving down the road. On the draining board sits the garishly green and yellow plaster doll, her pleated skirts swirling in a joyful movement, her head stuck back on.

He has the feeling that he won't be seeing very much of Velda any more.

AUTUMN

Important to treasure the rarities that the earth throws back up. The grey-green encrusted silverware of Mildenhall, Neptune with dolphins in his hair, pulled from the dark brown earth that is long-decayed oaks. The erotic charge of Bacchanalian revelry; the dishabille of Hercules in his cups, the perpetual energy of the unashamedly stunningly naked Saturnalian dance chased out in precious metal.

As if so much energy wheeled it out of the ground rather than being lifted out of the ground at the point of a plough share. Two children born a millennium and a half ago, Pascentia and Papittedo. Vivas! Long may they live, and so they did, both, for longer and forever in ways that the silversmith and their new parents could never envisage.

So how did life become a mean and grovelling thing through which we must shuffle as best we can?

Three hundred years flowering for the priory before the manifest sin, vicious, carnal and abominable living is daily used and committed among the little and small abbeys. Black-clothed Augustinians are made to move on.

M. Blatt

18

Cecily

She hasn't seen them since the fair a month and a half ago. Amelia had surprised her by saying that she would be going back with Tilly and Lizzie for a short while.

"Oh, why?"

"Don't look so hurt."

"I'm not."

"Look. Tilly's invited me to come back with her. Why not? I'll get out from under your feet…"

"But you're not under my feet. This is your home."

"I know. But I just need a break. What with Enzo and everything."

Cecily wondered what Enzo had to do with Amelia's decision to go and stay with Tilly but bit back any further comments, knowing that to protest would be futile and would risk exposing her as needy. Two into three just doesn't go; there is always one left feeling spare

"Yes. Of course. I'll see you, won't I, before you go back? If you go back."

"No decisions made just yet. But sure, only going for a few days."

A few days have turned into six weeks. Half a season has rolled by. Early leaves are crisping and falling in their ones and twos. Dawn comes later and dusk a little bit earlier. Sounds are different as the air cools and thins slightly. The swifts and swallows have gone. The year is beginning its long, slow backwards exit.

One curious effect of waking up next to Marcus has been to awaken certain memories. Of Henry. Of course of Henry. Who else?

She had been grateful when Marcus discreetly wrapped her sandal in a carrier bag and placed it behind the geraniums at the front door. So far they have managed to avoid any embarrassing encounters with each other, largely by staying on opposite sides of the street. Does he hold her in his gaze just that bit longer than necessary when their paths do cross? She isn't sure, but mercifully Marcus does not seem inclined to repeat the encounter.

Yet for all their mutual discomfort, Cecily does occasionally allow herself to imagine what it might have been like had they been more intimate. After all, Marcus is not bad-looking. Tall, a little too weedy and inclined towards the old-fashioned in his dress sense but he has a strong face. There is depth of focus in his eyes. His hands are rugged, and he pauses considerably before speaking.

She draws herself back from taking her imagination too far. This is partly out of loyalty to Henry. But she recognises it is partly out of fear too. The last time her imagination broke its bounds was eighteen months after Henry had died. A sorry little episode, in which to comfort the human was to insult the divine.

She'd met the stranger in the supermarket, of all the stupid, mundane, careworn, workaday places. His shopping had got mixed up with hers on the conveyor belt. After he paid for his goods, he stayed chatting to her while she packed her few meagre provisions. Perfectly obvious she was a woman on her own. Just one sorry mouth to feed.

"Fancy a coffee?" He pointed to the coffee bar behind them. Was he a checkout prowler? Was this his usual pickup technique mid-afternoon on a wet Wednesday? She'd glanced at the assistant but she gave no clue.

"OK. Why not?" Where's the harm? She didn't want to show herself up as cheap by pre-judging the situation.

At what point did she became culpable? At what point did the situation change, take on a totally different attitude? When she decided the slowly defrosting fish could take its chances? When he held her wrist, that's when.

They'd arranged to meet for a drink later that evening.

By ten o'clock, she was on her back having sex.

She met him again, by arrangement, two weeks later. It was exactly the same routine. A hard fuck. He was putting himself through his paces. 98...99...100 and turn. One...two...three... Sweat collected in his clavicle. She watched dispassionately as it pooled. What team did he say he supported? He gripped the headboard with both hands and arched his back, staring fixedly at the wall as he came. She wondered about the other half of the bottle of baby oil.

"Shall I see you home?"

"No. Really. Don't bother. Thank you."

As she got out of bed, she noticed a small rusty patch on the bottom sheet. It was her. She was either getting too old or too tender for sex with a stranger. She wouldn't even mention it. Let him deal with it. Sad thought, though. Her walls were getting thinner. Her colours were fading.

So it is in Henry's arms that she lies at night. For the past is safe, unchanging, guaranteed.

When Henry made love to her, he covered her like he was protecting her from an exploding bomb. He *was* an exploding bomb. She loved the size of him, the weight of him, the sheer bulk of her man. But he could pack a punch – a moment's rapture knocked off kilter by a pressing elbow, the compressions and bruises and awkward tilts of making love with a big and passionate and inventive man.

She wishes she could remember all the times they had sex. But then again, she doesn't. The greater the store of memories, the more there is to miss.

But there are the times she keeps on the top shelf of her memory.

The first time. On his office floor.

On their wedding day.

Saturday nights, in front of the log fire.

Sunday mornings, among the crumpled newspapers and toast crumbs.

The time he turned her over and pressed her face into the pillow.

But she can't recall the last time. How on earth was she to know it was going to be the last time? No sense of it being a valedictory fuck. A 'so long, farewell, thanks for all the good times' one. Or even, 'I will love you forever and take your heart with me'. So, was it a Tuesday – hey, what about it, girl, it's been a couple of days? A Friday – God, I think I've drunk too much but let's give it a go? Was there a deep, lasting connection as they looked into each other's eyes, bonded, one on one, forever? Or had she felt like an old nag that had been mistakenly entered for the Epsom Derby?

One thing was for sure though. Every night during their time together he pulled her to him, pulled her into the curve of his body and held her tight until they both fell asleep.

Perfect.

Henry always said she was steadfast, irreproachable. Those were his words. They were hard words but she tried her best to deserve them. More than anything, that's what she wanted to be as Henry's widow. Steadfast and irreproachable. But she had failed. She had failed, even as Henry's wife.

The sense of disloyalty was not just to do with Supermarket Man. If she could forgive herself that, then so might Henry if that wasn't a totally daft notion given that she'd met Supermarket Man long after Henry had died. No, it goes far deeper than that. Right to the spot that Mandy accesses with each piercing, quizzical look. Right to the spot where she had to make the hardest decision of her life. Right to the spot where she broke faith with Henry, broke faith in his ability to love her and cherish her even in the long years after his death.

"You'd think you'd somehow be protected from crazy stuff happening at a time like this."

Six years ago, Dr Bam looked at her from his standpoint of bitter experience. There was, nonetheless, a gentleness in his eyes. "I'm afraid nothing gives us immunity. The universe just doesn't work that way." Cecily shrugged and took his proffered letter of referral. "It is entirely your decision, of course, but my advice would be at least go and have a chat. I'm sorry to say this, Mrs Marchant, but your age doesn't work in your favour and with everything you've got going on at this time…" He left the rest hanging in the air, together with the unspoken thought that, of those who entered the clinic's doors, very few left 'unburdened'.

So, that was it, she thought, on the drive home from the surgery. Dr Bam had become her moral arbiter. She'd almost missed the signs, put the fatigue down to caring for Henry, the loss of appetite to the ever-present anxiety, her breasts feeling like they'd been hit by wet sandbags and a deep down yearning ache to change-of-life stuff.

Standing in the chemist's the previous week, waiting for Henry's steroids and stomach pills, the sudden thought that she might be pregnant nearly folded her in two. Someone had helped her to a seat and offered a glass of water.

Shakily she took Henry's medication and paid for the kit. Later that evening, after she'd helped Henry to bed, she took the test into the downstairs loo. There was his two-day-old newspaper leaning against the frosted window, a scallop shell that served as an ash tray and a scrunched-up cigarette packet on the window sill. The room was cold, a harsh light from the brash bulb reflected off the white tiles. Specks of fag ash dusted the seat where Henry had emptied the ash tray into the loo. She knew she ought to do the test early in the morning but maybe if she skewed the test she might buck the result.

No such luck. She was pregnant.

That awful discovery coincided with Henry's prognosis. He had nine months to live. How could she possibly deal with anything else? That was the thing that made everybody gasp in pain and bewilderment. She would have to deal with any other underlying issue herself.

And that is when the grotesque dummy, its oversized foetal head, its shiny, waxy skin, its open, screaming mouth moved in, to remind her of her loss of faith. Now, instead of holding Henry's growing child in her arms, she sits alone in her empty house. And by all accounts, Mandy fares no better. Does she feel the same pangs of guilt when she sees Cecily? Is Cecily her reminder of how different things might have been? As Mandy is to her, is she Mandy's prowling, untrustworthy conscience? She'd even given the grotesque haunting creature a name – Vernix.

Maybe she needs to talk to someone. Heave off the crushing burden from her back, drop it onto the floor, walk away from it, leave it. How simple and how beguiling. Maybe she could talk to Tilly or Amelia. Which one would understand? But wasn't there a danger that that might change things? With the secret out there, would she somehow be diminished, lose rank? Bright daylight might suck the air from the dummy's mouth, remove the malevolent gleam from its eye, stop its rattling chatter. It might defy Mandy's menace. But confession might also rob her of her sisters' respect. Could she take that risk?

Tilly had sent a text a couple of days ago. "Checking out college for Lizzie. Can we stay?"

"Doh! Need you ask? Who? When?"

"Me, Melly, Lizzie. Midday."

"Lovely!"

They arrive as one hectic, chaotic unit, reaching their arms through the front doorway to pull Cecily into strong, repeated hugs. They bring with them laughter, noise, fun. "We've got enough luggage here for a cruise."

"We've brought Australian Crunchies."

"Bliss. Come on in. You're in your own rooms. Lizzie, I've put you in the spare room. I'll give you a hand up with your cases and then we can catch up."

As Cecily brews coffee in the kitchen, she listens to the roar of feet on the floorboards above. The house is alive again. They are like the pet ducks they had in the garden as children. "Four bodies, one brain," Mother used to say as the Indian Runners hurriedly and randomly switched from one direction to another and then to another. How can she offer that comparison without it sounding like she is insulting her sisters and niece? Tilly would know. If Tilly said that they were marauding about like a gaggle of ducks, Amelia would laugh and agree, getting it straight away. Lizzie would laugh because her Mum and her two giddy aunts were laughing. Cecily could say it and she knows it would just come out too loaded with anxiety and awkwardness to be funny.

Do other sisters have the same stresses? Do they worry, individually, they are too much of this and not enough of that? That the others have got the secret, magical ingredient, whatever it is? Are there alliances, jealousies, inadequacies in every family? Or is she being just far too edgy? Shouldn't she just get on and enjoy their company?

"Coffee's ready," she shouts from the bottom of the stairs.

"Great."

"Coming."

"Bliss, sis!"

She stands close to the newel post as, collectively, they charge down the stairs and into the kitchen. "Do you remember those ducks we used to have?" But nobody hears her. They are already on their way to pouring the thick oily coffee and carving up the crisped rice and coconut squares covered in dark glossy chocolate icing that had been Mother's recipe.

*

They sit dabbing the last of the crumbs and tilting the last of the coffee. There is an air of expectation around the table.

"We've got something to tell you," says Tilly, Cecily looking at her with concern.

"Good or bad?" she asks quickly.

"Good. On the whole." Lizzie looks up sharply. "Yes. Good. Definitely good."

"Go on then."

"Do you want to tell Aunt Cecily?" Tilly asked Lizzie.

"No, you say."

"Right. Well. The thing is. Lizzie is pregnant."

Cecily doesn't know what to say. Lizzie sits stock still with her hands in her lap, giving no clues as to how she wants her aunt to react.

"Right. That's…that's… Sorry. I'm at a loss what to say. But it's good news, right?"

"No, it is good news, Aunty Cecily, it just takes a bit of getting used to."

"Of course, my darling. But if you're happy then we're all happy. Aren't we?" Cecily looks round at her sisters for confirmation.

"The thing is," continues Tilly, "Lizzie is pleased. We are all pleased. But there's one big complication. Nothing medical or anything like that. Lizzie is doing really well. The baby's fine. It's just that she really shouldn't stay at home. With the sheep. Risk of spontaneous miscarriage if she's around sheep. Especially at lambing time. And mine have already gone to the tup. So, we're already on for next season."

"Tell me you're not going back to that caravan. Or living with that…" She wants to call him a dickhead but, fearing that she might be insulting the father of her future grand-nephew or grand-niece, settles for, "bloke?"

"No, that's all over," Lizzie mutters from beneath her fringe.

"We were wondering whether you might let Lizzie come here." Tilly puts her arm round her daughter's shoulders and pulls her close. They both look at Cecily with the same clearwater eyes. "The baby's due end of January. She can defer her return to college. It would only be for a few months. Know it's a massive ask, but she, they, can come back to the farm in the spring. It's just that you've always said that this house and you are here for the family." Cecily puts her hand on Tilly's to slow the rapid rattle of words. "Think about it?"

"No need."

"Sure?"

"Sure." Cecily looks at her dear sister's face now flooding with tears. She would miss out on this most rare and exquisite time with Lizzie, but she was entrusting Cecily to be her daughter's helpmate. How could she ever doubt that Tilly loves her?

What an amazing time lay ahead.

She looks up the table at Amelia, who is smiling, but as one who is leaving.

Later that afternoon, they all sit out in the garden. Seed pods are closing round the bright gaudy shades of summer. Gladioli, lupins, foxgloves and hollyhocks are putting their costumes away for another season. In their place, crocosmia waves its orange bills at the reddening mountain ash and the baby-fist apples in the orchard. The sun is harvest hot. Trueman emits a groan of contentment from underneath Cecily's deckchair. Tilly is playing games on her phone in the next deckchair.

"Listen, Tils. There's something I need to tell you. It's been burning my mind for such a long time." Tilly puts her phone back in her jeans pocket and turns her full attention on Cecily.

"Go on."

"I don't really know why I have to tell you. It doesn't affect anybody but me. It doesn't change anything. It's just that I really, really have to tell somebody. It's too much to carry just on my own. When you said you were all coming down today, I'd made up my mind that I would tell you."

Even as she speaks, Cecily is still undecided whether to tell her sisters about the abortion. If she confesses, it might lessen the pressure inside her heart. But it might taint the day. Could she bear to be the brunt of their disapproval? No. She can't. She loves them dearly but knows that when Tilly and Amelia fight, they fight with sharp blades.

Tilly is silent.

"And then we have Lizzie's wonderful news." Cecily looks out into the garden.

Tilly nods, still silent, holding out her hand to take Cecily's.

Cecily takes a moment.

Steadfast and irreproachable.

Maybe with Lizzie's baby on its way, the mistakes and regrets and fuck-ups of the previous generation, and the one before it, would no longer matter. This could be a fresh start. She could forgive herself. It could all just slip away. No longer important. No longer relevant. Powerless. Hidden. Buried. Out of sight.

Lizzie and Amelia, so similar to each other, are sitting on upturned logs, knees and lower legs flattened to the ground, soles upright. They are chatting away quietly, almost conspiratorially. They are so alike. Lizzy looks well. Still painfully young.

Suddenly, seeing them side by side, she sees the obvious.

"Oh my God, Tils, is Melly...?"

Tilly nods. "She was going to tell you later."

"Enzo?"

"Of course. But he doesn't know."

"What's she going to do?"

"You know Melly. She'll tell us when she's ready."

"Oh my God!"

"Ssshh. Let her tell you herself."

It is turning out to be quite a day.

"Anyway. What were you going to tell me?"

"Doesn't matter. Now's not the time."

Later that evening, after supper, she will slip out to the churchyard. Wherever he is, maybe, just maybe, Henry is holding a small baby-apple fist in his own.

Maybe that is the greatest gift she can give him.

Reconciliation.

And then she might just call in on Marcus on the way home.

Four seeds in a hole;
One for the rook, one for the crow,
One to rot and one to grow

Lightning Source UK Ltd.
Milton Keynes UK
UKOW01f1203260916

283829UK00001B/62/P